Gillian Slovo was born in South Africa in 1952. In 1964 her family was forced into exile. They settled in London, where Gillian Slovo still lives. Since the birth of her daughter she has been writing full time and is the author of three detective novels featuring her character Kate Baeier. *Ties of Blood*, her first novel set in South Africa, was published in 1990, and in 1992 Virago published her second, *Betrayal*. In 1995 Virago will publish her fourth Kate Baeier novel, *Catnap*.

GILLIAN SLOVO

Façade

Published by VIRAGO PRESS Limited May 1994
42–43 Gloucester Crescent, Camden Town, London NW1 7PD

Copyright © Gillian Slovo 1993
First published in hardback by Michael Joseph Ltd 1993

A CIP catalogue record for this book is available from the British Library

Printed in Great Britain by Cox & Wyman Ltd, Reading, Berkshire

Spring

CHAPTER ONE

1992

Laura was suddenly, unaccountably, awake. She lay still, waiting for her breathing to die down, listening for the noise.

Nothing. The night was hushed; all sounds, save only for the city's background hum, utterly deadened.

It was a dream, she told herself. But getting out of bed anyway, she went quickly to the window.

The courtyard, far down below her, was lifeless. It was a dream, she told herself again, a dream with side effects, with sounds that merged into reality; with the power of an ambulance's siren slicing through a foggy night. Foggy? She looked out and saw a shallow haze spreading around the courtyard's lights. Not fog, she realized, but a spring mist.

Spring, she thought. Thank God winter is over. She was no longer frightened. She walked back to her bed and, making sure she didn't disturb Steven, sat down on it. Then, quietly, as quietly as she could, she moved the pile of books from the adjoining shelf.

Planning to bring out what was hidden there, she stretched her hand forwards. But then there was a movement, faint, beside her. She shoved the books back into place. That done, she slid into bed and lay there, quietly, beside Steven, waiting for sleep.

The shriek of an electric alarm jolted her from sleep. She stretched out a hand to silence it and in doing so realized that Steven had gone. She was alone. She yawned and flexed her back and, revelling in the luxury of the silence and the spaciousness as well, glanced idly at her watch.

'Oh shit.' She flung the covers aside, jumped out of bed and, running, negotiated the length of her living space. With one hand she filled the kettle while the other threw a slice of rye into the toaster. There was a note from Steven lying on the counter. She glanced sideways at it. 'Didn't want to wake you,' it read. 'You looked like you needed the extra. Hope I set the clock for the right time. Later, Steven.'

Bloody Steven, she thought fondly, trust him to think twenty minutes is enough.

She opened cupboards, grabbed knife, plate, jam, butter and then put the coffee on. While it was percolating, she washed her hair so rapidly that she was still regulating the water temperature during the last rinse. She was ferociously in motion: throwing a towel over her hair and brushing her teeth, applying lipstick, blusher, eye shadow and mascara, all in rapid succession. Then she dressed as quickly as she had done everything else and went to eat.

Biting into a piece of toast and swallowing it with swigs of coffee, she summoned up a vision of the line of journalists she was about to meet. In her mind's eye they merged and became one: a hunter, snarling, ready to trap his prey. She grimaced, and then she shook her head. Oh well, she thought, I'm used to it. She cleared the breakfast debris away and went to the mirror for one last dispassionate assessment.

What she saw met with her approval: a woman in her prime, green eyes, curly black shoulder-length hair, peach complexion, a woman who was still beautiful, whose age lines served to give her face more character. She nodded gravely at herself and checked the time. She had made it with minutes more to spare.

She used the time diligently, sitting on her pastel sofa and recreating flashes of her latest TV role – Elizabeth, the woman she had finished playing and was now promoting. She sat quite still and concentrated on her breath, rooting her body to itself just as she did before every performance. She set aside herself, the essential Laura, and moved into the other – the actress acting her public persona, selecting parts of herself that she was prepared to show, concealing all else. The public were not concerned with the real Laura Weber, what they wanted was the star, and it was the star that she would give them. She was good at it. She'd had lots of practice.

The harsh buzz of the entryphone punctured her tranquillity. She jumped up, suppressed a momentary panic and, pushing the entry button, embarked on one full day's worth of promotion.

CHAPTER TWO

'It's a bit like being a prostitute,' Laura said.

Claire Totley, personality interviewer to the quality press, raised one feathery eyebrow. 'Acting?'

Acting, Laura heard, and frowned: what could Claire mean? Not that Laura really cared. She felt a yawn surging. As she raised her fist to her mouth she shot a surreptitious glance at her watch. Four o'clock – six hours of constant interviews and the end was finally in sight.

'Do you mean that acting is like prostitution?'

Laura sighed. 'No,' she said as patiently as she could. 'I wasn't talking about acting. You asked, if you remember, whether I minded being interviewed and I said that there's something promiscuous about it. Brief encounters and all that.'

'Oh.' The word delivered without inflection. A pause. 'And I suppose the payment is the article.' Another pause, and then the bland voice spoke again. 'Tell me about your latest part,' it suggested. 'Tell me about Elizabeth.'

Nodding, Laura set herself on automatic pilot. 'Elizabeth is an interesting woman,' she began. 'Her vivaciousness, her vibrant sense of humour make her appear lightweight but she is in fact involved in a serious struggle.' The sentences, delivered for what must have been the fifth time that day, were flowing smoothly out, detached from conscious thought. 'Elizabeth is, in a sense, torn in two. She's tied to her children by a cord that must be broken if she is to survive. Her dilemma is that if she severs the connection she may end up annihilating herself. The joy of playing her was –'

6

'You've never had children,' Claire said, cutting right through Laura's set piece.

'I beg your pardon?' Laura blinked.

Claire's eyes met Laura's green. 'I asked if you'd ever had children.'

'No, I haven't,' Laura said. 'But did I miss something?'

'I was just wondering,' Claire said, 'how easy it is to act a mother when you have never chosen to have children.'

Chosen, Laura thought. How does she know I ever had the choice? She smiled. 'I don't think one has to have lived one's character's life in order to portray it realistically,' she said. 'I'm sure you'd agree that I wouldn't have to want to kill myself in order to play a woman on the brink of suicide.'

'Oh yes, I heard you were offered Hedda Gabler at the Haymarket.'

Laura's open palm curled into a fist. The Hedda negotiations were supposed to be confidential!

'Are you going to accept?' she heard Claire asking.

Nail touched skin. Calm down, she told herself, calm down. 'I haven't made up my mind,' she said softly. She smiled. 'And I'd prefer you didn't write about it, in case I say no.'

No reaction: Claire Totley was not one to take prisoners. 'It must be difficult,' is what she said, 'returning to a live audience after all the television you've done.'

'Difficult?' Laura said. Who had Claire talked to? 'It is a change of pace.'

'So you're going to refuse.' That look again, dispassionate, cold.

Laura met it head on. 'I'm juggling with my schedule,' she said, 'to see if I can free up sufficient time.'

'You're inundated with offers, are you?'

'I'm not complaining.' Laura sat back, composed again, and gestured with one arm towards her desk on which stood a teetering pile of scripts. 'I'm even getting wacky offers,' she said. 'Wacky but lucrative. American cops and robbers stuff, *Miami Vice* lookalikes with parts for English roses.'

The eyebrows again.

'Well, if not roses then accents,' Laura said and her voice

tilted in laughter. Inwardly she recoiled. She no longer knew which of the two she despised more – the woman opposite or herself.

'People say you've been lucky to inherit your looks from both your parents,' Claire said.

Your parents, Laura heard. Not again, she thought. She smiled sweetly. 'Shouldn't we be talking about me, rather than my parents?'

'Well, they are in the public domain,' Claire countered.

Like documents, Laura thought.

'Your mother was modern,' Claire said.

Modern – an odd way to describe Judith. Laura frowned.

'My piece,' Claire explained. 'I thought I explained. It's one in a series of profiles of modern women. Modern marriages, home versus work, you know – that kind of thing.' She glanced down at her notebook as if there was something she wanted to check, but when she spoke what she said could not possibly have been written there. 'Must be hard having a father like Leo Weber.'

'Hard?' Laura's frown deepened. 'Why?'

'Because he's something of a hero,' Claire said. 'Selfless, dedicated, charismatic. He could have done many things, but he chose to work with the United Nations Aid agencies, devoting his life to alleviating suffering.'

'And so?'

Claire shrugged. 'A difficult act to follow.'

Which is why I didn't, Laura thought: which is why I went on the stage.

'Your father remarried a few years ago,' she heard Claire saying.

She glanced up sharply. 'Four years ago.'

'Does that bother you?'

Silence, while Laura counted to ten, and then: 'I am thirty-nine years old, an adult,' she said, painstakingly enunciating each word, 'as is my father. Why on earth should his marriage bother me?'

'Because you are thirty-nine and his new wife is only forty.' Claire Totley's eyes narrowed, her face almost predatory. 'In fact she is the same age as your mother when she' – a pause – 'when she died.'

8

When she died, Laura heard and nearly hit the roof. How dare you? That's what she felt like yelling. How dare you? What right did this woman have? What right to let these nasty insinuations come slithering in? She leaned forward, ready to let loose.

But seeing how carefully Claire Totley was watching her, Laura bit back her surging bile. To react at all, she realized, would be to play into her opponent's slimy hand. She didn't speak immediately, she sat quite still using all her energy to help camouflage her reaction. It worked: when she eventually did speak her voice was on an even keel. 'Margot and I are the best of friends,' she said. 'I introduced them, I was present at their wedding, I proposed the first toast and I continue to see them regularly. And now' – she got to her feet, smiling – 'if that's all?'

Claire Totley's face did not register defeat. 'I liked the series,' she said as she also stood. 'I thought your Elizabeth was marvellous.' And then, having tossed a perfunctory thank you in Laura's direction, she left.

Laura stood at the window, waiting until the other woman disappeared. From far away, Claire lost her sting. She walked, her shoulders slightly bowed, her hand tightly clutching at her briefcase, her sensible shoes striking at the cobbles. Laura watched her go, feeling slightly sheepish at the way she had almost overreacted. When the phone rang, she grabbed for it.

'Darling.' It was Maya, her agent, her voice, as usual, pitched too loud. 'I hope I'm in time to warn you about that ghastly Totley woman.'

With the receiver wedged on her shoulder, Laura turned her back on the window, kicked off her shoes and sank down into the sofa. 'Too late,' she said. 'I've already bumped her off.'

'I don't blame you,' Maya said. 'She looks like a nineteenth-century governess but she keeps knives in that twin set of hers. I was grilled on two abortions and a miscarriage. And you?'

'Margot.'

'Margot. Oh well – you must have been able to handle that.'

Laura shrugged. 'I did – sort of,' she said, thinking that her inner reaction had been far too dramatic.

'Anyway,' she heard Maya saying. 'Don't let it worry you. La Totley's sadism is a strictly private affair – she doesn't dare follow through in print.' Maya paused momentarily before veering off track. 'Have you decided?' she asked.

'Decided?'

'She really did make you lose concentration, didn't she?' Maya drawled. 'Hedda, darling, Hedda.'

'Oh . . . Hedda,' Laura said. 'You know what – I need alcohol. And no, I haven't decided and yes I know I should have and why don't you come over and make me a margarita instead of making me feel guilty.'

'On my way,' Maya said.

1952

As Judith and Leo Weber walked into the room the buzz of conversation was momentarily stanched. It was Judith's evening, her first exhibition, and all eyes were drawn to her. She stood there, tiny against the immensity of the stark white walls and the boldness of her sculptures, almost too small for both. She was quite obviously scared, twisting to left and right.

But Leo would not let her go. His hand tightened on hers and he bent to whisper something in her ear. Whatever it was he said, it made her smile, and when she smiled, her face lit up, and colour came flooding into it, lighting the room with its exotic beauty. The moment of awkwardness was over: the conversation swelled again, words surging through the curtain of hanging smoke.

'Judith.' It was Heloise, a neighbour and close friend, who embraced Judith warmly. 'I was beginning to think you weren't coming,' she said.

Judith pulled a face. 'I nearly didn't,' she said. 'Leo had to drag me here.' She turned to him and smilingly removed his hand from hers. 'I'm OK now,' she said. 'Heloise will look after me. You are released.' She gave him a gentle push in the direction of a knot of people waiting to receive him.

He kissed her lightly on the forehead and went away. She turned, still smiling, back to Heloise. 'Poor Leo,' she said fondly, 'what he has to put up with.'

Heloise did not return the smile. 'What does he have to put up with?' she asked.

'The fact that his wife's a bitch.'

'His wife's an artist,' Heloise said. Judith flushed. 'And she's going to be a good one too.' Heloise linked her arm to Judith's. 'I'm proud to be your friend,' she said. 'Come and see.' And with that Heloise began to lead Judith around the room, pointing out those pieces which had been reserved, and others which were arousing interest. 'You are a success, my dear,' Heloise concluded when the tour was almost complete.

Judith shrugged. 'For today perhaps.'

'For longer than that,' Heloise said. 'Believe me, this I know.'

Judith smiled. 'What are you? A fortune teller?'

'No – I have a good eye, that's all,' said Heloise simply and then she stopped. 'I have a good eye,' she said again, 'and the piece I would like does not seem to be up for sale.' She pointed a finger at the corner.

Her finger had targeted a brooding figure which, standing separated from the rest, had a spotlight playing on it. Many of Judith's pieces were long and thin, figurative variations on the human shape, but this one was entirely different. It was a woman, sculpted from carefully rounded stone, solid, massive but without an aura of either smoothness or solidity. For Judith had chipped dangerously near one edge until it seemed as if the woman's hand jutted out, creating a shadow and at the same time a harsh black warning.

'That,' Heloise said, still pointing, 'that is the piece which shows some of what you will one day achieve.' She stared at it a moment longer before turning and looking straight into Judith's green eyes. 'Don't you agree?'

'I could never sell her,' Judith said.

'You call her Façade.' Heloise paused. 'Because she must deceive . . . the fact that she is pregnant?' she suggested.

A nod.

'And you as well?' Heloise's question was hesitant and she was ready to withdraw it. No need though: Judith flashed her an open smile.

'You're the first to notice,' Judith said. 'Apart from Leo, of course. Nobody else has guessed. I suppose it's because they don't believe I could actually be a mother.'

'And you,' Heloise said. 'Do you believe it?'

Judith shrugged. 'Rachel was hardly the world's best mother.'

'But she had Max to contend with,' Heloise said. 'Whereas you, you have Leo.'

Judith's face softened. 'Yes,' she said slowly. 'Yes, I have Leo.' And at that moment she caught sight of him across the room amongst a laughing crowd. She looked at him, her husband, so handsome and so relaxed, a beacon for others, a man who could make anybody feel at ease. She looked and as she did so she thought she felt something stir inside her. She touched her belly.

He must have felt her eyes upon him because at that moment he turned and smiled and raised a glass up in her direction, and as she lifted a hand to salute him, a flash light popped, a bulb ejected, and Judith Weber was caught for all posterity, smiling on the eve of her first show.

CHAPTER THREE

1992

It had been years since Laura had been in Leo's inner office but now she saw that it was substantially unchanged. His desk, a huge polished construction, was where it had always been; in the centre, dominating the space, making the other pieces look like mere irrelevancies. She followed him across the dusty pink carpet and while he sat behind the desk, she chose a chair in front.

He reached for a pair of spectacles, which were not part of her childhood memories and to which, therefore, she would never grow accustomed. He was all business: he opened a drawer, pulled out a set of papers and passed them over. 'Sign where I have indicated,' he said.

She lifted an eyebrow. 'Without reading them?'

'You should never sign anything that you have not read,' he said, his expression stern.

She smiled, thinking that since he always treated business with a rigour that excluded even the slightest hint of humour (it was the Prussian in him, she supposed) it wasn't worth trying to tease him.

'Come now, Laura,' she heard him cajole.

She pretended to look at the document although she knew there was no real need. Leo had already told her its purpose – it was connected with the loan of Judith's work for the forthcoming retrospective at the Whitechapel gallery. She let her eyes wander, unseeing, down the print and then, after what she hoped was a respectable enough interval, scrawled her name across the bottom. That done, she returned the lot to

Leo, watching as he stowed it away. Business over, he visibly relaxed. 'How's Steven?' he asked.

'He's well,' she said. 'And Margot?'

He nodded. 'Working as hard as ever. Of course she sends her regards.' His voice began to tail off. 'She was talking about extending an invitation,' he said as his eyes lost focus.

Laura laughed. 'I'll give her a ring,' she promised, knowing that Leo, who was so in control at work, found it hard to keep the many demands of his social life in his head. It had been worse before Margot. Margot: thank God for her, because when she married Leo she became both his wife and his social secretary.

'Laura.' Leo sounded aggrieved.

'I'm sorry,' she said. 'I was miles away. What did you say?'

'I was inquiring what your next project will be.'

She shrugged. 'The new serial's about to come out – I've been fool enough to say I'd do some promotion for it. I've also got a quick cameo to do but apart from that there's not much of interest on the horizon.'

Leo nodded.

'Except Hedda,' she said quickly.

Not quickly enough. 'Hedda? You have been offered Hedda Gabler?'

Here we go, she thought, knowing what was coming next.

She was right. 'You will naturally take it,' he said.

She looked away.

He knew her too well. 'You are surely not thinking of refusing?'

'Who knows?'

'But, Laura –' his voice was uncharacteristically loud – 'Hedda Gabler is a role made for you.'

He had touched a rawness in her. 'What?' she said flippantly. 'A suicide – made for me?' And bit her tongue, hard down, so hard she drew blood. She tasted the bitterness of it, thinking to herself: Was that supposed to be a joke?

A joke – how stupid of her. She looked across at her father. She saw his eyes misting over before he dropped them. 'Judith loved you, you know,' Leo said.

Judith. The name that stood between them, the name that these days was rarely mentioned.

His face was sad, so sad. 'You were too young to under-stand,' he said and then opened his mouth again as if he was about to say something else.

She didn't want to hear it. 'I was fourteen,' she protested.

'Too young,' he continued. 'I always regret . . .'

He was cut off then: the door to his office was flung open by his secretary. 'I'm sorry, Leo.' Dorothy seemed flustered. 'Jack is on the line. He insists on talking to you.'

Insists, Laura noted and sat there, watching a flash of irrita-tion – or was it anger? – jolting Leo's face. 'Again?' he muttered and, stretching out a hand, grabbed the receiver. 'Yes, Jack,' he barked, 'what is it now?'

As Jack started speaking Laura's disquiet mounted. What on earth's the matter with Leo, she thought. She had never heard him speak this way to Jack. She looked more closely, saw him gripping the phone so hard that his knuckles were stretched taut.

'No,' she heard him saying once, and, 'No,' again, and after that a longer invective. 'I refuse to be drawn into this nonsense,' he finished, almost spluttering with rage. 'It is a point of principle with me.'

'Principle!' Jack shouted the word loudly enough for Laura to hear it.

That was all she did hear: Leo rammed the receiver closer to his ear and said, 'Hold on, please, Jack.' That done he put the receiver down. 'No need to bore you with this,' he said, lever-ing himself up. 'I will take it in the other room.'

To bore you, a phrase which Leo had always despised. And yet using boredom as an excuse he had left the room to speak to Jack Carmichael, his opposite number at the United Nations and a long-time family friend. She frowned, thinking it made no sense. She contemplated getting up and walking over to the door to see if she could hear anything more. But no – she made herself sit still – she would not, could not spy on her father. And, she thought, it's my own fault he's acting like this, I should never have mentioned suicide.

She nodded – it was her fault – and sat there planning the wording for a subtle apology which might help return them to what should have been.

But there was no need for that. When Leo returned, he was

his usual urbane self, his melodic voice filling the office, delivering Jack's regards to her along with a riveting story of international intrigue and double-dealing. When he talked like this she saw the public Leo, the orator who brought so much texture to his words that his passions were passed on to others. She sat back, letting his eloquence flow over her, thinking that she would check later with Dorothy to see if anything was wrong.

But when he finished speaking and she got up, he forestalled her. 'I will come with you,' he said. 'It is such a glorious day.' And so he accompanied her downstairs, ensuring that she had no time alone with Dorothy.

But if this was what he had intended, he showed no signs of it: as he walked across Regent's Park with her, he seemed entirely carefree. He linked his arm with hers and guided her towards Great Portland Street tube and the sense that something was going awry was lifted. It's only Hedda, she thought as she kissed him a fond goodbye, dark Hedda, obsessing me.

CHAPTER FOUR

The voice spoke directly into Laura's ear: 'That's it, you're done.'

She opened her eyes. Too quickly – the light dazzled her, forcing her eyes immediately shut. When next she opened them, she did so carefully, her pupils slowly emerging to face the oversize mirror and its border of bright bulbs. That's better, she thought, but was still too dazed by sleep to face the studio. She bought time by looking around the room. Mayhem is what she saw, dusty pots of pink and brown, half-used tissues smeared different shades of red, delicate brushes lying disordered, a paint tray of rainbow colours, all littered along the bench.

'What do you think?' she heard Sally asking.

She looked back at the mirror and saw reflected there not herself but someone other: a woman tailored for the TV cameo she was about to play, a woman of an uncertain age whose passions were buried far beneath the surface. She nodded. 'It's good.'

'Of course it is,' a deep voice drawled, 'Sally's the best.'

She looked quickly round the high back of the chair. She saw a man, a stranger, standing by the door, leaning against the wall, his arms folded, his blue eyes shining, his generous mouth smiling. American brawn was what first occurred to her, and then she thought something else. Not thought exactly, for what happened was that she felt a surge of attraction welling up.

'I didn't want to interrupt,' he said. When he straightened up she saw how tall he was and, despite her first impression of bulk, how trim. He thrust a hand, a smooth, strong hand, at her. 'Tom Hooper.'

Tom Hooper – of course, her co-star. She put her hand in his. 'Laura Weber,' she said as what she had heard of him came back to her. Tom Hooper had a formidable reputation, was deliciously photogenic – so the word went – and intelligent as well; an American who understood the British sensibility and yet who (probably because he was American) brought a kind of wildness to the screen.

To the screen and to the bed – that's what Maya had said.

She smiled. 'Nice to meet you.'

'Likewise.' Silence, which he withstood while she thought vaguely that he was still clasping her hand.

'Ready for you, Tom,' she heard Sally calling.

The moment was broken: she withdrew her hand. 'I've been looking forward to working with you,' she said weakly. She cleared her throat. 'I'm surprised our paths haven't crossed before.'

He nodded, shrugged. 'Catch you later,' was all he said.

The studio in Hammersmith was like all its fellows. Unpainted walls dominated the space edged by uncarpeted floors, which were criss-crossed by cables, black eels converging on one corner of the room. In that corner perfection reigned. A tidy three-piece suite was placed against faded floral wallpaper; two standard lamps whose shades were pushed slightly out of shape defined the boundary of the furniture; and above them space lights hung menacingly – metallic monsters ready to strike.

It was all so tacky and yet, seeing it, Laura began to smile. 'Home, sweet home,' she muttered as the first assistant director came to guide her into place. She stood contented where they put her, tolerating the bustle, the hand that came and grabbed a piece of her flesh and moved it to one side, the man who stood in front of her and talked about her profile as if she weren't there. She stood as she had long learned to do, patiently, sealed up in a space she had created for herself, listening to the hubbub but separated from it. The rehearsal was brief and devoid of passion but she didn't let that worry her. It was the camera that mattered here.

'Right. Let's go for a take,' she heard and a light blazed. 'Quiet, please,' another voice called and then, into the sudden silence, 'Action,' and Laura began to move.

It was a small part she had, a cameo, but it was a beauty and for once everything went right. From the first, the crew was with her and she could tell by the quality of the silence, the speed of each successive take, the laughter after each was over, that things were going well. 'Couldn't be better,' the director whispered in her ear, but was soon proved wrong. For, when Tom Hooper arrived, and when they did their scenes together, well, that was magic. It was a match they had, a strange, almost chemical bonding that made each separate scene so easily surmountable. And it was also, Laura thought as they moved on to the next take, it was because Tom, the star of the broader piece, used his performance to add to hers.

'Great,' the director kept saying, and, 'Great,' again, and it wasn't hyperbole. Eventually she called a reluctant halt. 'Great,' she said, grinning at the repetition. 'Take five, every-body.'

Laura had stopped to discuss a wardrobe detail and so, reaching the canteen, found the rest of the cast and crew already seated. She stood in the entrance, her gaze drawn involuntarily to Tom. She was no longer protected by the vast crew or the all-seeing camera and, remembering the effect of his first touch, a warning bell went off. I won't sit next to him, she thought as deliberately she counterposed the memory of him with another vision, an image of Steven, his capable hands caressing her skin, his body joined to hers.

She turned her head. Tom was staring at her. He knows what I was thinking, she thought. She blushed.

He raised a teacup and his eyebrows also.

She berated herself for being so adolescent. Of course he hadn't known, he couldn't read her thoughts. She pushed herself into motion, into going over and sitting down beside him.

'Thanks,' she said as she lifted the cup to her mouth.

He grimaced. 'I'm afraid it's not worth any thanks,' he drawled.

She took a sip and nodded. 'Yeuch,' she said, returning the

cup to its cracked saucer, and, as the lukewarm brown liquid slopped over the edge, looking across the table. He had pulled a small silver hip flask from his trouser pocket, and he held it out to her. The hair of the dog, she thought, and licked her lips, but the warning bell sounded faintly again and she shook her head. He lifted the flask to his mouth, threw his head back and took a long, luxurious sip.

She found that she was staring, fascinated. She was sure she looked quite brainless; she forced herself to speak. 'What I really meant,' she said, 'was thanks for your generosity.'

'You're welcome.' He had resurfaced. 'It was freely given.' He grinned and drank again, wiped his mouth with the back of his hand, capped the flask and returned it to his pocket. 'And received as well,' he said, and for a moment he looked straight at her, and in that moment she felt that she had been wrong before, that he could indeed read her thoughts.

But the moment went, broken by Tom who, as if deliberately easing the sudden tension, began to talk of other film sets and of disasters that had occurred on them. He was, like Leo, a good storyteller and as each successive tale grew more ridiculous, she found herself laughing. I like this Tom, she thought.

He in the meantime had grown serious. 'I envy you, you know,' he said. She raised an eyebrow, wondering what she'd missed. 'You don't have to put up with TV. You've got the stage.'

The stage, she heard and found suddenly that she was trembling. She smiled, trying to cover up both her reaction and also the fact that she didn't understand it. 'So do you,' she said.

He shook his head. 'Not I,' he said. 'I majored in stage fright at college and, after so much screen work, I guess I've qualified for a PhD in it. Even the thought of going live gives me hives.' He paused and smiled and she saw how his straight teeth gleamed. 'Literally,' he said.

'I know what you mean,' she said, and was surprised to find that her voice was calm.

He frowned. 'You do?'

'I've had stage fright,' she said.

He was looking intently at her, his face strangely serious. 'But you use stage fright productively,' he said.

Productively. She remembered how she had almost refused to go on stage. *Productively*, she thought: how could he know?

'I've watched you come out on the stage,' he said, 'when you were full of fear.'

He was there, she thought.

'During *Private Lives*,' he said.

That was it; that was the only time.

'I saw you hesitate,' Tom continued, 'and then I saw you harness the fright and present it to the audience. You were dangerous when you did that. And brilliant.'

Brilliant, she heard, and a part of her knew that he was right – that night she had been brilliant. She was frightened suddenly, that this stranger should know her so well.

He did something then she had not expected. He reached his hand across the table and touched her arm.

'Let's move,' a male voice called.

The moment was over, the spell broken. Tom's hand was by his side and he was already slowly beginning to rise. 'We'll have to continue this later,' he said.

'Yes,' Laura said. 'We will.'

Stretching her arms up high and wide, she sloughed off some of her body's accumulated tension. 'OK,' she heard the first A.D. saying. 'That's a wrap. A good day's work, everybody. Thank you.' Grinning, she began to gather belongings up.

'Wonderful, darling,' the director whispered in her ear and then, muttering something about rushes and producer's meetings, hurried off.

She was ready and sauntering towards the exit, slowing down when she saw Tom waiting for her there. He smiled. 'A drink?'

No, she nearly said, although she knew no reason why she should say no and knew also that what she wanted to say was yes. 'Well . . .' she began.

'Give my regards to Steven,' someone called out, shocking her. How could she have been so careless? Of course there was a reason why she must say no, a simple reason – she'd arranged to meet Steven. She glanced quickly at her watch. Six-thirty. He would be waiting for her. 'I'm afraid I'm due elsewhere,' she said.

Tom's answering smile was so nonchalant that she told herself her anticipation was entirely of her own making. Except: 'Another time?' he said, forming it into a tentative question.

'Yes, I . . .' she began, but seeing that he had already detached himself and was about to move off, she shut her mouth.

'Well,' he said shrugging.

'Well.' Smiling, she mirrored his shrug and then she walked away.

She spent the short journey to the pub berating herself for an infatuation which, now that she was away from it, seemed like just another commonplace film-set fantasy. It's over, she sternly told herself, completely over. She walked into the pub.

But seeing Steven, she knew it wasn't over. It was the second time in almost as many days that she had watched him unobserved and the very thing that had made her feel her love before was now a cause of irritation. It was a small thing – merely that he was sitting alone, quietly, unbothered by her lateness. He's so stolid, so sure of himself, she thought contemptuously as a memory of the touch of Tom's ethereal hand flickered and began to flame.

She shook herself. Stop it, she told herself as she walked closer.

He looked up, straight at her, smiled, and gestured to a glass: whisky. He had got her one already, the malt she particularly enjoyed. It was just like Steven, so considerate – and yet she frowned, thinking that his foresight prevented her from drinking something other.

'Bad day?'

Bad day – what could he mean?

Oh yes, of course, he must have caught her frown. She shook her head, squeezed out a smile, sat down beside him, sipped her drink. And then, as the alcohol slid down her throat, her hostility faded. I love Steven, she thought, not Tom, and she put her hand over his, feeling its familiarity, its strength and elegance combined.

He smiled. 'Got any ideas for this evening?'

She shrugged, thinking it was his familiarity and his thoughtfulness that made her love him.

'A meal?'

No, she shook her head, she wasn't hungry and besides there was something else she suddenly felt like doing. 'Let's drop in on Leo and Margot,' she said.

He looked at her quizzically, but 'Good idea' was all he said.

'I always forget,' she heard him saying as he held the car door open for her, 'how close together our anniversaries are.'

'Whose?' she asked absently, bending down.

'Ours and your father's.'

She blinked, suddenly annoyed. No, she nearly snapped, that can't be – we're a long-established couple. But held her tongue for she realized that Steven was right – she had introduced Margot, Judith's aspiring biographer, to Leo in the same week that she had met Steven.

'Perhaps we should have a joint five-year bash,' he said as he shut the door. God forbid, she thought, but did not need to say it for he was walking round the car and when he finally was beside her she changed the subject.

CHAPTER FIVE

'Laura!' Leo's arms were open wide. 'How wonderful.' His embrace stretched wider. 'And Steven too – a double treat. Come in, come in, Margot will be pleased.' He fussed about them, ushering them inside. 'Margot,' he called as he stowed their coats away. 'Look who's here.'

They didn't have long to wait: the kitchen door opened and Margot appeared. For a moment, she stood motionless, framed against the light, her brown hair fluffed around her spherical face, her full red lips at rest. She's cross, Laura thought.

But Margot smiled. 'What a nice surprise,' she said, and began to walk, still smiling, towards them. As she came closer, her appearance was transformed: stationary, she had looked pretty but also pretty ordinary, but now that she was in motion she projected something extra, something that made one notice her.

And not just anything, thought Laura wryly, but rather a raw sensuality.

'We were about to eat,' Margot said. 'Do come and join us.'

Eat. Although Margot had spoken cheerfully, Laura was embarrassed. Of course Margot and Leo would be eating: it was unthinking of her to have insisted on dropping in at suppertime. She took a step backwards. 'We didn't mean to gatecrash your meal,' she said.

'Nonsense,' Margot said. 'It's only pasta. It can be easily stretched.' She plucked the bunch of flowers from Laura's hand. 'How gorgeous,' she said and, turning, led them all into the kitchen.

*

Margot was a proficient cook and 'only pasta' meant fresh, home-rolled tortellini, a rich, garlic-infused tomato sauce and a large salad dotted with home-made croutons. In no time at all two extra places were laid and the meal summoned up in front of them.

'Come,' Margot said, 'don't let it get cold.'

Laura smiled, wondering why, in the face of Margot's generosity, she was feeling so uneasy.

She lifted some tortellini up and, as she put it in her mouth, the answer came: I'm tired, she thought, that's all. She began to chew, trying to push away fatigue by listening to the others, but as their conversation flowed across the large table, her mind started wandering.

Until: 'More?' she heard and, blinking, saw Margot looking at her. She shook her head and smiled and to show she meant it, put down her fork. Margot turned away. 'Steven?'

While Steven held out his plate for more, Laura gazed down at the table, thinking that it had stood in the kitchen for as long as she could remember. Idly she ran a finger along the oak, tracing out the grain. She felt it smooth against her fingertip, and she felt, too, the darkened knots of wood, centres of whirlpools which had no pull.

This table: it had once been the pivot of her home. Around it her parents had gathered with their friends, talking long into the night, eating at odd hours, their laughter ricocheting up the stairs. And, later, when all the guests were gone, Judith used to stand by the table, her brows knitted in fierce concentration as she moulded shapes which would eventually be cast in bronze and iron. Laura remembered it as clearly as if it were happening in the now: coming back from school and standing quietly by the door while her mother worked with an intensity that brooked no interruption.

I wanted so much to stand next to her, Laura suddenly thought. She shivered. And heard a voice: Margot's voice. 'Laura,' Margot said sharply.

Laura started. 'I'm sorry – I was lost in thought. What did you say?'

Margot smiled. 'I said that the anniversary is coming up.'

Anniversary? Laura thought and, remembering what Steven had said before, thought, Not Margot as well?

But no: 'Judith's anniversary,' Margot said.

Judith's? Surely Judith's birthday has already gone? Laura frowned, looked round the table, saw the others waiting expectantly for her. Her mind meshed into gear: anniversary – of course what Margot was referring to was not the anniversary of Judith's birth but rather the anniversary of her death.

It was. 'It will be twenty-five years,' Margot said.

Will it? Laura nearly asked, but bit the question back. If Margot said so it must be true, for on the subject of Judith and the events in Judith's life, Margot, who had started on Judith's biography, was always right.

And anyway, Laura thought, the anniversary must of course be the reason why a major retrospective had been planned. How absent-minded of her not to have realized!

'I thought it might be nice to celebrate the occasion,' she heard Margot saying.

'Celebrate?' Laura asked, more curtly than she'd intended. She saw Leo looking at her, bewildered, and she told herself to tone it down. She didn't manage to. 'Why on earth would we celebrate a death?' she said, sounding just as angry.

Margot blushed. 'What I really meant,' she said, 'was it might be nice to commemorate Judith.'

Nice, Laura thought, thinking that it might be anything but nice.

But Margot was talking, faster now, one word clambering over the next. 'Of course there's the exhibition and the fact that Judith's reputation has never been higher,' she was saying, 'but I thought those who were close to her could come together and remember, not the artist, but the woman.'

Close to her. Laura thought that Margot, who had never even met Judith, had no right to talk about closeness. And anyway, she thought, it's such a mad idea – a party on the anniversary of a death! Twenty-five years – a kind of silver dying anniversary. It was ridiculous. She looked across the table. Surely Leo would say no?

He was still looking at her but now she saw that he was nodding. She frowned. 'Do you think it's a good idea?' she asked, her voice rising at the end, in disbelief.

He shrugged. 'It is fine by me,' he said. 'But it is entirely up to you. If you do not wish the event, then so be it.'

'But Leo . . .' Her voice was still too fractious; they were all looking, intently now, at her – Steven especially. She met his eyes but could not read his gaze, and that, in turn, disturbed her. All she knew was that nobody understood the vehemence of her reaction – not even herself – and that by flying off the handle she had destroyed what had been for the others an enjoyable evening.

'It is for you to decide,' she heard Leo telling her.

She nodded, thinking sadly that once he would have put it differently – for once they had decided all such things together. But then, she thought, those times have changed: I've left home, and Leo has remarried. Perhaps, she thought, that's why she'd got so cross, because she was jealous of Margot.

She smiled – how absurd – but found her smile fading. For the truth was that something precious, something she and Leo had shared, had been lost, and the fact that such a loss was inevitable, and part of life, didn't make it easier to take.

'Laura?' she heard: Margot nervously prompting her.

She was no longer sure how she should react. She chose to buy time. 'Can I think about it?'

'Of course.' Margot smiled. 'We have a few months anyway in which to decide.'

That was it – end of conversation. They changed the subject smoothly, talking of architecture and of Steven's latest building, and of matters that might have interested her if she didn't feel so tired. For the second time that evening, she let their conversation waft over her, pushing it away. She sat silent for so long that she began to think she would actually fall asleep. I'll go wash my face, she thought, and, yawning, got up.

'Back in a moment,' she said and the others, absorbed in their conversation, nodded absently-minded in her direction. Oh well, she thought, and padding over to the kitchen door, walked through.

She shut the door and stood by it, her feet sinking into the lush, fawn carpet, breathing in the fragrance of a house that had once been hers. Once – long ago – and now it was transformed. She looked about seeing the unfamiliar hat stand, the freshly painted walls, the brightly coloured poster, and there, directly in front of her, another new addition – a pottery urn filled with a frenzy of purple and pink dried flowers.

'*Dried flowers!*' she heard Judith's voice exclaiming. '*If God had wanted dried flowers he would not have invented rain.*'

Laura smiled, thinking how, even after all this time, both Judith's voice and her remorseless honesty were still so potent. But potent for Laura, not Margot, for by the changes in the hall it was obvious that, four years into her marriage, Margot was chipping away at Judith's icy grip. Maybe that's what the anniversary is about, Laura thought: the laying to rest of Judith. And maybe, a small voice said, you should follow Margot's lead.

To bury Judith properly – it was tempting. Tempting and terrifying as well. She shook her head. She was tired: she would not think of it, not now. Water; she needed water to splash on her face. There was a bathroom down the hall – she could wash there. She walked towards it.

At the end of the hallway were two doors side by side, painted in soft blues and intertwining whites, two doors which both looked equal. But they weren't equal. One led to the bathroom, the other to an altogether different kind of place. It beckoned to her, that place. I don't really need water, she thought, and put her hand on the other doorknob, turning it, half hoping that it might be locked.

The room was slowly revealed. Unique, it was, a space in which heaven and earth had been joined. It was like magic, even to one who knew all its tricks. Standing on its threshold, Laura's eyes were drawn to the ceiling and to the vastness of the night sky. She knew that concealed cantilevers supported the dome and yet her heart did not believe it. It *was* magic, pure and simple. Seeing it, she felt momentarily euphoric, as if she could spread her arms and fly.

She dropped her arms, pinned them mentally to her side. Webs of glass had made this room but her mother had worked with stronger stuff, with stone, rock and marble. Judith's spirit filled this place with its uneasy presence. Judith's spirit, unchanged, defying human scale, convention and even nature. It was this legacy that made the room untameable.

Untameable. And yet it had been so long. So long.

Twenty-five years, she heard Margot saying.

She closed her eyes. She would not think of it, not here, not in this room. She walked quickly down the hall but hearing the rumble of conversation issuing from the kitchen she passed it by. She began climbing the stairs.

She was on the first-floor landing when she heard Margot calling: 'Laura.'

She twisted her head. 'I'll be down in a minute,' she shouted. She continued upwards.

She was in a room, looking at a portrait. Judith looked back, her eyes flashing green, her open smile framed by flowing black hair. It was a powerful picture. Laura wondered what Margot must feel, living under its influence.

Not living, she realized, but sleeping. This was Margot's bedroom, the one she shared with Leo. Laura shouldn't be there, not without an invitation. She should go.

She was rooted to the spot.

Of all the rooms in the house, this one had been the last to change, but it had changed the most. Here Margot had cast out Judith's shadow. It had once been completely white; white walls, white curtains, a snow-white carpet and a white bedspread: but now all that was gone. The room was now a riot of colour, the walls canary yellow, the sheets and duvet royal blue, toned exactly to the deep-pile carpet.

Laura blinked. A white bedspread, she thought, and something other. She blinked again, her eyes misted; she knew exactly what that something other was – a figure sprawled, a trailing arm, a face waxen against the white.

She shook herself and then, as if she knew what she was doing, she walked past the bed and built-in cupboards and into the adjoining bathroom. Over to the bathroom cabinet she went, and looked into the mirror. She saw her own face reflected there, her ageing face. She put her hand under her chin and pulled the skin, tightening it, grimacing at the years she'd just removed. She made a face before destroying her reflection by opening the glass doors of the bathroom cabinet and inspecting the neat array of bottles. She was quite methodical, she let her eyes range from left to right until they found their target. She picked up a small pill container.

'L. Weber,' its white label said. 'Take one at night when required.' L. Weber, she thought: it could be me.

She took the bottle from the shelf, unscrewed the cap, turned the bottle gently so that one pill dropped into the flat of her waiting hand. One baby blue pill, strong Valium. She closed her fist around it thinking how well it would fit in her collection, its blue laid beside the tiny yellow Lorazepam eggs or the bright red Seconal. Yes, it will fit nicely, she thought, amongst the others in their hiding place behind the books. Slipping the capsule into her pocket, she replaced the cap and bottle and carefully closed the mirrored door. Then she left the room and slowly went downstairs.

'More coffee?' Margot asked as Laura walked into the kitchen.

Laura smiled and shook her head no. 'I did make a decision though,' she said gaily. 'Two in fact.' She heard her voice, too shrill in the expectant silence, and she modulated it. 'First,' she said, 'I think Margot's idea for a commemoration is good. Let's do it.' *Let's do it*, she heard her own voice saying.

'And secondly?' Steven was staring at her.

'And secondly,' she said brightly, 'I'm going to do Hedda.'

It was only when she said the words out loud that she knew she meant them. Yes, she thought, I won't be frightened by any ghosts, and, hearing Leo's energetic congratulations and Margot's echo, thought again, I'll play Hedda.

She smiled and glanced at Steven. She saw his eyes on her, his expression unfathomable. She frowned. 'Steven?'

He looked away. 'It's time to go,' is all he said.

They were in the car and he was driving. She waited for him to speak but when he didn't she broke the silence. 'Did I do something wrong?'

They were nearing Tower Bridge and a muddle of road-works. Steven slowed the car, concentrating on joining the long tailback.

'Did I?'

The car stopped. He turned and looked at her. 'You're doing Hedda.' She nodded. 'I don't think it's a good idea,' he said.

His words served as a catalyst: she felt herself going rigid. 'Why on earth not?'

His voice, in contrast to hers, was calm: 'I've told you. I worry that you're too exhausted for such a demanding role,' and saying this took the sting from her reaction. She had no right to be angry. He loved her, this constant man, and he was thinking only of her.

Even so, he was wrong. 'I have to do it.'

'But why?' He had turned, taken his hands off the steering wheel and was facing her.

Until that moment she hadn't known the answer but in that moment it came to her. 'Because I'm scared,' she said.

'Scared? Of what?'

She looked away, out through the window, followed the path of a piece of paper as the wind scuttled it along a dirty pavement. The paper blew out of vision. She bit her lip.

'Tell me,' Steven said.

She squeezed her eyelids hard.

'Tell me.' His voice was louder.

She turned and looked at him. 'I'm not scared of Hedda,' she said haltingly. 'I'm scared of what playing her will do to me.'

'Then don't.' He smiled wryly. 'Listen to the slogan. Say No.'

She blinked. 'If I say no,' she said carefully, 'then I will have given in.'

'Given in!' His voice was mocking. 'That's a bit macho, isn't it?'

Macho? Perhaps it was. She lowered her head. 'I can't say no,' she said.

'Why?' He was impatient.

'I can't explain it,' she said, almost pleading. 'I can't explain it but I know one thing. I know that after the near débâcle on *Private Lives* if I now refuse to play Hedda I'll be opening the floodgates to my fear. It will be the end of me. I have to play her or she will defeat me.'

She felt the tears brimming. Swallowing hard she looked at Steven. And saw him smile, so gently. She watched the lines around his eyes crumpling and she wanted to reach out and touch his skin.

His arm embraced her. 'It's OK,' he whispered. 'It's OK.'

She was crying.

Behind them one car horn hooted, and then another and another, a wave of impatience pushing its way towards them, but Steven ignored it. 'You can say no,' he said. 'You're just tired. You need a break.'

He was trying to help but he was still wrong. She shook her head. 'I have to,' she said. 'Or else I'm finished.'

Summer

1954

As Max Cohen's coffin shuffled slowly across the rollers, his widow, Rachel, began to sob. She started softly enough but soon accelerated until, by the time the coffin had vanished behind the curtains, she was bawling out her grief. The congregation gave a collective nod. This was how it should be.

Except not all members of the Cohen family were acting as they should: Rachel's daughter Judith, tall in contrast to her mother's dumpiness, calm in contrast to her mother's explosion, stood rigid, her eyes fixed on the drooping black curtains. And, as those who knew each other in the congregation later agreed, it was even worse than that – her eyes were narrowed and a small, grim smile could be seen playing along her bruised red lips.

'He was a good man,' Rachel sobbed.

A good man, Judith heard and her eyes twitched; dry lashes touching lower lids before raising themselves to expose pupils as still and as hard as emeralds.

'Come.' A whisper from the left. Leo began to steer his mother-in-law down the aisle while Judith stood and watched the couple go. She saw them stepping past the rank of Max's friends (fellow dentists and their wives) and his few remaining relatives. Discomfort was at a premium; feet shuffled and eyes were focused downwards. Judith frowned: the ceremony was over and yet the others wouldn't move. It's almost, she thought, as if they are waiting for someone.

Oh yes, she understood: they were waiting for her. She must pass them also, must walk away from death and from the thing that had once been her father, must hold up her head and enter the bright summer sunshine.

She did that, trailing behind her stocky mother and her elegant husband. Bringing up the rear, she thought, like a bridesmaid.

With a photographer outside, as well. The sun had gone in but not the photographer's bulb. It flashed once and then ejected, landing with a chink on the gravel. As the photographer bent to retrieve his detritus, his partner pushed his way to Leo.

'Thompson, Daily Mail,' he said. 'Would you care to comment on the increase in military activity in Kenya?'

Leo scowled. 'This is a funeral.'

The journalist's smile was an insincere flashing of decayed yellow, accompanied by too much gum. 'You're a difficult man to contact,' he said.

Leo, normally so mild-mannered, clenched his fist and took a step towards the other man, almost as if he were about to hit him.

Of course he couldn't. Rachel was in the way, turning her head rapidly from one man to the other. 'What's this?' she muttered.

What's this? Those familiar words, those words she'd used when, opening the kitchen door, she had found her husband and her daughter locked in combat. *What's this – as if her ignorance could keep the nastiness from creeping past the doors in her Hampstead Garden Suburb home. She looked to her daughter. 'Judith,' she said plaintively.*

Sighing, Judith spoke above her mother's head. 'Give him a quote and get rid of him,' she told Leo.

Leo pulled the man aside. 'The Land Freedom Army –' Judith heard Leo saying.

'The Mau Mau you mean,' the journalist interrupted. 'The terr –'

But Leo kept on going. 'The Land Freedom Army,' he said firmly, 'is composed of peasants who were first driven off their land and who have now been driven underground.'

'So you support the terrorists then?'

'Today's terrorist,' Leo said loudly, 'is tomorrow's mediator. It is happening already. Kenyatta, the man you call a leader

into darkness, will soon become respectable. In the meantime thousands of poor people all over the colonial world . . .'

'Judith.' Her mother was tugging at her sleeve.

Her eyes were drawn downwards until she was staring at Rachel's moon face. Silence; and in that moment Judith thought, not for the first time, of how unfamiliar her mother was. Unfamiliar, and oh so different: they could be strangers. When Judith looked into the mirror she never saw Rachel's features. Instead what gazed back was the other – that dark, malevolent image of her father.

'He loved you, you know.'

She nearly laughed out loud. Max had never loved her. He had loved a fantasy, that was all, a fantasy of a compliant little girl. As soon as she was grown he had rejected her; rejected her just as he rejected everything which could not, like ageing molars, be pinned down and drilled by steel.

'He was happy you married Leo,' Rachel said.

This time the laugh could not be stanched. 'Happy!' It erupted to the surface, sounding like a cry. 'Happy! He hated the fact that I married out. And don't forget that Leo is German – Max would never forgive that. A man who cares more about the Schwartzen than the sins of his own relatives, that was what my darling father called Leo.'

She was talking loudly and, out of the corner of her eye, she saw the journalist looking inquisitively in her direction. She dropped her voice. 'Come on,' she said.

But Rachel stood her ground. 'That's what Max might have said,' she insisted, 'but that was not how he felt. Believe me. I knew. I knew what was in his heart.'

Judith, listening to her mother, felt the fight go out of her. That was how it had always been. Rachel relating what had happened, Rachel interpreting her Max to the world. That's how it had been and, now Max was dead, that's how it would still continue.

'He was a proud grandfather,' Rachel said. 'Thanks to God at least he lived long enough for that.'

A grandfather, Judith thought bitterly, who refused to see his granddaughter.

'And now he's dead,' Rachel said, and she began to sob, theatrically, almost choking on her sorrow.

Dead. It was over. At last, it was over.

'I must get Laura,' Judith muttered.

Laura, her daughter, the one who would not now be tainted by Max's savagery. She was standing, Judith saw, in the distance, clutching Heloise's hand. Now, as Judith walked towards her, Laura looked uncertainly up at Heloise.

A nod was all she needed and she released her hold. 'Mummy,' she shouted. She ran at Judith. 'Mummy.'

And Judith stooped low and waited, arms outstretched; waiting to receive her black-haired, green-eyed child in her embrace.

CHAPTER SIX

1992

There was neither bell nor knocker, so Laura pushed at the massive door. When it swung slowly open, she followed it in. She was plunged into darkness – momentarily blinded. She stood patiently until her eyes adjusted; what she saw was a line of boarded windows, a bleak corridor and a narrow flight of uncarpeted stairs. Welcome to the glamour of the theatre, she thought, and began to climb the stairs.

At the third floor was a door whose top half was wired glass. Like everything else in the building, it was covered by a layer of thick grime. Laura stood on tiptoes, peering inside. A familiar sight greeted her: a shabby space, dark green linoleum, sludge-green walls, a group of rickety chairs arranged in a circle and one other item – a samovar propped up in a corner. She smiled. It looked like an unimaginative set design – pre-Revolutionary Russia circa 1907 – but was in fact a cheap rehearsal space. Her smile widened. This was where actors did their real work.

Actors – she could see them, too, circulating amongst the bric-à-brac, their elaborate social dance getting under way. She was late and the usual rituals had already been activated – lips pecked cheerfully at cheeks, words bartered in exchange for smiles, one individual weaving past the next as each joined the process of merging with the team. It was all so reassuringly predictable that Laura did not need to hear the actual words to know that the conversation centred on what had happened when they had last met. The venues would be varied but also uniform: so and so's party, or their preview, so and so's funeral, 'how dreadful', or even such a room as this, a clone in which each past rehearsal could merge into the next.

All of this, a collective courtship, and Laura the missing link. She need only open the door and it would flare out and suck her up, its outer skin rapidly resealing.

Thinking this, her throat unexpectedly constricted. The decision to play Hedda was behind her but now she was on the threshold, she was infested anew by doubt. She clenched her jaw and her fists as well. Hedda. The role might be too much, it might prove her undoing. Perhaps Steven was right: perhaps she should have gone travelling.

She stood there silent, thinking longingly about what might have been; about white sands, calm blue seas, distant sounds. 'It's not too late,' she told herself. But it was too late. A figure had already separated itself from the eye of the storm and was crossing the room. Laura took a step backwards. Just in time: the door was flung open.

'Laura.' An ebullient voice, arms spread wide. 'Our Hedda.' The disembodied warmth of a tropical beach evaporated as Gareth's arms enfolded her. Her face rubbed up against his rough tartan shirt and when he kissed her, she felt his beard scratching her cheek. She felt this and something more important: she felt her misgivings retreat. This, she thought, as he twirled her round, this is where I belong.

'You're looking great, as usual,' Gareth boomed. 'Come – everybody's dying to say hello.' And with that he led her into the room, his prize, his lead whose fame had made the leasing of a large theatre possible. 'Our Hedda,' he said again.

What she had expected next came to pass: she was surrounded by her fellows, sucked into the centre of the group. But contrary to her imaginings, instead of being frightening, the sensation was only reassuring. 'Our Hedda,' Gareth had said, setting her – as the star – apart. Yet that was not what really mattered here – what mattered was that she had stepped across the invisible boundary and joined them. Maybe, she thought, as pale lips fluttered across her face and as another hand pressed into hers, maybe what Maya had said the previous week was right. Maybe actors were just grown-ups searching for a family.

'OK, kids.' Gareth clapped his hands. He was standing by the circle of chairs and, as the general conversation faltered, he pulled one from the outside. Taking it to the centre, he planted himself on it. 'If you'd all make yourselves comfortable,' he said, 'then we can begin.'

They read through the play getting its general shape. When that was over, Gareth, who for such a big man was surprisingly agile, jumped to his feet. 'Great,' he said, rolling the 'r' melodramatically. 'And now I suggest we spend some of our precious time outlining the play's central features. Any problems with that?' He moved his large head around the circle, making eye contact with each one of them. When nobody responded, his eyes came to rest on Laura. 'Since Hedda is the motor which drives our play,' he said, 'perhaps Laura would like to sum up the action?'

Laura frowned. Sum up? she thought. Surely that was the director's job? She looked away, buying time; looked at Peter, her husband in the play, and saw that, when their eyes met, he shook his head. Just once, that's all, but there was intensity in the gesture. Her frown deepened.

She had a moment's grace, for Gareth, who had intercepted the exchange, was looking sternly in Peter's direction. In that moment, as Gareth's moist brown eyes hardened, old rumours came bubbling into memory. Gareth's trick, she remembered someone telling her, was to manoeuvre his actors into saying what it was that he felt needed to be said. He had a reputation as something of a bully, who dealt with a new generation of assertive actors by bending to their demands – by bending, that is, but never breaking. 'Persuade him to come right out with it,' her adviser had told her. 'Saves a lot of time and heartache.'

So that's what Peter's gesture meant. She smiled and, seeing that Gareth, who had silently disposed of Peter, was looking at her, said sweetly, 'Why don't you do it?'

'Fair enough.' His expression, puppy-dog friendly, made her think she had misjudged him. And then he began and she stopped worrying about motive and tactic and listened carefully to what he had to say.

'Our play,' he said, so softly that Laura found herself straining forward, 'centres on one woman – on Hedda Gabler.' His voice was louder now. 'And who is she, this enigma?' he asked. 'Is she, as some would say, a woman who controls all events around her or' – he smiled and dropped his voice again – 'or is she its opposite – a woman caught in the midst of forces entirely beyond her control?' He paused, waiting for his question to sink in before beginning once again to speak. 'We will have to uncover our vision, our conception, of Hedda's culpability in her fate. But in the meantime, what do we know of her?'

His hand, formerly engaged in tugging at his beard, was lifted. 'One,' he said, holding up one broad digit, 'Hedda is twenty-nine years old, the hitherto indulged daughter of General Gabler who has died and left her penniless.'

A second finger joined the first. 'Two: Hedda has, as she herself puts it, "danced herself out". She is no longer young; she needs a husband. Before the play starts she marries Jörgen Tesman, a man who, although he professes to love her, can neither understand nor satisfy her.

'Three.' As his thumb anchored his little finger, the remaining three digits stood straight together. 'She has returned from a dreary honeymoon to start a life that she despises and, worst of all' – here Gareth nailed Laura with his eyes – 'she is pregnant. OK, OK,' he said quickly, 'before Laura interrupts, I know that this is a contentious point – Hedda's pregnancy is implied but never confirmed. We will discuss it later. But' – his expression was quite ferocious now – 'she is pregnant. I am convinced of that.'

His eyes skipped past Laura and began ranging round the circle. 'Four.' His little finger was released from bondage. 'Into this stifling world comes Ejlert Lövborg, a man for whom Hedda feels deeply. It is not clear what she feels for him – it could be either love or hate – but there is no doubt that passion is involved. And yet when Lövborg appears he is a changed man, transformed by Mrs Elvsted' – Gareth nodded here in the direction of Lynn who was playing Mrs Elvsted – 'a woman bound by convention, the kind of woman in fact that Hedda most despises. And yet it is Mrs Elvsted' – the thumb sprung up – 'who has tamed Hedda's wild immoral Lövborg.'

Gareth's eyes alighted on his hand and he frowned as if he

could not understand what it was doing in the air. He let it drop. 'Three other people share Hedda's short life on the stage,' he said, nodding at each as he pronounced their characters' names. 'Berte, the maid, who moves the action on; Juliane Tesman – Aunt Julle – a virtuous woman whose very presence drives Hedda to distraction; and Brack, the judge, a man who knows his Hedda and who is determined to possess her. In this company, and over a short space of time, we see Hedda railing against her fate; trying to change it by reinventing a Lövborg who better fits her own desires; and then, when all her attempts end in ignominy, shooting herself dead. That, in brief is our story.'

And that, thought Laura glumly, is why the part is so scary.

'Frightened?' Gareth said loudly. He smiled. 'No need to be. We have time: we will manage it. But first let us leave nineteenth-century Norway behind and join Britain circa 1992. Tea, I think?' And with that he left his place inside the circle and, marching over to Laura's side, held out his hands. When she put hers in them, as she was meant to do, he pulled her up. 'Come,' he said. 'You're shivering. Come and warm yourself in the sunlight.'

Five o'clock and Laura was on her way to her father's house. Over Primrose Hill she went, her stride long and loose, her thoughts nowhere in particular. Although that wasn't quite right, for if any emotion were dominant it was a feeling of satisfaction. Yes, that was it. A burdensome obstacle had been removed. She felt – and this was the only way she could explain it to herself – she felt free.

I've survived; but even as the thought occurred, she knew that it was wrong. She had gone one better than mere survival – she had actually enjoyed herself. One short day of rehearsal and it had returned to her, not only her love of the theatre but also confidence in herself. The premonition of impending doom, which had been with her for some months now, was gone. I can do it, she told herself, and, thinking those words, knew that she didn't mean only that she could do the work. Everything had changed, was simpler and so much clearer. She could do it, the work and the rest as well, could make a go of it with Steven, could understand that what had recently seemed like nagging was merely a sign of his love and his concern.

She had reached the crest of the hill and she stopped, looking out on a London which stretched far into the distance. It's like a model, she thought, a tourist London without traffic or bother, a London to feast the eyes on. Except it wasn't quite like that: the sky was clear, the air still and yet the outlines of the buildings were all slightly blurred, covered by an almost invisible sheen that was slowly turning red. Pollution, Laura knew, but despite that, it was pretty. She smiled, thinking once again that everything was now all right.

A hand was thrust into her field of vision. A hand, extended so hard that it had become a claw. It flashed through the air, past Laura's face and out of sight again.

'Hai!' a voice shouted. The arm that controlled the hand was next, striking through the air so fast that it summoned up a breeze. 'Hai!' Again that word.

Laura turned, watching as a foot was slowly, slowly lifted until it hung, suspended in mid air. Then down it suddenly went, a jerky stride completed. Another foot, the other one and then the hands again as the black-clad scarecrow figure moved, jerkily, away. 'Hai,' she shouted as she went, a woman whose bloodless face was concentrated on fighting phantoms that only she could see.

Laura walked in the opposite direction, making straight for Leo's. Arriving there, she pushed the bell. When there was no immediate response she turned away and looked, past the gathering traffic, towards the hill. What she saw was lush green, tinged now by the sun's slanting rays and as she looked at it her sense of goodwill returned. Freedom: it was catching and she wanted to grab it. She had a desire, suddenly, to go to it, to throw off her shoes and feel the grass against her skin, to encompass all that space and then embark on her own mad form of t'ai chi.

For a moment she was lost in this fantasy, forgetting where she stood. Not for long though. A cough, coming from behind, pulled her back into the present. She turned and saw Margot, dressed in a below-the-knee flowered skirt topped by a crisp white blouse, standing beaming in the doorway.

CHAPTER SEVEN

Standing by the large picture window in Margot's attic study, Laura gazed out at the garden. In the background she could hear Margot muttering. Laura was here to help her with the guest list for Judith's party but when, not even stopping for a drink, they'd climbed up to Margot's office, Margot found that she had mislaid her tentative list and had begun to search her desk.

Not that Laura had minded; she let herself relax as she gazed out, her eyes gradually drawn to the large ash which towered above the garden's end. It made her smile for that tree had once been her second home. And my first theatre, she thought, remembering the plays she'd dreamed up there, and performances she'd given, too – dangerous events, herself the star teetering on a makeshift stage, rough planks nailed to a few of the intersecting branches. Thinking of those days, her smile widened. It had been a special time, preserved intact in memory, a time of peace and tranquillity. She looked up, smiling, as a cloud passed in front of the setting sun.

A voice intruded. 'Where on earth is it?'

Laura wasn't sure what happened next. She turned, that much she knew, intent perhaps on helping Margot. But as she turned something unexpected happened; she saw a vision. It was drained of colour, in sepia almost and in shadow, the sight of a woman bent over a desk, rifling through an open drawer. A woman . . . The colour came flooding in, making the woman's long robe transparent, showing the outline of the woman's legs. And in the shimmering of that vision Laura's heart began to pound, her breath came fast, her legs were trembling.

'I'm sure it was here,' she heard.

She fought to regain control. It's only Margot, she told herself, and saw that of course it was only Margot scrabbling in a drawer. And yet despite the insistence of her rational mind, she could still feel the shuddering of her own anxiety, the vague sensation that the woman in the scene she had just witnessed was not really Margot. She shut her eyes.

'Here it is.' Opening her eyes, Laura saw Margot smiling, waving a single sheet. 'Leo helped of course,' Margot said, 'but I'm sure we've left some people out. Do feel free to add to it.'

Feel free. Anger, unreasonable anger, came flooding in. *Feel free* – as if Laura were the outsider. 'I will,' she snapped.

Margot's eyes twitched and her two front teeth snagged her pink lips. 'Well . . .' she began.

'It won't take me long,' Laura said, softening her tone.

'Of course.' Margot said. 'Make yourself comfortable. I'll just go and get something from downstairs.' Awkwardly she thrust the paper at Laura and then left.

Laura was coming down the stairs and rounding the final bend when she caught an unexpected glimpse of Margot. The sight was puzzling somehow – enough to make Laura pause. She looked more closely. Margot was standing by the open door, holding it with one hand, and the strangeness, Laura realized, was in the awkwardness of Margot's demeanour. Intrigued, Laura went a few steps closer.

She saw that Margot's arm was tensed and that Margot was leaning her weight against the door, trying to stop someone from pushing it open. Her interest intensified. She looked more carefully, straining to see who Margot was barring from the house. She could make out only the general outlines: a tall man whose grey hair was blanched against a flaming red sky-line and whose skin was closer to yellowing parchment than to either black or white.

'You must go.' Margot's voice was as brittle as slate.

Must go, Laura heard, and thought suddenly how strange it was that she had not heard the bell ringing.

'I cannot go,' the man said. There was something un-English in his pronunciation. 'You have to understand . . .'

'I mean it.' Margot's hand pushed against the door without avail; the man's foot was in the way.

Slowly, quietly Laura moved closer.

'You must believe me,' the man's voice floated up to Laura. A voice formal in contrast to Margot's hushed anger, in an accent alien in contrast to Margot's rounded English vowels. French, Laura thought suddenly, but not native French.

'You must go,' Margot was saying. 'He'll be back soon.'

He?

'He'll be furious,' Margot continued.

There was only one explanation of 'he': she must mean Leo.

'You have spoken to him?' This from the man.

A toss of Margot's head, a gesture that could be either yes or no.

'You promised that you would.' The voice was almost hissing and there was a strange quality about it, a combination of seduction and of threat. Is it possible, Laura thought, that he and Margot are having an affair? But no – she shook her head – no, surely not, not with this man.

However: 'I was wrong to trust you,' she heard Margot saying, louder now, and more hysterical, while the man's reply was prompt and self-assured: 'As we have discovered, we have much in common, you and I.' He dropped his voice and said something other, something that Laura could not hear.

She was hooked, she must hear more. She took another step. Too loud. They both heard her, she could see it in the way Margot's hand tightened and the way the man's head loomed momentarily into view. Margot was quicker than he: she used the moment of surprise to push his foot away. 'Goodbye,' she said and closed the door.

But she did not turn. She closed the door and stood there, her hand still on the lock, her head hanging down. Laura paused, holding her breath. What she saw was unexpected: Margot swooning forward, clutching at the door-handle for support.

'Margot?' Laura walked fast towards her.

Margot's recovery was impressive. Laura got one glimpse of an ashen face before Margot pulled herself together. Her cheeks went red, two bright red spots which then diffused, turning to a general pink. And then Margot was also in motion, making straight for Laura.

'A salesman,' she said. She giggled. 'That's the trouble with writing at home,' she stuttered, 'they're always ringing on the bell.'

Except, Laura thought, this one did not.

'Some of them are very insistent,' Margot continued.

Especially if you keep them waiting in the kitchen so long, Laura nearly said, knowing it was the truth, knowing that Margot had been with the man when she'd arrived and that this explained Margot's failure to offer her a drink.

'How was it?' she heard.

She blinked. 'It?'

'The list.' Margot had progressed on to patient smiling, as if Laura were being slow.

'Oh. The list.' Laura blinked again. 'Fine,' she said. 'Not one omission.' She paused, and then: 'I crossed some names out,' she said. She was looking closely at Margot. She saw Margot's face darken.

Or thought that's what she saw. But when Margot spoke her voice was even, her expression composed. 'Good.' She nodded. 'I'll send the others off then.' She was herself, truly herself, efficient and unbothered by the encounter on the doorstep. Except as Laura watched Margot swallowed, her face suddenly serious, and then she opened her mouth. 'Don't . . .' she began.

Tell Leo, that's what she was about to say: Don't tell Leo.

'. . . worry about the arrangements,' is what Margot actually said. 'I have them all under control.'

CHAPTER EIGHT

Four hours later the scene on Margot's doorstep had lost its sting, but then four hours later Laura was surrounded by friends. She was at Maya's, dressed in low-cut black, a polished silver necklace glistening on her neck, flashes of silver glimmering through her hair. The debris of one of Maya's exotic meals had been cleared away, only coffee and cognac remaining.

There was laughter in the air. The conversation had veered on to tales of the casting couch after one of the guests was foolish enough to assert that such barbarity no longer existed. He was showered by anecdotal denials and, as the cognac did the rounds, the stories grew increasingly wild. Eventually Maya picked up the thread of the conversation and ran with it, leading them through a set of labyrinthian stories featuring Laura, ending finally in one Gothic description of Laura stealing the shoes and the trousers from a certain, and infamous, producer, before locking him in the bathroom. She was a skilled storyteller and had her guests in stitches.

'I don't believe it,' a man to Maya's left was saying, clutching his stomach in mirth.

With a straight face Maya turned to Laura. 'It's true isn't it?'

'Of course not,' Laura laughingly protested. 'Of course it isn't true.'

'It is, I promise you.' Tossing her head, Maya appealed to the other guests. 'She likes to pretend she's angelic, but I ask you: is she?'

And got the answer she expected. 'No.'

Laura, mock innocent, held her hands palm up. 'All right,

all right,' over gales of laughter which were gradually dying down, 'so it is partially true: I did lock him in the bathroom.'

'You see!'

'But it's not true that I took his shoes –'

'His trousers,' Maya interrupted. 'His trousers – that's the point.'

Laura grimaced. 'It isn't true that I took his shoes and his trousers with me. I left them there.' She smiled, dipped her head in Maya's direction. 'Satisfied?'

Jumping to her feet, Maya waggled a reproving finger in Laura's direction. 'That's sneaky. What Laura's not telling you,' she told the others, 'is that when she says she left his trousers she means that she left them on the window ledge. And' – Maya's voice rose above the sound of laughter – 'she locked the window – it was that kind of hotel – and took the key with her.' Back to Laura Maya whirled, her face and posture both schoolmistress stern. 'That's how it was, wasn't it? Come on, admit it.'

Laura shrugged. 'OK.' She shrugged again. 'But he did say he wanted to get naked.' And then, with laughter almost hysterical, she pulled another face and said: 'I was only trying to be obliging.'

With the punchline, the end of Laura and Maya's double act, the laughter ran out of control. Almost the whole group was possessed, laughing helplessly, clutching at their stomachs, while Laura sat and watched them and, smiling, thought how very lucky she was. This was her circle, her closest friends, and here she could relax and here all her dreary suspicions, her imagined conspiracies, even the specifics – her fears about what Margot was up to – here they were all cut down to size. It wasn't the wine speaking (she'd hardly had any), it was something else – a feeling of belonging, an escape from the world outside.

'. . . the other room?' she heard.

She looked up, startled, saw that the others had risen and were being ushered by Maya into the living room. I'll join them, she thought, and rose. She bumped straight into Steven who had walked round the table and whose hand was stretched out as if he were about to touch her. She smiled quizzically at him.

'I saw you lost in thought,' he said. 'All right?'

She nodded. Of course she was all right.

'Actually,' he said softly, his lips level with her ear, 'you looked so gorgeous that I had to come and tell you,' He moved his lips, and his tongue grazed her ear, flicking quickly within. She shivered. 'Let's go home,' he whispered, his arms around her waist.

'Mmm.' She snuggled closer, placing her hands on top of his.

'We could sneak out now,' he said.

But Maya was upon them. 'Come on, you two lovebirds,' she said. 'Come into the light where we can see what you're doing.'

They lay side by side, she and Steven, looking into each other's eyes, although that wasn't entirely correct – to look into another's eyes implies separating whereas Laura felt as if she and Steven were joined together. Her limbs were heavy, sated, sinking into the mattress; his arm was touching hers or else she was still partially lying on him, she wasn't sure which. She didn't care; she lay there, hearing her breath sluggish, feeling a smile playing on swollen lips, feeling herself at one with him. She lay there thinking idly that all of Steven's many accomplishments paled in comparison with the way he made love. Made love – that's what he truly did, he gave love with his hands, with his penis, with his entire body and with a generosity which seemed limitless. In bed he expressed a side of himself, the wild, unrestrained, emotional face of a man which was hidden again once his clothes were on. She sighed.

And heard his breath sounding a response and felt him moving. She blinked, saw his brown irises as separate now, saw his cheek muscles moving as if he were about to speak. She shook her head, slowly, slothfully, and touched his lips with hers, silencing him. And then, in that position, her skin sticky against his, her hair damp, trailing the pillow, she sank into a dreamless sleep.

'A penny for them.'

Startled, Laura looked up. Steven, she saw, had woken and was already out of bed. He smiled. 'So what were you thinking?'

'Let's see,' she said. She yawned and stretched and then shrugged. 'It's gone,' she said, yawning again. 'I was in a daze.'

'I'm not surprised.' Steven's eyes flicked over to the clock. 'Bit early for you, isn't it?'

'What do you mean?' she asked, feigning indignation. 'You know me – up with the lark.'

Steven grinned. 'Some lark.'

She turned her hands into playful fists and, standing up, jabbed one at him. 'Are you casting aspersions on my time-keeping?' she asked as, fists still at the ready, she began to dance lightly round him.

'Would I?' He had been smiling but as she jabbed again, he grabbed her. Immobilizing her hands, he slipped one arm round her waist and, drawing her to him, kissed her on the lips.

'Mmm.' She pulled a hand free and hooked it round his neck, drawing him closer. 'Mmm,' she said again and a distant echo of what had happened the night before engulfed her. And him as well, she guessed, for she felt his arm tightening, his body coming closer and through his dressing gown she could feel his swelling penis. For a moment she thought that he was going to lead her back to bed and in that moment she would have willingly complied.

Except he didn't do it. What he did instead was gently disentangle himself and, smiling, using the back of his hand to wipe his brow mockingly, say, 'Coffee?'

'Coffee. That's a new one!'

'Well, in that case . . .' He moved closer.

'No.' She dodged out of his way. 'I'd love some coffee. I'll take a quick shower and come out for it.'

His eyes twinkled. 'Promises, promises.'

'The coffee, I mean.' She turned and began to walk away.

She was already by the bathroom door when she heard him speak. 'Wasn't that lovely?' he said. His voice was soft. She stopped and, although she did not turn to face him, she nodded. He didn't, couldn't, leave it there. 'Wouldn't it be nice . . .' she heard him saying.

She willed him to change course.

Without success. He finished the sentence, just as she had expected. '. . . if it could be like this every morning.'

She turned and looked at him, saw him standing a long way away, their feet separated by an expanse of burnished wood. She looked at him but did not speak any of the sentences that sprang unbidden to her lips – the ones he had heard so many times before. Like: 'I'm not made to live with anybody,' and, 'It's going so well, let's not push it,' and the angry ones as well, like the one she had last used, the: 'I told you the limits of what I could offer when we first met and you agreed – you said it was what you wanted too.'

She said none of things because if she did, she knew exactly how he would reply, knew that he'd accuse her of being scared, of being unable to be close, and would sum up by saying that she was destroying their relationship.

'Laura?'

She wrinkled up her nose. 'Go on, darling,' she coaxed, 'make the coffee.'

He tried to follow her lead. He wriggled his eyebrows, Groucho Marx-like. 'In exchange for what?' he challenged.

'In exchange for my scintillating conversation,' she said and when his eyebrows continued to move upwards she added quickly, 'All right: in exchange for my adorable and, let's face it, rather rare morning appearance at the kitchen table.' She turned away.

Too late, however, to miss seeing the disappointment and sadness on his face. She steeled herself against it. It's not my fault, she told herself, and, opening the bathroom door, beat a rapid retreat.

Under the shower she went, closing her eyes, feeling the water washing over her. Over her body only – it could not wash away her thoughts of the memory of Steven's expression. She turned, tilted up her head but the image followed her, and with it came a sudden uneasy feeling that he might be right, that if she did not commit herself to him, then she would lose him. She dropped her head. Lose him as she had lost everybody else; as she had lost Judith and Leo as well.

Lost Leo. She had never thought of it this way but it was true. For what she'd once had with Leo, a closeness that matched no other, was now gone. And the reason for this? Well, that too was obvious. She had lost Leo because of

Margot. She could trace back the progress of the loss: it hadn't happened immediately, not in that first year when Leo was still trying to adjust to living with another, but now, three years on, Laura could clearly see that it was to Margot that Leo turned, and on Margot alone that Leo spent his love. She nodded, thinking as she had done sitting at Leo's table that the loss was weighing on her, a lump of unacknowledged sorrow which she carried with her always.

Not that Margot was at fault. It was Leo and his work which took so much out of him that he had little time to spend on any relationship. What he had he naturally gave to Margot – after all, she was his wife.

Except, Laura thought, frowning as she remembered the man on Margot's doorstep, if Margot is betraying Leo's love . . .

At that moment she heard Steven's voice sounding over the gushing water. 'Coffee.' She licked her lips. Pushing her thoughts away, she turned off the shower and, wrapping a towel around her, went into the kitchen.

Once at the table, she worked overtime, chatting pleasantly of things (other of course than her and Steven) which might interest him. And found that, despite herself, she was suddenly engaged. She had started to talk of Hedda and had been taken by an idea which made fresh sense. 'Do you think that Hedda is so convinced she's on the brink of catastrophe that she plunges herself into it in order to get it over with?' She frowned. 'That's not tautological is it?' she asked.

But playing with motivation – either fictional or real – was not something Steven had ever found easy. 'I don't . . .' he began.

'Doesn't matter,' she cut him off, smiling to show that it really didn't. And in that silence, gave him his opportunity.

'It's not as if I'm suggesting marriage,' he said.

She bit her lip.

'All I'm asking' – each word issued slowly from his mouth – 'is a little more commitment.' His face was impassive but his eyes were sad. 'It's been a long time,' he said.

Five years, she nearly said; not that long. But she didn't because she didn't want to hurt him.

If only he knew how much she wanted to say those simple words that would soothe him. But the words – they would not come, they were stuck deep inside her throat. If only she could have said them, if only she could have told him that she loved him as much as he loved her and that not living together was more to do with her own craziness than with reality. But no; she couldn't say that, because she wasn't sure that it was true. So all she did was nod and, 'I'll think about it,' is all she could bring herself to say.

He dipped his head gravely and got up. 'I'd best be going to work,' he said. He rose and turned away.

She was on her feet as well. 'Steven.' When he turned she saw how his jaw had tightened. 'Steven,' she said again and, running up to him, she stood on tiptoes and searched out his lips. 'I do love you,' she murmured, wondering again whether it was true, and then kissing him hard, kissing away her doubts equally with his, feeling him kiss her back as between them was formed a kind of passion, bittersweet in its intensity.

CHAPTER NINE

Get back, Laura silently told the yawn.

'Of course Hedda's fascinating,' Gareth was saying, 'but we should focus on her symbolic rather than her individual value. She represents . . .'

The yawn came surging out, a mother of a yawn. Gareth was appalled. He turned and glared at her but the yawn was stronger even than he, leapfrogging to Laura's neighbour and on again, moving around the circle from one mouth to the next. Successive hands fluttered up while Gareth waited, his feet transfixed, his eyes, surprisingly small in such a large head, tracing the yawn's progress. So long did it continue that Laura found herself giggling.

She was rewarded by a second angry glare. 'Something amuses you.' A statement, not a question.

She swallowed and, concentrating her vision on the scratched green linoleum, heard a chair scraping against it.

'Come.' Gareth was in front of her, one reddened hand extended. She hesitated. 'Come.' He beckoned impatiently with the hand. She got up. His hand grabbed hers. 'If you'd move the chairs back to the wall,' he told the others, while holding on to Laura.

She felt his grip tightening and, looking down, saw the pattern of his skin against hers and saw as well how his fingers were covered in fine black hairs. She breathed in deeply, tugged at her hand.

And easily released it. He didn't even notice, she thought: thinking that her revulsion stemmed from unfounded paranoia.

'Act Three,' Gareth said. 'After a long, wild night.'

Act Three? she thought.

'Hedda has sent her ex-lover off with her husband,' Gareth continued, 'telling him to come back covered in glory – in her words, with vineleaves in his hair.'

What was this? Plot workshops for beginners?

'She and Mrs Elvsted wait for their men to return . . .'

The others members of the cast had piled their chairs against the wall and were standing in a circle, listening.

'Morning has arrived and the maid appears . . .'

I can't believe this, Laura thought. He spent three hours lecturing us and now he's going to continue with us standing? She took a step forward.

And found that it was worse than that.

'Laura' – Gareth was smiling – 'has as usual anticipated me. If the rest of you could get your scripts we can begin. Don't bother about blocking, or anything like that. Just concentrate on the feelings behind the words.'

He's expecting us to do Act Three, Laura thought. 'Gareth?'

'Yes?' His face was bland. 'Yes, Laura?'

What if she were wrong? She hesitated, doing a quick mental calculation.

'You have a problem?'

She made her mind up. 'No,' she said airily. 'No problem.'

Act Three, when Hedda sows the seeds of Lövborg's destruction and of her own as well, is perhaps the hardest act of all – especially taken out of context – but although fear rose to Laura's gullet, she batted it away. Focusing her energy inwardly, she lay down on a set of chairs that had been lined up to make a couch, closed her eyes and waited.

She did not have long to wait. Hearing the maid's final line, she sat up, eyes open. 'What's that?' she, as Hedda, said.

And took off from that moment. As Hedda she continued; as Hedda spinning in ever-decreasing circles while one piece of disconcerting news was piled upon the next. She, Laura, was completely in control and yet the magic which issued from Hedda's mouth was not pre-planned. It was almost as if she were possessed; her performance so alive that the others were carried along on the crest of her special wave.

A wave which finally broke when as Hedda she burned her ex-lover's manuscript. 'I'm burning it –' she said in a low voice, 'burning your child.' She closed her eyes. Act Three was over.

Silence. Silence broken only by the sound of her faltering breath. It's like the last time when I saw Judith, she vaguely thought.

No. It could not be. The room sprang sharply back into focus.

'Good . . .' Gareth's voice intruded.

Good God? Or just good?

'Laura.' He was right next to her and he wrapped his arms around her waist, looking straight into her eyes. 'I'm speechless,' he said.

Speechless. Praise indeed from Gareth, although she thought she saw something uneasy lurking in his expression. 'That's not like you,' she said, smiling.

His face darkened. His hostility is real, she thought. He challenged me and when I rose to the challenge he didn't like it.

'And now . . .' Gareth said.

'Gareth.'

Gareth. They all heard it and looked together towards the door, to where a man, all six foot two of him, was standing. It was Tom Hooper, smiling expansively.

Laura's stomach lurched.

'Tom.' Gareth was in rapid motion. 'Good to see you.'

Meeting in the middle, the two shook hands. 'Likewise, Gareth.' Tom's powerful voice reverberated across the empty space. 'I haven't called at a bad time, have I?'

'Not at all.' Gareth shrugged while Laura, watching, thought that beside Tom Gareth looked shrunken.

And not only Gareth – Tom would have had the same effect on Steven. She remembered how several months ago, when she had last seen Tom, he had almost made her forget Steven. She shook her head. Stop it, she told herself. And found that she had lost touch with what was happening in the room. Both men were staring at her. 'I take it that's a yes?' she heard Tom asking.

A yes? To what? She grimaced apologetically.

'Lunch,' Tom said patiently. 'To discuss the cameo.'

Lunch, Laura thought, licking her lips. Yes, lunch would be good, but what cameo?

'Don't say you've forgotten.' Tom was smiling fondly as if forgetting was something she regularly did. He turned to Gareth. 'See what happens,' he shrugged 'out of sight, out of mind.'

'Surely not you, Tom,' Gareth said, his voice, in contrast to Tom's, uncharacteristically lightweight.

'So you won't mind if I whisk your leading lady off for a quick bite of lunch?'

'Of course not.' With one cursory nod, Gareth dismissed Laura as if she were irrelevant, his pawn perhaps, which he had handed on to Tom!

Typical men, she thought, but was distracted suddenly when she heard a muttering coming from behind. 'Bloody star,' was what she thought she heard, and then a muttered: 'Thinks she can waltz off whenever she wants,' but before she could find out who had spoken she felt Tom's arm touching her on the shoulder. Her resistance collapsed; she let him guide her across the room.

'What cameo?' she asked when they were safely out of earshot.

He shrugged. 'First thing that came into my head. You don't mind, do you?'

No, she thought, I don't mind. 'I'm starving,' she said and glancing at her watch saw it was already two o'clock. 'It's late,' she said, surprised, 'how did you know we wouldn't have eaten?'

Tom smiled. 'Gareth's predictable,' he said.

'You've worked with him?'

'I've had that pleasure,' delivered in a voice that brooked no further inquisition.

As they rounded the corner, she framed another question but he got in before her. 'How does Monsieur Patrice sound?' he asked.

*

Monsieur Patrice sounded initially flustered but quickly recovered. 'For Monsieur Hooper,' he said, 'anything is possible,' and Laura, watching, felt momentarily put out. Who is this Tom, she thought, who can charm everyone?

'This way.' Monsieur Patrice showed them into a private booth.

'I'm impressed,' she said despite herself.

Tom smiled. 'I come here often.'

'With a different woman each time I bet,' she said, the words spilling accidentally out.

His eyes flashed. 'I don't like to dine alone,' he said briefly, and picked the menu up.

A spark had passed between them.

No, Laura thought, that was wrong. The spark had not been mutual. Tom had thrown it as a warning and in the moment of its impact she glimpsed another Tom. The power behind the casual exterior, that's what she'd seen.

'Should I order? I know the menu well.' His voice was light.

She nodded.

'OK?' Tom asked after the waiter had delivered their food and gone.

She smiled. 'Perfect,' she said, and it was the truth – he'd ordered as if he could read her mind.

He began to speak: of mutual friends, of plays and of the business, and as she joined in she found her distrust waning. He led her easily from one topic to the next and she let him lead, laughing at his jokes, topping his anecdotes with her own and, gradually, felt herself relaxing.

Until he unexpectedly changed course. 'Tell me,' he said. 'Do you like Hedda?'

She was thrown off balance. 'It's a good role,' she said, but seeing him frowning added: 'You don't think so?'

He shrugged. 'It's good enough.' His blue eyes were twinkling. 'If you go for victims.'

'Victims?' She looked at him.

Their eyes had locked. 'Hedda is so bitter,' he said, challenging her.

Challenging her. Well, she could rise to that! 'Hedda's bitterness is not of her own making,' she said. 'She's a victim only because she is a modern woman trapped in the wrong century. And like many of us she rails against her mundane life.'

'Mundane?' Tom raised one feathery eyebrow. 'Don't you mean ordinary?'

Laura shrugged. 'Mundane – ordinary – what's the difference? The point is that Hedda's too ambitious to settle for less than she deserves. She longs for an extraordinary passion and she is prepared to take risks for it. I admire her for that.'

She was almost in full flood but Tom deflated her. Gently he did it, laying his fork down, reaching across the white, white tablecloth. 'What about you, Laura Weber?' he asked.

His hand encompassed hers. She felt the warmth of it, starting on her skin and radiating outwards. She leant forward. 'What about me?' Her words, swaying as they were between timidity and courage, were quite distorted.

'Do you long for the extraordinary?'

'Are you offering it?' She looked and saw his lips stilled. She wanted to stretch out and touch those lips, to run her finger along them. She lifted her hand.

But at the last moment she stopped herself for she saw vividly, there in her mind's eye, Steven. Steven as he had been the night before, concentrating on her pleasure; and Steven, the way he'd looked when he'd left that morning, his gentle face up close as they had kissed. What the hell am I doing? she thought. Steven – he was her man.

'Dessert?' Tom asked.

When she said no he called the waiter anyway, ordering brandy for them both. And then, as they sat and sipped the brandy, his manner was perfectly casual and uninvolved. So uninvolved, in fact, that by the time he'd walked her back to the church hall, she had begun to believe that she'd imagined the potential in his touch and was surprised to find that she actually felt disappointed.

They stopped at the bottom of the stairs and he held out his hand. 'Nice lunch,' he said.

She hesitated, seeing his hand hovering. The disappointment welled. 'Yes,' she said. 'It was lovely.' She stood, abruptly, on her toes, and kissed him, just as abruptly, on the lips. He smiled.

She smiled back through the quickening of her pulse. 'I . . .' Words would not obey her summons.

'I'm in the phone book,' he said. 'Give me a ring if you're ever at a loose end.' He touched her lightly on the nose before turning and walking off.

'Good lunch?' She was late; the others had been waiting for her and on several faces disagreeable scowls were etched.

She glanced guiltily at her watch. 'Sorry.'

Gareth clapped his hands together. 'In the circle, please,' he said.

As they began to move, picking up chairs and putting them in places that had so quickly grown routine, Peter spoke into her ear. 'Maya phoned,' he whispered. 'She'll meet you in the class at six-thirty. No excuses.'

They were in the middle of a line of sweating, groaning women. 'I saw Claire Totley's piece in the Sundays.' Maya said. 'It wasn't bad.'

Laura threw her arms up following an elaborate pattern of eight while muttering an uninterested 'umph'. She breathed out and her arms dropped down, twisting in the wrong direction.

Maya, careless of the patterns made by others, merely kept on going. 'So how's the Welshman?'

'Who?' Laura asked, thinking that Tom surely wasn't Welsh.

'Gareth.'

'Oh. Gareth.' Laura grimaced. 'He's about as Welsh as an aubergine,' she said. Looking in the mirror, she matched her jerky movements to the line reflected there.

'And as attractive,' Maya said.

'Oh I don't know.' Laura had almost caught up but they'd changed the step. 'I've always thought aubergines were very attractive.' There – she was finally in sync.

'To the right,' the teacher yelled against the pounding rhythm. 'The right.'

Maya was one pulse behind the others. 'So where were you?' she asked shouting above the music.

'Where was I when?'

Maya's eyes flared. 'When I phoned.'

'Lunch.' Laura skipped two paces to the right.

'Lunch?' Maya shifted out of Laura's way. 'With who?'

'Can't talk,' Laura hissed. 'I'm concentrating.' She did eight star jumps and then, turning with the crowd, began to jog.

But she could not run away from Maya's persistence. 'Who did you lunch with?' Maya said later, when they were both lying on mats.

Laura heaved herself up. 'Tom Hooper.'

'Tom Hooper.' Maya was motionless on her mat, her frizzy red hair splayed around her. 'I see.' There was a pause and for one blissful moment Laura thought Maya had given up.

No such luck. 'You want to talk about it?' Maya's voice hissed in her ear.

Laura launched herself into a further set of push-ups. 'There is nothing to talk about,' she said between gritted teeth.

'I see.' Maya had turned on to one side and was supporting her head with her elbow, no longer even making a pretence at working out.

'Ladies.' The teacher was by Maya's side. 'Less chat. More sweat.' She bent down and nudging Maya on to her back held her feet. 'Raise your arms and twist,' she said. 'That's it, keep those feet firmly on the floor.'

'Oh shit,' Maya groaned as she saw Laura laughing at her. 'Whose stupid idea was this?'

'Actually,' Laura said when the class was over. 'There is something I want to ask you.'

'Tom?' Maya's face was beetroot-red, her hair fluffed out so far that it swamped her small features.

'No.' Laura nudged Maya with her elbow. 'Come on, this is serious.'

'Serious.' Maya pursed her lips together.

'I wanted to ask you' – Laura was talking quickly, too quickly – 'to come with me to Leo's. You know – I told you about it – the mad party Margot's organizing in memory of Judith.' She was gabbling, she knew she was, but she couldn't stop herself. 'It's going to be a trip down memory lane,' she said, 'and I don't think I can bear it without a friend. A current friend.'

'Of course.' Maya was no longer joking. 'Of course I will.'

1957

There was a tree on Primrose Hill, Laura's favourite. The big one, that's what she called it – she was too young to know its proper name. She had only ever seen it in the daylight, from the living room or when passing underneath. But now she saw that in the dark the tree had a special look, huge and brooding as it stretched into the black sky. She sat on the stairs concentrating her thoughts on it, floating between sleep and wakefulness, merging with the comings and goings, the tree her reference point.

'Darling.' Her mother's arms were flung high and wide. 'Darling. Come on in.'

Under the hall light Judith stood, her burnished hair flashing black against a tight, bright, blue-green dress, while her talking, laughing friends surrounded her, heaping her with gifts, watching as she shredded at the wrapping paper.

'You shouldn't,' she squealed as she unpacked a silver brooch, and then again, 'Darling, how wonderful,' as another treasure came spilling out, whilst all the time Laura sat watching, revelling in her mother's gaiety. Again the doorbell rang and Laura saw Judith admit the next group of admirers, replacements for those who had begun drifting into the crowded sitting room.

'What this?' Judith cried, as she pulled a small embroidered jacket from a box. 'Darling, you're brilliant.' She flung her arms around her friend and as she did so the present, a jacket, fell. Watching, Laura saw a hundred tiny mirrors flashing and she couldn't stop herself, she clapped, her two small hands banging together.

The noise seemed so very loud. She put her hand up to her mouth, waiting fearfully for discovery. But only one of them had heard her: her favourite – Uncle Bernard – and he looked up and, seeing her, winked. 'Let's join the others, shall we?' he said, ushering his troupe away.

She was safe. She knelt, her head against the wall, and closed her eyes, waiting for she knew not what.

What woke her was the sound of the front door softly closing. Peering down the stairs she saw a dark figure bending. Quietly it bent, and intently collected up the remnants of Judith's cast-off wrapping paper. That done, a man's back was straightened, a hand lifted a suitcase.

Daddy, it was her daddy.

At that moment he looked up, saw her sitting there and smiled – his daddy's smile, long and warm. And then he was beside her. He scooped her up. 'What are you doing up so late?' he whispered.

She nestled into him, breathing in a familiar fragrance which was mixed with something other: fatigue and something acid, almost sour it was. 'It's Mummy's birthday,' she said.

She thought she felt him stiffen but no, she must have been wrong for when she looked at him he was still smiling.

'She got a lot of presents,' she said.

'Did she?' She was deposited on the ground. 'Well, I have something here for you. It comes from the country I've just visited.' A rustle of paper and then he placed it in her hands, a small object wrapped in tissue, which she slowly and carefully unwrapped.

It was a bracelet; tiny, fragile, silver, and it fitted her wrist perfectly. 'It's beautiful,' she said, turning her hand, watching as it caught the light. 'It's mine,' she said.

'Of course it's yours.'

Of course it's yours. A voice, not Leo's, had spoken out, and a body, not Leo's, was standing by her. Her mother's voice, her mother's words.

'You're back,' her mother's voice continued.

Laura was on the floor amongst their legs, her mother's meshed in silk, her father's covered in brown flannel on which dark, dried mud had stuck. His legs bent forward and she heard him kissing Judith.

'You're late.' Judith's voice was dead pan.

'There was trouble.'

'How drearily predictable.' A hollow laugh. 'Trouble in Ethiopia again.'

'In the Sudan.' His voice was gentle – and something other. Was it possible, Laura thought, was her father scared?

'The Sudan, of course, forgive me.' Her voice was cool. 'Are you coming down? I . . . we . . . have guests.'

'I brought you something.' She could see his hand pulling an object from his pocket. 'Happy birthday,' he said.

Judith didn't throw the paper away – not this time – and neither did she shout in glee. She exhaled, once only.

And then her legs bent and she was kneeling beside Laura. 'Look,' she whispered. She turned it in her hand. 'Isn't it beautiful?'

Laura touched the small carved green tortoise, seeing how tiny was her own hand, soft in contrast to her mother's strong, weatherbeaten one. And feeling too the coolness of the tortoise's touch.

'It's jade,' her mother said, 'look.' And something else she whispered: 'He remembered,' is what it sounded like. But could that be it? Could that be what she said?

And then her mother straightened up. 'It's lovely,' she said, her voice full of warmth. 'Are you coming down?'

Laura found herself picked up, contained by her father's strong arms. He hadn't been scared, she thought: he was far too sure and far too strong. She had imagined it.

'I'll put Laura into bed,' she heard him saying. 'And then I'll join you all.'

'Do that.'

She heard her mother's heels tapping against the stairs. And as Leo began slowly to carry her back to bed, his cheek resting against hers, she heard Judith open the door and heard a voice call out to her.

'Of course I am,' Judith's loud voice wafted up. 'Especially now that Leo's back.' And then Judith began to laugh, and her laughter reached up, encircling both Laura and her father.

CHAPTER TEN

1992

She had parked outside Leo's house and was getting out of her car.

'Miss Weber?'

The voice, a grating uneasy voice, unnerved her. She turned – too fast. She hit her head against the door and dropped her keys. Stars gyrated and then a man's head swam into vision, blocking out the light.

'Miss Weber?'

His face came gradually into focus, a gaunt, lined, brownish-yellow face set uneasily on top of a scraggy neck. As for the man himself, he was tall and spindly, the dominant impression being fragility. Fragility, that is, mixed in equal measure with aggression. He was by the car, hemming her in.

She searched for and found her voice. 'You're in my way.'

'Of course.' He stepped awkwardly away.

She bent down, retrieving her keys.

'I must apologize,' he said, his voice foreign, formal and also vaguely familiar. 'I did not intend to frighten you.'

She blinked. 'I wasn't frightened,' she said, using the moment to lock the door. She walked to the pavement and he followed, limping. She frowned. 'Do I know you?'

He bobbed his head. 'We have not had the pleasure of a formal introduction,' he said as he used one light tan hand to smooth back grey hair. 'I am a friend of Leo Weber's. An old friend. If it is not too impolite, I would say that I knew of you as a child.'

She shrugged, pushing the suggestion of intimacy off. 'You're coming to the party?' she said, thinking that she must surely have seen his name on Margot's list.

'The party? That privilege has not, unfortunately, been reserved for me. But I know of it, of course: that is why I have been lying here in wait for you.'

In wait for you. The phrase repeated itself on her. She was suddenly afraid. She turned.

He moved to block her exit. 'Please, do not misunderstand me. I mean no harm. You must believe me.'

You must believe me. Where had she heard those words before?

'I have something of importance to impart.'

Oh yes. Now she remembered, not only the words but the colour of the man's skin. Of course she had seen him before: he was the man she'd spotted from the stairs, the man who had been hiding in the house when she had visited. 'You know Margot,' she said, thinking that now he was in front of her and she could see how frayed were his clothes, how calloused his skin, her suspicion that Margot might be having an affair with him seemed absurd.

Except his pale pink lips twitched. 'I am acquainted with your stepmother, yes. Leo Weber is a fortunate man to be intimate with two such lovely women.'

The smile: it was more threatening than amused. Laura looked fiercely at him. 'What do you want from me?'

Her anger threw him off balance. He took one step backwards, his face crumpling, each wrinkle imploding into the next. She saw him anew, not as a threat this time, but as somebody old and poor, his clothes threadbare – particularly in comparison to her party finery. He means no harm, she told herself.

His eyes narrowed. 'Perhaps you would profit by listening.'

No, she had not imagined it. His malice was genuine. Walk away, she told herself: Walk away. She did not walk away. 'What is it?'

The man frowned and, pulling absently at the sleeve of his crumpled brown suit, revealed frayed white cuffs. 'Something that concerns your father. And your mother.'

'My mother? You mean Margot?'

The man's eyes narrowed. 'She as well perhaps, but the lady I was referring to was your true mother: Judith Weber.'

'Judith?' She sounded dim but couldn't help that. 'What about her?'

But at that moment the man's watery brown eyes slid away. 'I will speak to you another time,' he muttered.

'Wait –'

'I must go.' He was already moving off, almost lurching in his effort to get away.

His limp was so pronounced it slowed him down. I can easily catch him up, she thought, and took one step forward. From behind her a voice called out. 'Laura,' it called.

No – she would not be stopped: she must reach the limping man.

'Laura.' The voice was louder now.

She knew that voice so well. She turned. 'Jack,' she said.

Jack Carmichael, who tended to move faster than lesser mortals, was already by her side. 'Long time no see,' he boomed, and putting his arms round her lifted her clear off the ground.

Her feet were dangling in the air. 'Jack!' She was laughing and struggling too.

He dumped her back on earth. 'You're looking great.'

She dipped her head, thinking in turn that although Jack, a huge man whose face was almost as red as his thick hair used to be, had aged, he still managed somehow to look invulnerable.

'Come on in,' he said.

He *is* invulnerable, she thought as he steered her towards the house, and impossible as well.

As well as being no mind reader. 'Don't let me go back to the States without your autograph,' he was saying. 'My kids, you know, the second set, ordered it. They're addicted to that weird English soap – what's it called?'

'*Accident Hill?*'

'*Accident Hill*. That's the one! If they miss an episode there's hell to pay.' Jack pressed the bell before turning to her. 'You're doing great,' he said. 'Your daddy's proud of you. Me too.'

'Thanks.' Laura smiled but then, looking beyond Jack, she saw in the distance the man who had accosted her. The man, she realized, who had run from Jack. Her smile faded. 'Do you know him?' she asked.

Jack frowned.

'Jack?'

He shrugged, his immense shoulders heaving. 'Know who?' he asked, and then as the door opened he stepped inside, pulling her after him.

'Leo,' he roared. 'Look who I found.'

The hallway was in chaos, every surface covered with racks of hangers, empty boxes, vases stuffed with overblown summer arrangements, plates stacked perilously high, gleaming glasses arrayed beside them. And there, in the midst of this, amongst the bustling caterers, stood Leo, staring helplessly at a tray.

Seeing Laura, he set the tray down. 'Hello, stranger,' he said, walking over and kissing her on the cheek.

'Doesn't Leo look great?' Jack boomed. But Laura, comparing Leo to Jack, thought what Leo looked was grey. Jack stretched across, jabbing Leo in the stomach. 'If I'm this fit when I'm this sonofabitch's age,' he said affectionately, 'I'll be a happy man.'

Laura nodded, thinking Jack was right: after all there was a good fifteen years between the two men; she should never have compared them. She felt herself relaxing.

'If you wouldn't mind!' A man juggling a stack of chairs was trying to manoeuvre past them.

A courteous Leo pulled Jack and Laura out of the man's way. 'Let us leave these kind people to finish their work,' he suggested, nudging them towards the stairs.

Laura was closest. She started to ascend, hearing Jack still in full flood: 'I guess it's all Margot's influence,' he said.

Margot! Laura stopped and turned to Leo. 'Where is Margot?' she asked.

Leo, standing at the bottom of the stairs, was in shadow but Laura thought she saw his face darken. 'She's getting ready,' is what Leo said.

He doesn't sound angry, Laura thought. She must have

imagined the darkening of his face. Of course Margot would be getting ready – making sure that, on this day of Judith's party, she sparkled.

'Let us go to my study,' Leo said.

In Leo's study Laura could smell the stale vestiges of Jack's cigars and sense something else as well – a hint of static, perhaps. She shrugged it off. Leo was busy with drinks so she sat down, choosing one corner of the massive brown sofa. Jack lowered himself into the other as Laura looked around, thinking how much she liked this room and also how its heavy leather and mahogany furniture, its long velvet drapes and fading family portraits perfectly expressed Leo's Germanic origins.

She glanced up. Leo was beside her, handing Jack a whisky. She shook her head when he, by gesture, suggested she also have one. As Leo went back to his desk, Jack lifted his glass, held it up to the light, twisted his wrist and then, throwing back his head, downed the drink in one. 'That's better,' he said, winking at Laura. 'Malt – Jack's patent remedy for jet lag.' He smiled. 'So how's the acting game?' he asked.

'Fine,' she said. 'And the poverty relief business?'

What happened next was unexpected. Jack shrugged and then, in a voice tinged with unfamiliar hostility, said: 'Ask Leo.'

Leo was in the process of sitting down. He stopped and frowned, his frown deepening until it became an angry glare.

Silence. Laura's eyes moved between the two, watching as they faced each other, these two old friends, locked in soundless combat.

Jack leaned forward. 'Leo,' he said, and it seemed to Laura that proud, sure, fierce Jack was pleading with her father.

But Leo merely shook his head.

Angering Jack. 'Can't you see?' He sat abruptly back, was almost growling. 'Can't you see that this is no longer personal? At stake are years of work and the reputation of others as well.'

'You are worried about yourself?'

Jack's face flushed scarlet. 'That's unfair.'

Leo stayed calm. 'Yes,' he agreed, 'it was unfair. But please, my friend, do not concern yourself with this. I agree it is unpleasant, but I remain confident in the good sense of our colleagues.'

'Confident!' Jack was on his feet, his fists clenched tight. 'May I remind you,' he was shouting, 'that it was your confidence in others which set this whole thing off?'

Leo blinked. 'A low blow, Jack,' he said, quite softly.

Another long-drawn-out silence, until finally Jack, nodding, sank back into the sofa. 'The trouble with you, Leo,' he said, sounding uncharacteristically subdued, 'is that you believe other people will comply with your high standards.' He shook his head sadly. 'And they won't. If nothing else, surely this whole episode has proved that?'

Jack's soft words had an effect that his bluster couldn't. The antagonism faded from Leo's face and he turned his eyes downwards, focusing on his hands. Hands which were whiter than Laura remembered; which, covered in liver spots, began toying with a small green object.

'Hasn't it proved that?' Jack insisted.

She recognized that object. It was Judith's jade tortoise.

'Perhaps it has,' Leo said.

The tortoise which she had almost forgotten, the one which, as a child, she had coveted and which first Judith and then Leo had promised would one day be hers.

'You have lost your fighting spirit, my friend,' she heard Jack saying.

She saw Leo's hands slackening, and watched the tortoise slipping from his grasp. He looked across at Jack. 'Do you blame me?' he asked.

'No.' The heat had gone from Jack's face, and the spirit as well. 'No, I suppose not,' Jack said, and Laura was overwhelmed by sadness and by confusion. She had no idea what was going on or why these two old friends seemed on the point of becoming enemies.

She never got the chance to find out, because at that moment the study door was opened.

'My darling,' she heard Leo saying.

My darling, over-emphasized, out of relief, perhaps, that the conversation had been ended.

Jack was on his feet. 'Margot!' he thundered. 'Great to see you.' And Laura, watching, saw Margot engulfed just as the doorbell rang.

CHAPTER ELEVEN

'It's like an animated *Who's Who*,' Maya whispered into Laura's ear: 'Conveniently indexed.'

Maya was right. Looking round the living room Laura saw it jam packed with celebrities segregated almost exclusively by profession. She did a more detailed survey; saw that in one corner a knot of theatre directors and actors were exchanging raucous gossip, while opposite a group of Judith's contemporaries, many of them now famous artists, were more seriously engaged in drinking. Between them floated people plucked from Leo's world, dark-suited, urbane people accustomed to wielding power.

'It's beginning to give me the creeps,' she heard Maya saying.

'Don't worry. One more round and they'll start mixing,' she said, and noticed that this was in fact already happening – that brave loners were making forays across unseen barriers, blurring the boundaries of each group. 'Bizarre,' she said.

'Which bit?'

'This whole event. Speeches and all. It's bizarre.'

'Good speeches though,' Steven said as he plucked two glasses of wine from a passing tray.

Yes, Laura thought, the speeches had been good. There had been no shortage of volunteers. One after the other they had taken centre stage to talk of the genius which, now apparent in her wildly successful retrospective, they had always known was there. Images were produced: Judith shrouded in plaster dust, her eyes sparkling as one light touch transformed a piece, her words flooding out as she talked of the art that was her passion. Almost everything was mentioned: Judith the artist and the friend, the hours she had spent helping others, her intolerance of the elite or pompous, her work, her ambitions, her family life. Everything, in fact, except her death.

'Here.' One of Steven's glasses landed in Laura's hands. 'You've done great,' he said as, turning, he handed Maya the other.

Maya nodded. 'And you look a million dollars.' Maya's eyes strayed round the room. 'Margot's made a big effort as well.'

Following Maya's gaze, Laura saw Margot standing by Leo's side. No surprise that, Margot had spent the whole evening attached to Leo – almost, Laura thought, as if she were his shadow. Is she protecting him? Laura wondered. But Leo needed no protection. It must be that Margot was just too scared to separate.

'It must he hard on her,' Maya said.

'Hard?'

'Not Margot's natural environment,' Maya said, pointing at a particularly concentrated gaggle of celebrities.

And Laura, whose eyes flicked back to Margot, saw the uneasy stretch of Margot's mouth. She nodded. Maya was right – Margot with Leo removed would look out of place here. Even her clothes, her neat blue suit and matching pumps, her blue drop earrings and dangling necklace, proclaimed her difference.

'Don't be such a snob,' she heard.

She tore her eyes guiltily from Margot but found the conversation had moved on and that Maya's teasing words were aimed at Steven. Relieved, she turned away, letting her eyes range aimlessly round. They landed eventually on a face, a gentle, soft, familiar face. She stood on tiptoes; waved. 'Heloise!'

Heloise's face lit up and she began pushing through the throng, trying to get to Laura. When that proved too difficult she lifted a hand and pointed at the door. Laura nodded. 'I'll be back,' she told Maya and Steven.

They were outside in the garden, she and Heloise. In the distance was the blackness of the ash and above it silent clouds coasting darkly across what had earlier been a brilliantly lit sky. Laura shivered.

'You are cold,' Heloise said. 'We should go in.'

'No.' Laura shook her head. No, she thought, I want to talk to Heloise. She peered through the darkness. 'It's been a long time,' she said, thinking that Heloise, who seemed content to be on her own and childless, was nevertheless the most motherly of women.

A nod and then Heloise's melodic voice floated out on the shadows. 'How are you, Laura?'

How are you? A question asked of Laura dozens of times that night. 'I'm fine,' she said as she had done each time before.

Heloise's eyes, in the dark more grey than blue, did not waver. She doesn't believe me, Laura thought, and wondered whether she believed herself. She thought back on the day; on her arrival at the house; on the strange man who had accosted her and whom, in the general bustle, she had almost forgotten. And she thought too of sitting in Leo's study and of witnessing the argument between him and Jack. There had been no time to deal with that either for time had speeded up as people came flooding in; glamorous confident people who'd made speeches about her mother that might have made her cry – if, that is, she had been capable of any emotion.

'Laura?' Her name pronounced in that familiar way – the first syllable lengthened, the 'r' softened, the second syllable unexpectedly curtailed.

'I don't know.' The only honest answer she could think to give.

Heloise accepted that. She smiled and the tiny lines around her gentle eyes smiled with her. 'Memorials to the dead are all very well,' she said. 'But they can be hard on the living.'

Laura nodded. 'Yes,' she said, remembering why it was she had stopped visiting Heloise – because Heloise's contentment seemed to be fuelled by a determination to state emotional truths that always made Laura want to cry. She blinked and swallowed and looked away.

A movement distracted her. Through the kitchen window she saw Margot, released from Leo's side, walking into the light, leading in a small contingent of people. Laura watched Margot, suddenly animated, pointing at the wall. At one of Judith's drawings.

In that moment, Laura felt herself hardening. No wonder Margot's animated, she thought, she'd doing what comes naturally. 'She's the curator of Judith's life,' she muttered softly.

Not softly enough. 'Would it be better if she pretended Judith had never existed?' Heloise sounded angry.

Shifting her gaze from the tableau inside back to a night which was now almost jet black, Laura frowned. 'What do you mean?'

'A simple question.' Heloise was undeviating. 'Would you prefer it if Margot ignored Judith?'

Ignored Judith, Laura heard, and was suddenly invaded by longing and by sorrow. She felt the tears returning.

No. She had long discarded such pain, she would not let it in. She used words to repel it. 'Why on earth should Margot ignore Judith?' she said. 'After all, she is supposed to be Judith's biographer.'

'Ah.' A soft word fluttering through the dark.

'Ah what?' Her own voice, in contrast, venomous.

'Ah,' Heloise said calmly, 'so that is why you hate Margot. Because she never finished the book.'

No, that's not it, Laura thought. She shook her head. 'What makes you think I hate Margot?'

Heloise did not immediately answer. She shifted in the dark, her soft skin grazed against Laura's arm and her perfume, a soft musk honed by something sweet, was terribly familiar.

'Age changes us all,' she eventually said.

Except you, Laura nearly replied, thinking that Heloise was her second mother, had comforted her when Judith was too busy and held her after Judith died.

'But it has not made me entirely witless,' she heard.

Heloise knows how bad I feel, Laura thought; and thought as well what a relief it would be to reach out for Heloise, to hold on to her and tell her what she could not tell anybody else: that the ground was shifting beneath her feet; that Steven's demands, Leo's absence, Tom's siren's song, all of this and Hedda Gabler as well, were threatening to overwhelm her. She took one step closer.

'You were the one,' she whispered almost to herself, 'who stood by me.'

Heloise must have known what Laura meant. She looked at

Laura, something faraway in her gaze. 'I wonder,' she said. 'I wonder if I did enough,' and then she said something equally puzzling. 'I should have known,' she said, 'how hard it was for you – a mere child. I should have known, before I came to wake you and tell you that Judith was dead.'

To wake you? 'You didn't wake me,' she said. 'I called you.'

'No.' The past had claimed Heloise and she was talking almost as if Laura weren't there. 'That was the time before,' she said, quite absently.

The time before – what on earth was Heloise on about? Laura opened her mouth to ask, but at that moment a burst of laughter from the kitchen distracted her. She looked up, seeing Margot, confident now, her head thrown back, the centre of attention, her small teeth gleaming.

Laura felt herself deflate. She looked across at Heloise, saw her smiling and realized then that she could no longer confide in Heloise. Trust Margot, she thought, to stop me from getting what I want. And said the words, perhaps, out loud, for: 'Don't blame Margot,' was what Heloise replied.

She felt her chest tightening: Margot – insinuating herself into every conversation. She turned, stared at Heloise.

At Heloise who did not see the tears in Laura's eyes and whose voice as a result was stern. 'You must not blame Margot for things that you feel you have done,' she said.

'Me?' She raised her voice, pitched it for ridicule. 'What have I done?'

'I don't know,' Heloise replied. 'You tell me.'

Nothing, Laura wanted to say. Her eyelids were pricking. Nothing. She would not speak.

Heloise had no such scruples. 'Being difficult is not always a virtue,' she said.

Difficult – what on earth did Heloise mean?

'Sometimes being ordinary is what matters,' she continued.

There was a criticism inherent in this nonsense and Laura was stung into a reply. 'Ordinary . You mean like Margot?'

'I didn't.' Heloise sounded disappointed. 'But yes, we can talk of Margot if you like. You resent her, yet what would your father be without her?'

Lonely, Laura thought. Alone. 'Leo has had a hard life,' she said.

It was still there in Heloise's voice, that sense of an opportunity overlooked. 'He's not so easy himself,' she said.

And Laura, listening, felt some of Heloise's disappointment at the same time as she thought again that she could no longer turn to her. Those days had gone; she was no longer a child; and, besides all that, Heloise had indeed grown old.

'Laura?' There was concern in Heloise's voice.

But no, it was too late. When Laura spoke her voice was light and easy. 'Come on,' she said, linking her arm through Heloise's, 'this isn't like you. What's making you so snappy to-night?'

A pause. Heloise shrugged and squeezed Laura's arm. 'It's not always easy to get old gracefully,' she said, and her voice tailed off. 'Sometimes,' she said, so softly that Laura thought she might be talking to herself, 'sometimes I envy your mother because she didn't have to try.' She looked up to the sky. 'It's going to rain,' she said. 'Shall we go in?'

Laura nodded. 'I'll join you in a minute.' Her smile was solid, reassuring. And kept firmly on her face while Heloise walked through the garden and up the garden stairs. 'I'll be there in a minute,' she shouted in answer to Heloise's wave.

And then she turned and, as the first drops of rain touched lightly on her head, only then, did she begin to cry.

Autumn

1963

*A*rriving home from school, ten-year-old Laura saw her mother standing at the far end of the hallway. She saw Judith's black, black hair and Judith's burning green eyes, and even Judith's dusty work shirt rolled up to reveal Judith's strong forearms. Behind Laura the au pair bustled with their coats.

'Your father's in Togo,' Judith said.

Laura nodded.

'Togo is a stretch of land on the bulge of Africa,' Judith said. 'Leo probably wandered there from Upper Volta, which is where he was last sighted.'

The au pair, a skinny, unhappy Austrian, sidled across the corridor and out of sight.

'There's been a coup in Togo,' Judith said. 'Do you know what a coup is?'

A pulse was ticking, somewhere inside Laura's ear.

'It's when the army overthrows the government,' Judith said, and then, seeing Laura flinch, added: 'Don't worry, there won't be one here,' throwing out her crooked, imponderable Judith smile.

Laura swayed as an image from her biology lesson, a human body stripped of skin to reveal interlocking blood vessels branching out from an ugly central pump, possessed her. It was no longer two-dimensional, it was alive. She could feel it, could feel the pulsing of veins as crimson blood plunged thickly through.

Judith's voice swam through the reddened blur. 'He phoned and said that he was well. He sent his love and said to tell you he would be back within a week.'

Within a week, Laura heard and touched the wall. Just once, a gentle touch, and she was secure again.

'You're home early.'

'Not really.' *There. Her first words spoken in her young girl's pipsqueak voice.*

'So I'm early then, am I?'

A faint inclination of the head.

'Well, I suppose I should get back,' *Judith said but didn't move. Instead she smiled.* 'I've done enough today,' *she said.* 'Should we have tea together?'

'Yes,' *hoping that Judith wasn't joking,* 'I'd like that.'

Judith had meant it. 'Good. Marine Ices then,' *she said.* 'I'll get my coat.' *She turned, hesitated, and then turned back again.* 'Would you like to see what I've been working on?' *she asked, and seeing Laura nod gestured with her hand.* 'Come,' *she said, waiting patiently as Laura walked towards her, speaking only when Laura was beside her.* 'Poor love,' *she said,* 'do you feel that Africa has stolen your father?'

Laura nodded, swallowed hard.

'It's difficult, I know,' *Judith said.* 'But you're lucky in a way.' *That was all, she didn't explain.* 'Now, come on,' *she said.* 'Come and see how I've wasted my day.'

The door was opened and Laura stood momentarily inhibited by the sheer scale of the room. Above her was glass, greying somewhat in the dim autumn light, a scattering of brown leaves on it, while all around were works half formed and half unhewn.

'This way.' *Judith zigzagged through the chaos and then abruptly stopped.* 'There.' *She was pointing with her finger at a painting on the easel, a portrait of a thin-faced, green-eyed, ravaged man.* 'What do you think?' *she asked as if she couldn't bear to wait.*

Laura swallowed.

'It is hideous, isn't it?'

Yes, Laura thought, relieved, it is ugly. And familiar as well.

'It's Max,' *Judith continued.* 'Max Cohen: my father, your grandfather. You never met him.'

No, thought Laura, I never met him – and neither have you ever mentioned him.

'He died when you were about two,' *Judith was saying.* 'But *he refused to see you, even as a baby. Leo wasn't a Jew, you see.'*

No, Laura nearly said, I don't see.

'I thought that by painting him I could drive his phantom out,' Judith muttered. She narrowed her eyes. 'I should have known that it is not so easily destroyed.' She looked at Laura, said, 'You must find this hard to understand – you with your perfect father.' She blinked, her green eyes suddenly unfocused. 'Max was selfish, while Leo's dedication to other people is selfless. Do you know' – she looked down – 'sometimes it feels like two sides of the same coin.' And then – at last – she came back into focus. She smiled, as if she was genuinely amused.

'That will teach me to use oils,' she said. 'I never was very good with them. Come on – let's get out of here.' She turned and began to look vaguely round the room. 'Now – where did I put my coat?'

It was by the wall, hanging on a peg, obscuring a small mirror. She strode over to it, and pulling it down flung it over her shoulders. Laura waited, silently, for what came next.

Judith caught her reflection in the mirror and saw what Laura had also seen: a smudge of brown upon her forehead. Using the back of her strong hand she wiped at it.

'He stuck to me,' she muttered, laughing softly but without mirth. 'Just as he stuck to me when he was living.' And then she shivered and walked away, walked to the huge glass wall and looked out of it on to the browning garden. 'I wish Leo was back,' she said. 'I hate autumn.'

CHAPTER TWELVE

1992

Although she was late for work she felt too comfortable to move. She sat in Steven's car gazing absently out of the window. The day, which had begun gloomily with rain falling steadily from a grey shroud, was now transformed, the sky so blue that she wondered, briefly, whether she had imagined the dim light earlier.

It was almost possible, she thought, for the time between *then* and *now* was immense. So immense, in fact, that the two seemed unrelated. The *then* belonged to another era, an era when it was always grey, an era which had begun in Leo's garden during the party as a cold rain had begun to fall. But as for the *now*, some months later, well, it was different: it was about closeness, not isolation, about sanctuary not fear. And about Steven next to her, his hand casually resting on hers. She smiled. 'What you are going to tell them at work?' she asked.

'About what?' Perplexed, he shook his head.

'Your lateness.'

'Oh that.' His face cleared. 'I'll tell them the truth – that I was so busy making love with my honey that I forgot the time.'

'Oh yeah?' She stretched over and kissed him long and hard. 'I bet,' she said when finally she detached herself. He put his hand up to his brow and wiped flamboyantly at it. She opened the door and began to clamber out. 'Speak to you later,' she said.

'I'll call tonight,' he shouted as she crossed the road.

Waving her hand in acknowledgement, she made her way towards the church. She was nearly there when, glancing idly back, she saw that Steven hadn't yet pulled out. How old-fashioned of him, she thought, he's waiting to see me safe, and, waving once again, this time to release him, approached the wrought-iron gate. She put out a hand; began to push at it.

'Miss Weber.'

A stranger's voice and yet she knew it; a voice linked inextricably to the *then*.

'Miss Weber.'

She turned and saw the outline of that gaunt, angry spectre which had infiltrated her dreams. She swallowed, saying the first thing that came into her head. 'How did you find me?'

His thin lips curled up. 'We have friends in common.'

Margot, she thought, but pushing that thought away she spoke again. 'What do you want?' Her voice was ice.

His answer was a question. 'Have they turned you against me?' They? she thought, and looking more closely saw his face was thinner than the last time and streaked with grime. He was nodding. 'I see that they have.' His right eye twitched, and twitched again. He was different now than he'd been the time before: he was on the verge of collapse. He's dangerous, she told herself. 'They will go to any lengths,' she heard him muttering.

She asked, despite herself: 'Who's they?'

He smiled. 'I think you already know that.'

Who? she nearly asked again but stopped herself this time. This man was clearly mad.

'I think you know more even than you will admit to yourself,' he said.

She bit back a retort; said only, 'I am on my way to work,' and pushed again at the ageing gate. As it swung creaking away, his hand grabbed hers. She felt its coldness and looking down saw it, like a talon, its veins standing out an angry lilac. 'Let go of me,' she said uneasily.

He gripped her harder, holding on. 'You must not.'

Her knees buckled but she found the strength somehow to wrench her hand away. 'Touch me again,' she said loudly, 'and I'll scream.'

He did what he had done at their first meeting – as soon as she stood up to him, he seemed to collapse. 'Please,' he said, his voice pitifully low.

Move, she told her limbs. Move.

'Please.'

The gate was open. She walked through it, up the decrepit path.

His words pursued her. 'It's about your mother.'

Don't listen, she told herself. Keep walking.

'I was with your father when she died.'

She stopped.

'In Stockholm. We were in transit.'

Yes, she thought, turning, yes, that sounds right. Leo had been in Stockholm on the night that Judith took the pills.

'Poor Leo Weber,' the man said. 'He was a worried man.'

'Of course he was.' Her words came out unbidden. Walk away, she told herself.

'No,' the man continued. 'Leo Weber was a worried man before he knew of your mother's tragic death. He had something on his conscience.'

She was inching her way slowly back towards him. No, she told herself. Stop.

He knew he had her. 'But then of course,' he said, so softly that she went even closer, 'you know that. Why else did he take an early flight to London? An early flight' – he grimaced and the skin on his forehead stretched taut, exposing bone – 'but not early enough.'

She couldn't help herself. She found that, as his yellowed eyes inspected her, she crossed the gap between them. Run, she told herself, as she saw him stretching out a hand. She did not run. Closer she came, until she was upon him. His hand closed on her wrist.

'Leave her alone.' The shout, loud and forceful, startled them both. It was Steven, running hard across the road. 'Let go of her.'

The man's eyes glinted. 'Again,' he said softly; and then even softer, so that he was almost whispering: 'Ask your father where your mother obtained the pills that killed her.' He dropped her hand and turned.

'Wait.'

The man's head twisted round and his mouth smiled sadly at her. 'Or better still,' he said, 'ask your stepmother. She knows everything,' and then he began to walk away.

'Wait!' she cried.

But Steven was upon her. 'Are you all right?' she heard him

say. She had no time for Steven, she must talk to the man. She turned, but when she moved, Steven stuck out his arm and pulled her back, whirling her round until she was facing him. 'Are you all right?' he insisted.

She glared at Steven.

'I'm sorry.' He was no longer holding on to her. 'Did I do something wrong?'

Silence.

'I noticed him,' Steven continued, 'when we first stopped. I wondered why he was staring so intently at the car. So I waited to see what would happen.'

Words, she thought, spilling from Steven's mouth.

'I was worried that he was threatening you.'

All words, as she wondered what the man had been going to tell her.

Steven was running out of steam. 'I wanted to see that you were safe,' he finished lamely.

She was breathing more easily now and her thoughts had slowed down. She looked at Steven using fresh, calm eyes and saw that his face was reddened by the exertion of his run and flushed also with genuine concern. She felt her anger fading. Steven's not my enemy, she told herself. 'It's OK,' she said.

'Who was he? A fan?'

She shook her head.

'Who then?'

Tell him, she ordered of herself.

But no, she couldn't. 'Some madman,' she said, 'part of London's general deterioration.' She sounded genuinely cool – even she was impressed. 'I'll tell you about it later,' thinking that later, when she had had time to think it over, she would be able to tell him. He hesitated. 'I'm late,' she said. 'And you too.'

He nodded. 'I'll call you,' he said and, leaning forward, kissed her gently on the cheek.

'Do that.'

He was walking away but something in the tone of her voice, the hesitation, perhaps, the slight mistiming in her delivery, alerted him. He stopped. 'Are you all right?'

She nodded and smiled her best smile. 'I'm fine,' she said.

*

She stood in the entrance hall counting and it was a long time before she opened the door and peered cautiously out. Yes, she was safe – Steven had gone.

The nearest phone was blocks away. She walked slowly towards it, trying out different openings. None of them seemed to work. How could she broach the subject after so many years?

She reached the phone box but found, to her relief, that it was occupied. She stood a few feet away, thoughts churning, half hoping that the wait would stretch on for ever. But no, the someone finished, replaced the receiver and, having thrown one uneasy look in her direction, marched quickly away. The look made her smile; she knew she had provoked it, standing there arguing with herself. And all for no reason, for when had she ever had difficulty raising anything with Leo? She went into the glass cubicle and dialled Leo's office number.

'United Nations Aid Support Foundation.'

'Dorothy.'

And as she always did, Dorothy recognized Laura's voice. 'Laura.' She sounded pleased. 'How are you?'

'I'm fine. Can I speak to Leo?'

But no. 'He's not in today. Try him at home.'

At home. Of course she could do that.

'Well . . .' she heard Dorothy saying, 'if that's . . .' At home – she did not want to ring Leo there. 'Dorothy!' she said sharply to stop the other hanging up.

'Yes?' spoken so gently that Laura was hauled into the past, to the hours she'd spent with Dorothy, waiting for Leo to finish up, opening Dorothy's drawers crammed with multi-coloured tissue paper and sweets, blackcurrant pastilles and red-striped humbugs, all scented somehow by the lavender and violet that seemed to cling to Dorothy's possessions and to Dorothy herself.

'What is it?' she heard Dorothy saying.

'Do you still keep fruit pastilles in your drawer?' That's what she almost asked but instead what she said was: 'I met a man,' and she proceeded to describe him.

'Laura!'

That was all, her name, but there was something hostile in it. She hesitated until, hearing only silence, she knew she must continue. 'Do you know him?'

More silence.

'Do you know what he wants?' She was beginning to feel anxious.

When Dorothy eventually spoke, she was bellicose. 'I cannot answer this,' is what she said; and then immediately something else: 'You have no right,' is what it sounded like.

'I beg your pardon?'

'The man's psychotic.' Dorothy was speaking clearly now. 'He's out to ruin your father. You must not speak to him.'

'But, Dorothy . . .'

'You must not. That is all I can say.' A pause and then: 'I'm sorry, Laura –' sounding anything but sorry – 'I have work to do.' And the phone went down, leaving Laura standing slightly dazed on the pavement with the receiver in her hand.

She might have stood for quite a time if not for the fact that a woman, who had been waiting within earshot, stretched out her hand and, saying 'You finished then?' grabbed the phone.

'I must go to work,' Laura muttered.

'You do that, luv,' the woman said encouragingly and, turning her back determinedly on Laura, began to dial.

The cast was gathered in a circle; when the door banged shut, their heads whipped up. Nine pairs of eyes stared at her. Someone giggled and someone else muttered what sounded like 'Madame arrives' while Gareth separated himself from the group.

'You're late,' he said, striding towards her.

She nodded. 'I'm sorry.'

'I don't consider . . .' he began but abruptly changed course. 'Let's get on with it,' he said and, turning away, used his arms to regroup the cast.

'As I was saying,' he said, 'it will be changed.'

She stood there stiffly, with fragments – the man's face looming, Steven's concern, Dorothy's raised voice – clashing in her memory.

Ask your father – that's what the man had said.

Ask your father what? she thought.

Who gave your mother the pills.

She shook her head, pushing his voice away. Dorothy was right, the stranger was psychotic. Why should she ask Leo?

She didn't need to ask, she knew the answer, knew that Judith had collected the pills herself, slowly and furtively, stashing them until she'd got enough.

No – wait a minute. She shivered. That's me, she thought, not Judith. I'm the one who collects pills. She thought of them, those multicoloured capsules hidden by her bed.

I've got enough now, she thought.

No. She shook herself again, more vigorously this time. She mustn't think of them; not now, it wasn't time. Margot – she'd think of her instead. She frowned. Why had the man told her to ask Margot about Judith?

Because, an inner voice replied, because Margot knows everything. Margot: the keeper of the family secrets and the family keys.

'Laura,' Gareth's voice intruded. 'Join us.' An order, not a request, followed by an impatient: 'Coming?'

She uncurled her fingers, unclenched her hands and began to walk slowly over.

'We're waiting.'

'I'm sorry,' she said, but seeing Gareth wince, remembered that she had already apologized. 'I'm sorry,' she said again as Gareth's scowl deepened.

In the centre of the circle was a model of a stage. Oh, of course, Gareth had mentioned it might at last be ready. No wonder then that he was cross with her – he was peculiarly attached to the model, had been frustrated by the long delay in obtaining it. She craned her neck, looked more closely. What she saw was a miniature drawing room whose walls were painted red. Red, she thought, that's original.

'And it's the wrong bloody shade of red,' Peter whispered. 'That's why Gareth's in such a mood.'

'Yes. Thank you, Peter.' Gareth was glowering. 'Now if I could be allowed to fill Laura in?' A beat, then: 'Yes,' he said wearily, 'the walls are the wrong shade – maroon I specified, not scarlet. But never mind, Barbara here' – he waved a hand carelessly at the set designer – 'assures us that it will all be sorted out. The drapes will be . . .'

Don't tell me, Laura thought: red velvet.

'Red velvet,' Gareth said. 'As for the chaise longue and the other substantial pieces, they should be' – he flicked his hand again in Barbara's direction – 'and I emphasise the should, they should be dark green – closer to black than to green. The net effect' – he looked at Laura – 'is a room imploding on itself, a claustrophobic hell.'

The net effect, she thought, is one big cliché.

'So what do you think?'

His voice was distant and she was tired. She wanted only one thing: she wanted to go to sleep.

'Laura?'

Shit – must he always ask her? 'Since I've kept you all waiting,' she said softly, 'it might be better if the others had their say.'

'But I'm asking you.'

I'm asking you, she heard, and something else as well – a silence. A tight, suspended silence it was, a collective breath held in against the outbreak of a storm. Her eyes flicked along the circle but they were all, without exception, looking down. She was on her own.

'What do you think.'

She opened her mouth, simultaneously framing a smile. 'It's a good, inoffensive choice,' she said.

'Inoffensive?'

She shrugged. What else did he want?

Plenty. 'I'm beginning to wonder how far your commitment stretches,' is what he said. 'And I'm not the only one.'

'What?' The word spilled out involuntarily.

He smiled. 'I'm sorry, Laura,' he said, 'but your lateness is just another symptom in a chain of disrespect.'

Disrespect? What was he talking about?

'You think you're unique,' he said, his voice hewing into the deadened silence, 'but we're all equal here, and all equally important,' the words flooding out fluently out as if he had prepared them. He's setting me up, she thought, and her eyes narrowed. 'I can see you disagree,' he said. 'Well, go on, spit it out.'

She shook her head. 'I'm not sure what you want me to say.'

'I don't *want* you to say anything,' he said, sarcasm dripping. And then a transition: a moderation of tone, a piece of advice, delivered one comrade to another. 'But I think it would be better if you did.' A pause and the final gibe. 'Come on, Laura, you've never been a coward.'

She frowned. He was definitely goading her, but why? And why in front of all the others?

'You believe in equality amongst the cast, don't you?' He was so close his features were distorted, his eyes popping, his mouth a gaping cavity. 'Don't you?'

She stood her ground. 'Of course I believe in teamwork.'

'But also in the hierarchy of importance?'

She shrugged, thinking vaguely that she must be missing something. 'I wouldn't equate the role of Hedda with, say, Berte's or Aunt Julle's,' she said. Or, she nearly added, with any of the others.

Gareth was upon her. 'That says it all.' He was crowing. 'When they complained . . .'

They?

'. . . that you wouldn't take them seriously I told them that they were imagining it. But now' – his smile was ghastly – 'now I'm inclined to believe them.'

So that was it. The penny dropped. So that was what this public lynching was all about. Oh, she knew just which members of the cast had complained – Alison and Katherine, simpering women, both of them, looking for a scapegoat for their own inadequacies. She took a deep breath. 'Have you quite finished?' she asked between gritted teeth.

The first glimmer of uncertainty made Gareth's full lips quiver. She saw it, written in his eyes, the realization that he might have gone too far. But Gareth was a bully and he tried to brazen it out. 'I'm speaking as a friend, of course,' he said.

Of course, she nearly replied; and of course I'm walking out as one.

She smiled. She could do it – so easily. She could do it and it was time. She had spent months making excuses for him, for his petty tyranny and constant vacillation. Well, that was over now. She would walk out and leave Gareth to find out just how equal each member of the cast really was.

'Laura?'

The air was stiff with panic, alarm in every eye. Oh yes, they knew it also, that Gareth had gone too far and, oh yes, they could see what she was thinking.

'I'm . . .' she began. Going, she nearly said.

But found that she could not. She was standing immobilized, nine sets of eyes on her, fixated by an earlier time. A time when she had taken the decision to play Hedda and had told a protesting Steven why. *I have to*, she'd said, *or she will defeat me*. Now, as darkness encroached, she felt it even more strongly. She would not, could not, go. Not now. 'I'm fine,' she said.

CHAPTER THIRTEEN

Six hours later, she made her way slowly downstairs. 'A drink?' she heard Peter asking.

She turned, smiling, towards him. 'I'd love one,' she said breezily, 'but I'll have to take a rain check.'

Together they stepped outside. Dusk was falling on a world turning grey and damp. She felt Peter's arm on her shoulder. 'Tired?' She nodded. 'I'm not surprised,' he said. 'You were brilliant.'

She stopped and raised her eyebrows. 'What, with Gareth? I wasn't brilliant. I was pathetic.'

'No, not with Gareth.' He pulled a long face. 'Although thank God you didn't overreact.' His face cleared. 'No, I meant as Hedda.' She shrugged – she didn't really care. A pause and then, 'Don't let Gareth get you down,' Peter said.

'No. I won't.' She swallowed and, before she could stop it, a question came rushing out. 'Are people complaining about me?' She regretted it immediately. She had chosen Peter because he was her friend and because he wouldn't lie, but now, watching him struggling for an answer, she thought she should have been more compassionate. 'It's OK,' she said. 'You don't have to say anything.'

But he felt he had to. 'Some of the cast find you standoffish,' is what he said.

'Some of the cast. You mean Alison and Katherine?' He nodded almost imperceptibly. 'I thought so.' A surge of vindictiveness suffused her voice.

'They're a different generation,' Peter said. 'With a different training. They're not used to doing so much during rehearsal.'

'Sure, I know that,' she said bitterly. 'But why do I get the blame?'

Peter shrugged. 'I don't know,' he said. 'Perhaps they feel threatened by you.' He had gone further than he'd wanted and he sounded tetchy. 'You're not the easiest, you know,' he said.

So even Peter, she thought, Peter whom I considered my friend, even he has turned against me. She was speechless for a moment, gripped by sudden, searing rage.

'You could try being less impatient,' she heard him say.

The brightness that had obscured her vision faded and she saw him looking sympathetically at her. Her anger drained. He is my friend, she thought.

'Couldn't you?'

She found to her surprise that she was smiling. 'I could,' she said. There are some advantages in playing Hedda, she thought, for Hedda has taken all my anger. 'I'll be a better girl in future.'

'I'll believe that when I see it.' Peter was also smiling. 'You always were a rebel.' He licked his lips. 'Are you sure you don't want that drink?'

'I'm due somewhere else,' she said. 'Another time?' She raised a hand, hailing a taxi. As it stopped she kissed Peter on both cheeks. ''Bye, darling. See you tomorrow.' And then she was in the taxi with a driver who had twisted round and was waiting for her to speak. He wants to know where I'm going, she thought, her mind a blank, for, despite what she had told Peter, she had no plans. Oh well, she thought, I can just go home.

'Where to?'

She was fooling herself: she knew exactly where she was going. Leaning forward she spoke clearly at his wall of glass. 'Primrose Hill, please,' she said.

'Keep the change,' she told the driver and bounding up the steps rang the bell. There. She was committed. She need only wait.

Or so she told herself. But as the seconds passed, doubt began to gnaw. Is this mad? she wondered. The thought caught hold. It did seem mad, rushing over to ask Leo a question because of the stranger who had twice accosted her. It was mad. No good could come of it. She turned.

Too late. 'Laura,' she heard.

Back she turned to see Margot standing on the doorstep. 'Is Leo in?' she asked.

Margot shook her head. 'He's still at work.'

Laura, remembering what Dorothy had said, frowned. No he's not, she nearly said.

'Can I help?'

Laura shook her head, wanting to say no, but an internal voice intervened. *Ask your stepmother*, it said. So: 'Can we talk?' is what she said instead.

'Sure.' Margot was smiling. 'Come in. I'll put the kettle on.'

'So what's this about?' Margot asked as she held the kettle under the gushing tap.

She couldn't say it, not immediately. 'I was just passing,' she said.

Margot put the kettle down, punching in its plug. 'That's nice.' She turned. 'Tea? Coffee?'

Not tea, nor coffee, Laura thought. 'I'd prefer a drink,' she said. 'Would you mind?'

Margot smiled. 'Of course not.' She glanced at her watch. 'I'll join you. Whisky?'

Laura nodded. 'Great.' And then, as Margot left the room, she sat down, trying to compose her thoughts.

'Ice?' Margot was back, a bottle of malt in hand.

Ice – it would buy her time. 'Please,' she said, and continued sitting, watching as the bottle was plunked down and Margot fetched an ice tray and a bowl to hold the ice.

'Margot?'

'Hmm?'

'Where did Judith get them?'

'Get what?' Margot's teeth were gritted in concentration as she tried to dislodge stubborn ice from the plastic tray.

Laura took a deep breath in and, on the out-breath, 'Where did Judith get the pills that killed her?' issued from her mouth.

That killed her, she heard her voice saying and at that moment saw Margot bend the tray so hard it tore. Chunks of ice came spewing out, chunks which missed the bowl, hit the counter, bounced off and skittered across the floor.

'Shit.' Margot was on her hands and knees, trying to gather

the slithering fragments. Laura followed her, dropping to the floor as well. As Margot stretched out for ice, Laura watched.

Margot stopped, turned and looked at Laura. Their eyes locked. She's trying to outstare me, Laura thought. She let her own eyes relax, concentrating on Margot's brown irises while the periphery surrounding Margot's face she allowed to blur gently. It worked. Margot's eyes flicked sideways.

There was a shining ice cube within grasp and Laura saw Margot spot it. Laura judged her moment well. As Margot reached out her hand, Laura moved faster, grabbing for the ice. Margot snatched her hand away.

'Where did she get the pills?'

'Why ask me?' Their faces were so close they were almost touching.

Laura smiled. 'Because you know.' Her mouth straightened. There was no reason to be smiling.

Margot's eyes were moist. 'It's him, isn't it?' she asked.

'Him?' Laura leaned back, sitting on her heels.

'Ben.'

'Ben – so that's his name.'

A nod.

'Who is he?' Laura asked.

There was composure now in Margot's face. She began to rise.

'Who is he?' Laura also moved.

Margot was on her feet. 'If you want to know about Ben,' she said, 'you must ask your father. But as for the other question . . .' She turned and Laura could hear ice clinking. 'I can answer that.' She twisted her wrist and there was the sound of liquid pouring. 'The pills belonged to Leo,' she said. A clinking and then, turning again, Margot handed Laura a glass. 'They were part of a wager. Leo was furious at the way dangerous drugs were being dumped in the Third World. He bet a friend who worked for a major pharmaceutical company that he could pick up any drug he wanted. He did as well, his collection was comprehensive. The prize for winning the bet was a case of vintage champagne, duly delivered. Leo was going to produce it for Judith's fortieth.'

For Judith's fortieth, Laura heard, shocked to think that her father could have left pills for her mother to find. Looking up, she saw a look of what could only have been malicious glee crossing Margot's face. 'Why are you telling me this?'

Margot shrugged. 'You asked,' she said. 'And anyway, it's all on public record. It came out during the inquest. The coroner even commented that –'

'All right.' Laura banged on the wooden counter. 'That's enough.'

'You did ask.'

Her words hung flatly in the air, prim words which turned the pain on Laura and at the same time exposed the real Margot – the spiteful creature lurking behind the façade. 'Who is Ben?' Laura asked.

It worked: the light in Margot's eyes went out, replaced by something else. By alarm – that's what it was. Well, Laura would press home her advantage. 'Who is he?' she asked.

Margot's lips opened and then abruptly closed.

'I know you know him,' Laura said, her tone determined. She would not give up, she would not.

Margot took one step towards her. 'Ben . . .' She was almost whispering.

And never got the time to finish for: 'Margot!' the name sounded out. It was Leo's voice calling to his wife, not in endearment, but in rage. They moved in tandem, the two women, their heads swivelling simultaneously round.

What they saw was Leo in the doorway, his face darkened in displeasure. He was listening, Laura thought. I wonder what he heard. But then she stopped wondering that for, glancing across at Margot, she saw how Margot's eyes had hardened and saw as well something else igniting Margot's face – malice, that's what it looked like, so intense that it seemed murderous.

She took an involuntary step back.

And felt Leo's arm around her. 'This is an unexpected pleasure,' he said, smiling as he kissed her on the cheek.

He let go then and nodded at his wife – a nod which ricocheted off Margot to be just as curtly returned. Then he was smiling again, looking at his daughter. 'To what do we owe the honour?'

When Laura hesitated, Margot's voice supplanted hers. 'A drink?'

'Please,' Leo said. 'Gin and tonic.' His voice was pleasant

and polite but as Margot walked away his posture changed. What had been upright before, sagged; his smiled froze, becoming what it had surely always been – a grim pretence.

But then, before Laura could say anything, he turned to her. 'How are you?'

She could not make small talk, it wouldn't come. 'I need to ask you something,' she said.

'Not now.'

Not now, staccato and so unexpected that she whipped her head round to see if he was talking to Margot. But no, Margot had not yet returned.

'I'm sorry, darling.' He had modulated his tone. 'It's not a good time . . .'

. . . *not a good time*: words issuing from the present and from the past as well, from a time so long ago, when she had braved the dark night to creep into his study. To creep in and reach her hand up to his wet cheek.

'It's been a long day,' she heard him saying.

At least that phrase was new, spoken to the adult not the child. She heard it and she nodded and, looking straight at him, saw that although he wasn't crying, his eyes were heavy.

'I'm exhausted,' he said.

Perhaps, she thought, perhaps that is the truth. Perhaps it is fatigue and not pain making his eyelids droop.

'It's good to see you though.'

He was trying so hard to deny what her eyes could see – and failing so conspicuously. His smile, it was heartbreaking. She could not stop herself. She put her arms around him and whispered in his ear. 'Oh, Daddy,' she said. *Daddy*. When was it she had last called him that? 'I love you.'

And he – he did not push her off. She felt his hand, softened by age, squeeze gently round her upper arm. 'Laura,' he said. 'You are my life. You know that.' He breathed out once, long and slow, and she saw colour returning to his cheeks. 'I'm sorry,' he said, his voice now strengthened. 'What was it you wanted to ask me?'

'Gin.' Margot had returned. 'With tonic?'

'Please.' His eyes were still on Laura.

Who found she no longer had the heart to press him. He would answer now, she knew it, answer anything she might care to ask and yet she knew that what he'd said was true; that he was bone tired.

What did it matter anyway? She could ask him another time. She shook her head. 'Not now,' she said.

'More whisky?' This from Margot.

She was also suddenly tired. 'No,' she said. 'No, thanks. I'd better be off.' And when neither of them said anything to that she briskly added: 'I'll call a taxi.'

CHAPTER FOURTEEN

There was an insistent ringing in her ears. She turned over, trying to escape it, but the ringing persisted. The phone, she vaguely thought. She stretched an arm out; grabbed for it.

'Laura?'

The ringing had stopped.

'Laura?'

Where had she heard that voice before?

'*Laura.*' The voice would not give up.

She forced her eyes open, banishing darkness. Her arm was thick, clotted with corpulent lethargy. She grunted.

'Laura.'

The voice, it really was familiar. She pushed herself up, squinted at her clock. Three-fifteen, it said.

'Laura, are you there?'

Her hand tightened on the phone. Of course she knew the voice. 'Heloise,' she said.

A sigh. 'Thank heavens.'

'What's happened?'

A rush of memory, twenty-five years old, invaded. *What's happened?* She'd asked that then as, standing on the stairs, clad only in a thin, knee-length nightie, she'd watched strangers engulf her home.

'Laura.' Her name again. 'I am sorry but you must come to your father's house.'

'What's happened?'

'Just come, my darling.' The phone went dead.

This time she had no nightie to remove and this time she was a full-grown woman. She strode over to the cupboard, flung the doors wide open and paused for a moment, wondering which were the appropriate clothes.

Appropriate for what? she thought as grabbing a pair of jeans, a T-shirt and a sweater she pulled them on. *Your father's house*, that's what Heloise had said. Her keys were where they should have been, lying on the counter. *Your father's house*. That must mean, surely, that Leo was all right. She was outside already, standing under the vastness of a starry night.

Margot. It must be Margot. She heard her sneakers thumping on each successive stair. She was in the car and turning at the key. Too hard. The engine didn't spark, it clicked instead – just once, before it whined and died.

Died. Could Margot be dead?

Leo would be needing her, she must go to him. She must concentrate. She straightened her back and turned the key again, more slowly this time. The engine kicked itself briskly into action and she pulled off, calmly, carefully, deliberately.

She did something then that she had only ever done on stage: she constructed a barrier to her thoughts. A mental barricade, it was, which consented to directions. Just as sometimes she was conscious only of the play and the words the play demanded from her, this time she was riveted exclusively on each separate moment of the journey. She saw the face of each driver that passed, and the faces of their passengers too. She could have closed her eyes at any moment and counted backwards, and she could have known how many lampposts she had passed. She was thoroughness itself, her driving flawless and precise. She took the most direct route and each traffic light seemed to have been forewarned for each was green. She drove fast, efficiently, and the only extraneous thought she allowed herself was a flash of sudden hope that the journey might take for ever.

But like a performance the journey had its own momentum and like a performance it had to end.

She had reached Leo's house and she stopped the car. She was vulnerable again. Blue lights were what she saw, flashing against the dawning of the day. She left her car and walked past them, and past a knot of people, their faces a mournful ghastliness against the rotating blue. The door, the front door, was open wide. She passed over the threshold. And felt a hand, grabbing at her elbow. 'Out,' a rough voice ordered.

She almost did just that, almost turned and conveyed herself out. It was so tempting; she yearned to do it. But no.

'Leave her.' Heloise was coming fast towards her, her soft face streaked with the grey pallor of distress. 'It's his daughter.'

His daughter, she heard, knowing what that meant. She shook her head. No, it could not be. 'Is it Margot?' she heard herself asking as she looked down the hall. There was a woman halfway along it, slumped on a chair, her head between her hands. A woman – Margot.

Heloise took hold of her. 'No, darling. It's your . . .'

Your . . . father, that's what Heloise was about to say, just as she had once said 'your mother'. Laura pushed Heloise away. 'Where is he?'

Heloise inclined her head, gently, in the direction of the kitchen.

'And is he . . .?' Saying those words she took one step forwards and, saying those words, she knew they were unnecessary.

Heloise was in her path again. 'Don't go in there, my darling.'

Don't go in there. That's what they'd told her that time before. *Don't go in there*, as if they thought that they could undo what she had already seen, as if the image of that woman, the kernel of what had once been her mother, sprawled untidily across her bed, would ever, ever leave her.

'What happened?'

'It's too soon to know. The police are there. And the ambulance men too.'

She did not bother pushing Heloise aside, she merely circumvented her. She was fast and she was determined. A few steps and she was past both Heloise and Margot, one more and her hand was on the doorknob, another two and she was in.

There were – she didn't know, she couldn't count – there were many, many people in the room and all of them were men. Men in uniforms and casual clothes, men in blue and men in white, men chatting lightly to each other over this, this scene of death.

Live men, and in their midst was Leo.

But it wasn't really Leo. It was the shell only of what had once been Leo. It – he – was on the floor, his arm outstretched, his mouth agape, lying in a pool of dark, congealing crimson. Lying there, his shirt had been ripped open, he was lying there and he was dead, his face distorted. That face which she had seen so recently and which had smiled at her, its wrinkles crinkling. Now those wrinkles were irrelevant – he was no longer aged, but ageless, and the wrinkles had been frozen into an unfamiliar pattern. He was transformed. This was not the face that had once been streaked with tears, the face that as a child she had reached up and touched.

She touched her own cold, cold cheeks and felt that the wetness had been transferred to them. Men's voices came distantly to her. 'Who let her in?' Voices asking pointless questions. 'What's she doing here?' Men's rough hands were on her, tugging her upright and pushing her away. 'Get her out.'

A woman had her now, a woman leading her from the room, nudging her along the hall. Heloise. 'Come, my darling, come sit down.'

Heloise, thought Laura, who always arrives in times of pain, who housed me that night when Judith had died.

'Would you like to wait next door?' Heloise's face was looming alarmingly.

A quick shake of her head and then: 'Where's Margot?' The question, it was pointless. Margot was clearly visible. She hadn't moved; was sitting on the same straight-back chair across the way. Sitting fully dressed, every detail catered for – everything down to her tights and polished shoes.

Everything in its place, Laura thought, for Margot will be for ever suburban. A suburban housewife but with one exception: she had blood all over her.

'What happened?'

Laura turned and saw Steven standing by the front door. Someone must have summoned him. He looked, she thought, ridiculous – his clothes crumpled and mismatched, his hair badly tousled. Seeing her, his mouth opened.

She beat him to it. 'Yes,' she said. She turned her head. 'What did happen?'

And Margot, who had made no sign since Laura's arrival, responded instantly. She raised her head and Laura saw that her face was blank and insipid. 'I think he had a heart attack,' she said.

CHAPTER FIFTEEN

'Is he all right?' This from Steven.

'He's dead,' Heloise murmured.

He's dead, Laura thought, and of a heart attack. That's why he was lying in a pool of blood – the same blood that stained Margot's neat clothes.

'Oh no.' Steven's arm went round her shoulders.

Her muscles tightened. A heart attack – she almost laughed. So that's why there were policemen crawling everywhere! A heart attack, she nearly said, give me a break. She felt Steven's arm tightening.

And felt another arm, her father's embracing her. Her father, coming up to her and whispering in her ear.

What was it he had said?

How could she have forgotten? *You are my life.* That's what he had said. *You are my life* – and he was dead. He had been her world, her comfort for so long, and he was gone. She was alone.

She heard someone crying; felt the arm again. Steven's not Leo's. Pushing it away, she looked at Margot. 'Why did you do it?' she asked.

Margot frowned. 'Do what?'

'Why did you kill him?' the words ringing out.

'Laura!' Heloise was scandalized.

But Laura didn't care. 'Isn't that what happened?' she asked, knowing that it was, knowing that the hostility she had witnessed yesterday had turned to violence, knowing that her visit and her questions had somehow been connected. She stood there, waiting, remembering how it had been: the expression on Leo's face and Margot's as well, the words unsaid, the unasked questions. And while all this kept racing round, she saw Margot's eyes widening, her pupils contracting her mouth opening, closing, and opening again. And then: 'He had a heart attack,' Margot said. She was on her feet and lurching forward, gagging as she hauled herself up the stairs.

A hand gripped Laura by the elbow, Heloise's hand. 'That was uncalled for,' Heloise said, her fingers jabbing into bone. 'And also most unwise.' Her grip tightened as she twisted Laura round. 'It will not help to turn on poor Margot.'

Poor Margot, Laura heard and looked up to where 'poor Margot', had stopped on the first landing, the same one where Laura, as a child, had often liked to sit. An image – a shining memory engulfed her. She shook her head, screwed her eyes up tight, shaking it away but it continued to assail her. When she looked up again she saw not Margot but herself a child, sitting on the stairs, her father beside her. Her father who, bending down, had picked her up and hugged her to him. Her father who'd come from such a long way away to make her safe. Her father – who was dead. She felt tears welling.

She heard a retching sound – Margot.

'I'll go.' Steven was already halfway there, scrambling to support the grieving widow.

She might have followed but she heard a door closing behind her. She turned and saw a man of medium build, a pudgy face, pasty complexion, thinning brown hair and a crumpled brown suit. 'Miss Weber,' he said. 'I am Detective Inspector Howard, the officer in charge of this case. My condolences.'

She shook her head, pushing this most cursory of official sympathy away.

'We'll soon be out of here,' he said, as if this might please her.

But she didn't want them gone. 'Can I talk to you?' she asked.

He nodded. 'Certainly. The sitting room?' He pointed at the door as if he owned the house and then, 'What can I do for you?' he asked as soon as she was seated.

'Tell me what's going on,' she said.

He had sunk wearily down into the sofa; now he nodded, pushed himself upright. 'We're waiting for the forensic examiner' – he smiled – 'sorry, in layman's terms, the police surgeon, to complete his inspection. When that's over, the coroner's office will arrange for transport of the body.'

She was suddenly alert. 'The coroner's office?'

'Routine. Don't worry, everything looks normal. Our preliminary assessment is that your father suffered a massive heart attack.'

A heart attack, just as Margot said. She did not believe it.

He missed the tightening of her face. 'Of course we will contact his GP,' he said, 'to confirm the existence of heart disease.'

She shook her head. 'There wasn't any.'

The policeman looked, for the first time, uncertain. He leaned forward. 'Mrs Weber said your father was ill.'

'He wasn't,' she said determinedly.

The policeman's eyes narrowed. 'You don't agree?' he asked, and added quickly: 'Do you have any reason to be suspicious?'

Suspicions – she had so many of them. She chose the only one she could put into words. 'The blood?'

'Oh.' He nodded. 'The blood, yes, you went to the kitchen, didn't you? Our working theory is that Mr Weber hit his head when he fell. The post mortem will of course need to confirm this – and the coroner as well.'

'And then?' Her voice was high, too high. She brought it down. 'That's it?'

He nodded. 'Sure – unless we find evidence of foul play, that's it.' He put his hand on the sofa, preparing to push up.

'What kind of evidence?' Her words cut through the air.

He stopped. 'I beg your pardon?'

'What would you consider evidence of foul play?'

He shrugged. 'Signs of a struggle, anything missing or out of place, eye-witness accounts, medical suspicions, irregularities in –' He paused, looked straight at her. 'Your stepmother says your father had a heart condition. Do you have any reason to doubt this?'

She kept quite still. What could she say? What could she? That she knew Margot had killed Leo, knew it for a fact although she had no facts to back her up?

'Do you?'

She shook her head. 'No.' And saw him smile, relieved, and rise.

'If there's nothing else . . .' He didn't wait for an answer; he left.

She followed him. Why not? There was nothing else to do.

Margot was on her way downstairs. It was quite a show. Having slowly negotiated one flight, she paused, stretched out a shaky hand and gripped the banisters. Support, that's what she was asking for, support and pity.

She wears his blood well, Laura thought.

Margot's next step positioned her directly under the light and her features were suddenly illuminated. In that moment, Laura saw how pale was Margot's face, and how bloodshot her eyes. Shocked at this unexpected sight of suffering, Laura looked quickly away. I shouldn't have been so hard on her, she thought. Out of the corner of her eye, she saw Margot moving. I must help her, she thought. She raised her head.

What she saw was Margot smiling. Smiling – at such a time as this. The sight, so obviously calculated, drove pity out. I can't pretend, Laura thought, bracing herself for the encounter. I can't pretend to be her friend.

She needn't have worried. Margot was smiling not at her but beyond her, at Heloise and Steven. Laura nodded. Margot was certainly a pro: Steven, Heloise, even the policeman, they had all been fooled.

All of them, that is, except Laura. Laura, who knew how to dissemble and who also knew that that's what was now required of her. She met Margot at the bottom of the stairs. 'I'm sorry for what I . . .'

'It's OK.' Margot, her hand raised, cut her graciously off.

Well, Laura was her equal. 'It must have been dreadful for you,' she said.

Margot nodded, tears leaking from those reddened eyes.

'Do you feel strong enough to talk about it?'

'Perhaps tomorrow.' Heloise's voice was stern.

'No,' Margot protested as Laura had known she would. 'No, I'd rather get it over.'

Of course you would, Laura thought, whilst you're still word perfect. 'Let's go to the sitting room,' she said.

They were in the sitting room, listening to Margot's tiny, trembling voice. 'Leo was late from work,' Margot said.

'Yes?' Laura prompted, remembering that, according to Dorothy, Leo had not even been at work.

'That's right, you were there.' Margot swallowed. 'After you left we had supper. Then Leo said he had more work to do.'

'So he went upstairs?'

'No.' Margot shook her head. 'He went back to the office.'

The office! Ridiculous! Leo never went there at night.

'He said he needed to redraft something he'd written on the computer. That's why he went to the office rather than staying here.'

She's worked out all the angles, Laura thought, except we both know that he had never learned to work the computer and that Dorothy did all his typing.

'He came in at one-thirty. I was worried: he was so uncharac-teristically late. I had waited up for him. He went to his study and then I heard him calling me, so I went up.' Margot's sniffs were getting louder.

'Margot. There is no need . . .'

'No.' Margot brushed Heloise off. 'I've almost finished.' She sniffed again, apparently stemming tears. 'He was furiously angry. I didn't know why – he wouldn't tell me what was wrong. He just kept shouting about something missing.' She paused. A big gulp for air.

At last, the transition from study to kitchen, Laura thought.

'He rushed downstairs.'

'You followed him?' Laura said, knowing that the answer must be no.

'No,' Margot shook her head. 'I stayed for a moment, trying to work out what had got him so angry. I couldn't – so I went downstairs.'

But he was already dead.

'But he was already dead,' Margot said. 'I went up and held him . . .'

Which, conveniently, is how you got the blood on you.

'. . . but I'm sure he was dead. I phoned for the ambulance.'

After you were sure that he was dead.

'And then when they arrived I phoned Heloise, asking her to contact you.' She was sobbing; tears splashing down her face, ugly streaks spreading, blotching her skin. Sobbing as if in genuine grief, while opposite her Laura looked on; looking at a woman the same age as her, a woman who had stolen and destroyed her father. A woman who had once pretended to be Laura's friend and who still had the strange ability to invoke friendship, for even as Laura's rational mind rejected Margot's extravagant display of grief, her hand was twitching, wanting to stretch out, wanting to offer comfort. She leaned forward.

But then she heard a scuffling coming down the hall. She knew what that must be. She was on her feet, running to the door.

They were taking Leo away. He was on a stretcher, encased in white plastic, and they were moving him carelessly, twisting the stretcher this way to avoid the stairs, and the other to set it straight. She could see through the front door; she could see a wooden coffin standing there. Rough wood – that's all he merited. He was nothing to them; he was dead. They were taking him and they were going to cut him up.

She stood there, hearing Margot keening now, hearing Steven and Heloise comforting her; comforting Leo's wife rather than his daughter. Well, Leo's daughter was made of stronger stuff. She stood there, head held high as they carried her father away.

CHAPTER SIXTEEN

A voice was picking at her – 'Laura, Laura' – Heloise's voice, summoning her, for the second time, from sleep. She shook her head. She would not be summoned. She was too comfortable, too warm and snug in bed.

'You must get up.'

No. She kept her eyes shut, knowing vaguely that if she opened them she would be engulfed by pain.

'I have brought you something,' she heard Heloise announcing.

I don't want it, she thought.

'Open your eyes.' Heloise sounded almost angry.

Her will was stronger than Laura's – she got her way. Laura did as she was instructed, opening her eyes, pleasantly surprised to find that she felt no particular pain. Curious, that's all she felt. Looking round she saw curtains drawn, the darkness filtering through. I'm safe, she thought, gazing in the half-light around Heloise's meticulously organized spare room.

'Here.' A bowl, dark and green, was thrust into her cupped hands. 'Try it,' Heloise said.

Why not? She brought it closer and breathed in, smelling fragrant chocolate.

She froze. Hot chocolate: a liquid conjured from the past, sweet in the acrid face of death and warm against the silence of the grave.

Memory overwhelmed her and when it did she no longer felt so safe. Heloise did the same last time, she thought, gave me chocolate in this bowl. I never told her, she thought, what happened after, how it came surging out, a stream of brown bile disgorged into the toilet.

She shuddered, thinking of the last time and thinking that what Heloise had said on the night of Judith's party was true: it had been Heloise who had woken her. She frowned. Of course that was what had happened, why did she ever think it otherwise?

'Let me help you.' Heloise, determinedly occupied, pulled the side table closer.

'I don't want it,' Laura said, trying to stop her.

It worked. Heloise, her onward motion suddenly suspended, looked carefully at Laura. 'That's OK,' she said at last.

That's all, two words, *that's OK*, but spoken so gently that they managed where something more momentous might have failed. For as those words were spoken, Laura knew it wasn't OK – and that it might never be.

Awareness of what had happened came flooding back, sweeping away numbness. Leo, her father, he was dead. Leo: for so long he had been her whole family, her father and her mother both, and now there was nobody, nobody else. She had no parents now. She was utterly alone.

She was gasping, suddenly, she couldn't breathe, her chest was caving in.

'Laura.' Heloise's voice was distant.

She felt the room spinning; she was plunging into blackness.

'Laura.' Louder, more alarmed. 'Breathe out,' insistently, 'breathe out.'

She did so, and on the out-breath made a sound, a groaning, almost bestial sound, which came spewing out.

'That right, breathe out.'

That sound again, abhorrent, unnatural, she must stop it. She thrust a hand into her mouth, biting down.

'Let it out,' she heard.

No. Heloise was wrong. She could not let it out, she must not. She was alone, she could not afford to let go. She shook her head.

And felt the bed suddenly shifting, and then Heloise was beside her, and her hand was taken from her mouth and Heloise's arms were round her, rocking her. Rocking. It felt so good. Silent tears began coursing down her cheeks.

She lost all track of time, felt only Heloise's arms around

her, and Heloise's gentle voice, and the stream of salt water annihilating vision until gradually, slowly, it began to die down and she found her voice.

'Why did you wake me?' Her voice, plaintive.

Heloise sighed. 'The police phoned. They'll be here at four.'

At four, she heard and, twisting her head round, looked at the drawn curtains, realizing then that the darkness she had taken for night was merely the gathering of dusk.

'The post-mortem is complete,' she heard Heloise saying.

She winced as an image of sharpened steel slicing into Leo's flesh invaded her. 'Where's Steven?'

A pause and then: 'With Margot,' Heloise said. 'He should be back soon.'

Laura stiffened. Soon – which meant, of course, that he'd already been gone too long. 'How is the grieving widow?' she asked.

The colour washed from Heloise's eyes, blue was turned to grey. 'Margot is naturally very upset,' she said.

'Naturally.'

She had done it now. 'Margot is not your enemy,' Heloise said, no longer patient.

Margot is nothing, Laura thought, thinking also that now Leo was dead, she and Margot had nothing in common.

'You should be there beside her.'

Oh yes, Laura thought, looking away, I should certainly be there. But not with Margot next to me.

'She needs your help. The press are besieging her; the phone will not stop ringing. She is not as accustomed as you to dealing with such demands.' Heloise took Laura's shoulders in her hands and twisted them round. 'Blaming Margot will not bring Leo back,' she said softly. She blinked and Laura, watching, saw that there were tears in Heloise's eyes. And tears in mine as well, she thought.

'It isn't Margot's fault,' Heloise said. 'It's nobody's fault.'

Nobody's fault. If only Laura could believe that. She looked away again. If only she could – if only she could hear of a death and not apportion blame.

If only she could.

She opened her mouth. 'Heloise . . .' She never finished. A footstep sounded and Steven was by the door. She closed her mouth. She couldn't ask Heloise, not now, not with Steven present. She couldn't ask Heloise for she knew not what – to be a mother to her, she supposed, to make it feel all right.

Steven. Shit, what timing. She shut her eyes, feeling the bed sagging as he sat down. Another movement and his arms were around her. His strong, comforting arms. Her senses were so sharpened, her hearing and her sense of smell as well, she could breathe his familiarity in, his slightly musty saffron warmth nudging at her anger. She felt new tears begin to rise. These are my friends, she thought, my family, I am not alone. She took a deep breath in.

She stiffened and sniffed again – just to make sure. Yes: there it was, that faint, familiar aroma. Her muscles contracted as she drew herself upright. 'I gather that "poor" Margot had time for full ablutions,' she said. 'Perfume and all.'

His reaction proved her right – as guilt flashed across his face, he pulled away, taking Margot's sweet stench with him.

She narrowed her eyes. 'Needed a lot of tender consolation, did she?'

'Laura!' That tone again, a warning while both their faces hardened.

How wrong she'd been before. They were not her allies. They couldn't be for they were completely gullible, duped by Margot's fierce cunning. She had no allies and there was no reprieve. She was on her own. 'I have to go,' she said.

She left the room, moving with precision. Even though it was years since she'd been in this house, she knew just where to go: down the hall, down one half-flight of stairs and straight into Heloise's bathroom. Two steps and she was by the basin, but it was too mean, too small. Over to the bath she went; knelt down, turned the cold tap full on and shoved her face into the path of the streaming water.

It did its work, the water, it swept away her fury until, at last, she was finished – subdued and shivering. She got up, pulled a dressing gown from the door, threw it on, knotted it tightly round her waist and padded back to the bedroom, rubbing a hand towel energetically through her hair.

The room was empty, the bed made, and beside it on the back of an easy chair lay her clothes, all freshly washed and ironed, cleansed just like her emotions.

She dressed and went downstairs; found Steven and Heloise sitting at the small kitchen table. They looked up when she entered but neither spoke. She knew immediately what that meant: with silence – that's how they had decided to cope with her – with silence and understanding. Well, she didn't mind. She didn't mind anything. She smiled when Heloise poured her coffee and she even managed to down a slice of buttered wholemeal toast. And then, when she was done, she spoke.

'We should go next door,' she said.

They walked beside her, each holding one arm, as if she might escape.

But no, that was wrong. They were holding on to her so that they could protect her, for a crowd had gathered outside Leo's front door and as she came closer a flash went off.

'Laura,' someone cried. 'Laura. This way.' She turned. Another flash. 'What happened, Laura?' A second voice. 'Was he murdered?'

The front door opened and she was propelled inside. She felt Steven's arm bracing as her knees began to buckle. She gritted her teeth, locked her muscles, forcing herself upright. She was on her own. She could not afford to lean on Steven.

'Laura.' A pale-faced, black-clad Margot, was hurrying towards them, her face full of serious concern.

Well, Margot was not the only one who could play that game. 'Margot,' Laura said, matching Margot's pathos with her own. 'How are you?'

CHAPTER SEVENTEEN

She stood, immobilized, outside Leo's study. Her hand – she wanted it to turn the doorknob, but couldn't get it to – it wouldn't move. She tried again – again, no joy. Don't be silly, she told herself – and stood there.

'Don't be silly.' She said the words out loud, goading herself to action. It worked. Her hand stretched out and grabbed the knob. But did not turn it. The hand had no more power; it was shaking. Shutting her eyes, she let it drop.

She continued to stand there, arguing silently with herself. The worst is over: Leo is dead. The worst is over. What else is there to fear?

And knew the answer suddenly. Leo's ghost. That's what scared her. The strange thought that it might have possessed his study.

She frowned, thinking that it was absurd. Leo, who'd dwelt determinedly in the here and now, would never dream of coming back a ghost! She shot her hand out, grasped the doorknob and, twisting it, forced the door open.

The room was abruptly revealed, darker than she had anticipated. Darker – of course, it had been night when Leo died and, with the curtains still drawn, it looked as if night had come again. Pulling the door shut behind her, she took one tentative step forward.

A ghost, there *was* a ghost inside the room – not Leo's but another, her mother's – Judith's. She stood and watched it, that thing, her mother as she had been that night, bending over Leo's desk. Bending, scrabbling, muttering to herself, rooting through Leo's possessions as on the floor an upturned light shone through her nightie, illuminating her legs. A ghost which, hearing Laura enter, turned round, a savage look upon its face. No – she took one step backwards. No – Judith could not return; not now, not ever. She closed her eyes, shutting the vision out.

When eventually she reopened them, she found, of course, that the ghost was gone. No – she shook her head – not gone, for it had never existed. Her hand shot out, the light clicked on.

She looked around the room, seeing it with fresh eyes. It made her feel so sad; it was like a mausoleum, frozen, its furniture heavy with age, the patterns on its coverings so dark they looked like shrouds. And worse than that there was the smell – Leo's smell – linked so inextricably with the smell of death.

Death and loss – that's all this room could offer – death and loss. She turned, about to leave, but remembered suddenly what she was doing here. The jade, the tortoise that both her parents had meant for her, she must get it before it fell into Margot's hands. She turned again, walked quickly to the desk.

It isn't there, she thought, almost panicking, it isn't there. But then, telling herself she could not know, not after one cursory glance, she slowed and began to search the desk top more carefully.

Her first impression had been right: it really wasn't there. She shook her head. She wouldn't give up, not now. Inside, she thought, that must be it, Leo must have put it in his desk. Walking briskly round, she sat in Leo's chair – in Leo's leather chair, old even in Judith's time, precious to Leo because it was one of the few family possessions to leave Germany. She ran her hands along the leather, stroking its softness, knowing that the chair had belonged to Leo's father, her grandfather, who had been a long time dead.

They're all dead, she thought, a chain on both sides, going back for generations and ending decisively with me.

She leaned forward, opened up a drawer. It was so neat, this drawer, so orderly – her eyes filled with tears. She looked at the pencils lying in a row, all newly sharpened, the paper clips in their separate, labelled box, the envelopes graded carefully according to size.

No jade. She shut that drawer and opened the one below. So

she searched them all, the secret one included. And when she'd done that, and when it was all over, she knew the jade was gone. She frowned.

Perhaps it never was here? she thought.

But of course it had been here. It always had – ever since Judith's death. And she had seen it recently, she was sure of that, had seen it lying in Leo's whitened, ageing hands. Her eyes narrowed, remembering the policeman's dutiful enunciation of what he would consider grounds for suspicion. *Anything missing or out of place* – that was one.

Well, something is missing, she thought. I must tell him, I must tell him now.

'Miss Weber.'

The voice, that same policeman's voice, made her jump. She turned and saw to her relief that the voice was real: the policeman was standing in the doorway.

Her moment's terror must have been openly displayed for, 'Miss Weber?' he said, sounding concerned as he took one step towards her.

She got up and, reorganizing her expression, offered him a reassuring smile. 'You gave me a fright,' she said by way of explanation.

He nodded and seemed to relax. 'You weren't downstairs,' he said.

Downstairs? She looked at her watch and saw it was long past four. 'I'm sorry.'

Another nod – forgiveness – and then straight to business. 'I've come to tell you that I won't be bothering you any more. Your father's death was as a result of a coronary thrombosis,' he said and then, seeing perhaps her incredulity, added: 'The wound to his scalp was superficial, consistent with his head hitting the side of the kitchen counter as he fell.'

'But there was so much blood!' she protested.

He nodded. 'It looked like a lot, it always does. But if you ever had the misfortune to attend a pub brawl you would know that the scalp area is heavily supplied with blood vessels. The coroner's court will, naturally, have the final say, but between you and me, I don't anticipate any problems.'

'A heart attack.' It came out involuntarily, and angrily as well. 'It can't be.'

His face hardened. 'Miss Weber,' he said, sounding aggrieved. 'Your father was sixty-nine years old and in poor health. And yes, before you ask, we did check with his GP and he confirmed that Mr Weber's heart defect had been detected six months earlier.'

No. She shook her head. It wasn't true.

'The condition was serious enough,' the policeman continued, 'for a specialist to recommend by-pass surgery. Mr Weber decided against this.'

It couldn't be true, for if it were, she would have known. 'No,' she said.

He frowned, making no attempt to conceal his impatience. 'I'm sure that your father's GP would be happy to confirm what I have told you. And now, if you don't mind ...' He didn't bother tying up the sentence, he turned and began to walk downstairs. Down and round he went. She watched him go.

Until, suddenly, she was in motion too. 'Wait.' He had almost reached the hall. 'Wait!' He turned. 'A sharp blow, you said?' A nod. 'Could it have been caused by something other than the kitchen counter? Something small?' Another nod. 'I know ...'

The living-room door had opened and Margot emerged. Margot who, seeing Laura on the stairs and the policeman down below, looked puzzled from one to the other.

'Miss Weber?' The policeman was waiting for her to release him.

'I know what it was,' she said, watching Margot. 'And so does Mrs Weber.'

A gentle smile played across Margot's unsuspecting lips. 'What do I know?'

'What happened to the jade, of course.'

She was right, she knew it, for she saw dismay flashing across Margot's face. But the policeman had been looking only at Laura. 'What jade?' Taking one faltering step backwards, Margot swallowed. 'What jade?' she asked, louder this time.

Laura's eyes were fixed on Margot. 'There was a small jade tortoise on Leo's desk, wasn't there, Margot?' Across Margot's face a myriad different expressions were separated out – confusion, terror, guile, deceit – each in turn.

Speech – Margot was struggling for speech – and here it came: 'I didn't know . . .' she stuttered, but was too clever to risk an outright lie. 'I didn't know where the jade was kept,' she said.

Yet what she said was still a lie, for she must have known. 'It was on Leo's desk,' Laura prompted. 'But now it's gone.'

The policeman, his interest finally aroused, turned. 'Is this true?' addressing Margot not Laura.

'I . . .'

Got you, Laura thought.

Margot shrugged. 'I know of the piece,' she said softly. 'Although I haven't seen it for a while. In fact, I'm not sure,' she continued, letting a frown gently deepened, 'if I ever saw it on Leo's desk.'

'Ah.' The policeman's expression relaxed and he nodded, once only, but in that moment Laura knew she had lost him. He wanted to believe Margot so much that there was no point arguing – not without some more evidence.

But she couldn't stop herself. 'How can you say that?' The words burst out of her. For how could Margot? If Laura had seen the jade then so had she. And Laura *had* seen it. 'How can you say that?' She was almost screaming.

She had lost control and lost the policeman too. He looked at Margot and then at her, and when he looked at her she saw contempt. Hysterical – he didn't say the word, but that what's he was thinking – hysterical in the face of Margot's calm. 'I'm sure it will turn up.' That's all he said and then, pausing only to shake Margot's hand, he left the house.

1964

It was the most glorious moment that Laura could remember, a moment studded with happiness. There they all were, alone on the steep hillside, the three of them together, her parents and her.

It was autumn and inhospitably cold. They had known it was freezing and had decked themselves out with coats, hats, gloves, scarves and even earmuffs, but these now all lay discarded – multicoloured fragments of protection no longer required.

'Watch!'

Laura turned from her grinning father and looked down the hill.

'Here it comes.' Her mother's cry carried on the wind. Laura, standing on the crest of the hill, saw her mother run forwards and, just at the right moment, let go, flinging her hands up.

It was perfectly, precisely, timed, Judith's gesture. The string tightened and the crimson kite was lifted by a gust of wind.

'Let it out.' She needed no instruction, the spindle was already turning in her hands, its nylon string lengthening as the kite flew up, heading straight into a chaotic sky.

It was tugging hard at her, too hard. 'Help me,' she called, half panicked.

But Leo, who was standing to one side laughing at the antics of his two women, shook his head. 'You are doing it by yourself,' he called. 'And doing it very well.'

In that moment, as Leo's voice sounded, everything was changed. There was a sharp tugging upon the rope and then the kite begun to duck and weave, spiralling above Laura. 'Help me,' she called again, meaning it this time.

The kite was out of control. 'Hold on.' Judith was coming closer. 'Hold on,' her voice urgent. But Laura could not hold on. She felt the string slicing through skin, its former fragility now causing solid pain, and she gasped and then she couldn't help herself, she felt her hand go slack.

The kite was free, rising above her, borne by a furious wind. Straight up it travelled until it suddenly began to duck and weave, its string trailing behind.

'No.' She could not bear it. No, it must not be lost. Not this – this magnificent thing that her mother had made for her. She closed her eyes. Her ears were hurting and she felt the tears stinging her wind-scorched cheeks. And felt suddenly something else as well, a rush of wind beside her, a rush that was warmth itself.

She opened her eyes. Leo had passed her and was running, running down the hill. Against the buffeting of the elements he ran, lurching down, his arms up as he tried to grab the string, sprinting over obstacles, squelching through mud that did not seem to slow him down, running, running to catch the object of Laura's desire. She, too, was suddenly in motion, her legs moving without prompting, pumping twice to her father's every stride, so that she was plunging down the hill, seeing at the same time how Judith was also running.

And so they ran, the three of them – Leo in front, Judith gaining and Laura at the back. She was invulnerable: her foot hit a rock and she sprawled forward but, stretching an arm out, she broke her fall, pushed herself upward and continued running. Straight and fast, feeling the panting of her own breaths, running until . . .

They had stopped, the two of them, her parents; had stopped and were standing gasping at the foot of a tall tree. A tree which had imprisoned Laura's kite, its branches entrapping the brightly flashing construction. There was no time to register disappointment, no time at all, for Leo was in motion again and Laura found herself watching, her mouth agape, as her father, her dignified, righteous, gentle father began to climb the tree.

'Hey. Go it, Leo,' Judith called and Leo climbed faster. He

was so sure-footed, displaying a vigour that contrasted with his habitual calm dignity.

'Yay, Leo.' He was on the highest branch, his hand stretching out. He freed the kite, let it drop down. Judith caught it, held it tight as Leo released the trapped string from its spiky cages and then slowly, much more slowly than he had ascended, Leo came down. His face was flushed but his voice was its normal poised and courteous self. 'Let us get the string in order,' he said.

Laura saw the kite resting in her mother's strong hands, and saw that it was broken – an ugly gash across its crimson expanse. It was beautiful, she thought wistfully, remembering how she had watched those hands of Judith rapidly fashioning this kite of tissue and of wood.

'What do you think?' she heard. She looked up at Judith, at Judith's flushed skin and flashing green eyes. There was silence as mother and daughter gazed at each other, and in that moment Laura could swear that a single thought passed between them. The kite – that's what they were thinking – the kite had served its purpose.

'Here. You do it.' Yes, Judith had done what Laura had been hoping she would do; had thrust the kite into Leo's hands.

And he, her father, had guessed just what to do, had reached into his pocket and, withdrawing his key, had used it to slice across the string, freeing the kite from its restraints. And then, when the next gust tore through, the kite was launched into the air. High it went – not spinning but straight upwards – high into the sky, a gash of bright red against a darkly changing world.

CHAPTER EIGHTEEN

1992

'It's time,' Laura heard Steven saying.

She didn't respond. She continued sitting motionless, staring at the blue sky.

'It's time.'

She blinked, thinking idly that there was no kite out there – it was gone, just like Judith, and Leo, too.

'Are you ready?'

She nodded. Yes, she was ready, would leave this room in Heloise's house and join the cortège.

'Coming?'

Cupping her hands together, she dropped her face into them.

'Laura?'

She breathed in once and out again, and then moved her fingers, circling her eye sockets and her forehead too, pushing down hard against the dryness.

'We'll have to go.'

She nodded wearily and got up.

It was one of those bright, autumnal days which do not seem like autumn. Except, she thought as she emerged, it is autumn, the bare branches matching the crowd's dark funereal wear. The crowd – it was bigger than she had imagined, the row of looming black saloons fronting a queue of cars that stretched round the corner. Mourners were milling out in front while the strangers who had been gathering since early morning were contained behind steel cordons.

It was like a show to them, the strangers. As she made her

way slowly down the stairs she heard a collective gasp of recognition; saw fingers pointing. She stood for a moment motionless, her tight black skirt hugging her figure, her black jacket open to reveal a crimson silk shirt. It wasn't only strangers who reacted so sharply. Margot and Dorothy had been standing close together deep in conversation, but when Laura's feet touched bottom they each looked up, directly at her. She frowned: Margot – Leo's murderer and Dorothy his secretary, who had been so brusque when Laura had phoned the office. Margot and Dorothy: could there be collusion between them?

At that moment the two women separated. Dorothy walked over to Laura and as she came closer Laura saw how red-rimmed were her eyes. Of course, Laura should have known. Dorothy could not possibly be implicated, she had been with Leo so long and she had loved him.

'Oh, Laura.' Dorothy's eyes were misted, her voice on the verge of breaking. 'And to think that you phoned on the very day and I told you he wasn't there.'

'It's all right,' Laura said softly.

'He came in soon afterwards, you know.'

Laura's eyes narrowed. Why was Dorothy bothering to tell her this – unless of course that's what Dorothy and Margot had been doing, making sure that Margot's story added up?

'. . . I told him you rang. He said he'd try you later. He said . . .' She was sobbing so hard that her words became inaudible and she was reduced to stuttering until Laura put her arms around her and hugged her tight.

'Oh, Laura,' Dorothy said before another voice, Steven's voice, intervened. 'The car,' he said. Laura looked up, following his gaze, and saw that the door of the second car had been opened and that Margot was waiting by it. It was time. Kissing Dorothy on the cheek she pushed her gently away and walked towards the car.

They drove to the cemetery, she and Margot, with Jack Carmichael between them and Steven sitting opposite. No words were exchanged; even Jack was silent, sitting staring straight ahead, each hand squeezing at one of the women's.

When they arrived, the mourners divided into two halves, one on each side of the empty pit. Margot went one way and Laura the other, Leo's two women standing almost opposite each other. At their head was a large tree, its branches jagged and bare; and under it the coffin, a ponderous, shining, over-blown thing complete with brass spine and handles; and by its side – Jack.

When the crowd was all at rest, Jack began to speak.

At first Laura caught every word but gradually Jack's voice started phasing out on her. She felt so restless, her eyes wandering around a crowd which seemed drearily homogeneous.

'Sometimes we would talk of death, Leo and I,' she heard Jack saying, 'and then I discovered that death had no power to frighten Leo.'

How could it? she thought: he lived with it.

'He was a man whose convictions burned strongly,' Jack continued. 'All his working life he fought against the injustice which brings premature death; against famine, war, poverty . . .'

Her eyes were stinging. She looked away. The symmetry of death, she thought, has joined Leo with those he tried to save.

'. . . a man,' Jack said, 'who was unquestionably, unfashion-ably moral, an honourable man who never shirked the truth. He would not let either changing fashion, or' – and here Jack paused and looked around – 'political expediency affect what he knew was right.' Another pause as Jack passed his hand across his eyes. 'The world without Leo,' he said more softly, 'will be a darker place.'

She looked more closely at him, saw that the expression on his face was more uncertain than it had ever been and that his normally vibrant skin was dulled. It's as if a light has gone out. And yes, she thought, a light must indeed have gone out. Jack and Leo, Leo and Jack: they had been inseparable, bound together by a common passion. But it was more than that, more than theory, for they had loved each other, Leo and Jack, that much was certain.

Love. So many people had loved the undemonstrative Leo. It could not be feigned, their love; it clung to the words that had been written about him and to the faces of the many who had travelled to his funeral.

'His personal life was not always easy,' Jack was saying. 'He came from Germany, before the war, and although he was too young to have been implicated, his life was blighted by the knowledge of the horrors committed in the name of the German people. And when later tragedy struck, when his first wife, Judith, died by her own hand, Leo wavered. He went on always with his work, but it was many years before he smiled again. It was his daughter, Laura, who became the mainstay of his life: for her he continued . . .'

Did he really? Laura thought. Just for me? She shut her eyes abruptly and Leo's face loomed up, Leo's gentle, tired, familiar face. She watched it numbed, this inner image, watched as it opened its mouth. *You are my life*, she heard. *You are my life*: words of love and meaning pronounced even as he gently pushed her away. Her eyes were pinpoints, squeezed shut against her skin, against her nose, tiny whirls amongst a sea of wrinkles.

While Jack had got to Margot: '. . . at last found happiness again . . .' he said.

And yes, Laura thought, Leo had found happiness with Margot – at least in the beginning. She remembered it so well, that look on Leo's face as he'd told his daughter of his love for Margot, that childish, embarrassed look which made her want to put him out of his misery, she who had after all introduced them and who knew exactly what was going on. He had blushed then, when she had laughingly teased him about young love.

Oh yes, he had loved Margot. So what had happened to change all that?

'. . . only to have it summarily cut off . . .'

Her throat constricted.

'. . . we can at least give thanks' – Jack paused, looked briefly round – 'that death came quickly for Leo, such an active man, would never have made a good invalid . . .'

She was gasping and the tears were flowing – not lightly but in hot splashes spilling down her cheeks.

'. . . so, Leo Weber, my friend,' Jack said, his head drooping, 'go in peace. Just as in your lifetime you worked so tirelessly for peace, may you now find it. Go then, in peace.'

In peace, he said, and choking turned away, his massive shoulders heaving.

In peace: the words reverberated and as they receded the sound of grieving took over, while Laura stood, tears coursing down, forcing herself to bear witness as the ugly casket was lowered into the moist earth. As jerkily one side touched ground, and as the long, wide supporting strand was pulled from under it.

And only when that was over, the coffin finally at rest, did she look up. Up and over – her eyes were drawn across the grave, to Margot. Margot who, seeming to feel the tug of Laura's gaze, lifted her head.

Their eyes locked – Laura's green and Margot's brown – and in that moment Laura thought she could see a swelling of sorrow that crossed the gaping cavern, so intense that she was no longer sure whether the misery she saw in Margot's dull eyes was Margot's or her own reflected back. And in that moment Laura believed what everybody had been endlessly repeating: that Margot would never have harmed Leo, that she had loved him fiercely and that she was grieving for him. Grieving just as Laura was.

The thought, a tiny ray of hope, expanded and Laura wanted to reach out and clasp Margot's hand and ask for forgiveness for her behaviour since Leo's death, for her coldness at the inquest and her bitterness when the coroner had pronounced a verdict of death by natural causes.

And perhaps she would have done so, she would have stretched across and spoken, if not for the fact that Margot broke contract. Suddenly – just like that. Her eyes came into focus and she looked at Laura, looked coldly; no hint of friendship in that gaze. Then she blinked; not once but twice she blinked and, haltingly, began to move.

Leaving Laura's sympathy turning back into hostility. They're wrong, she thought. Margot's grief isn't real, it's studied.

Margot stumbled. And now she's going to throw herself into the grave, thought Laura.

But no, Margot stopped in time and, leaning briefly down, she grabbed a handful of dirt, threw her arm out, throwing dirt upon the coffin. There were pebbles amid the dirt and they slid across the polished wood, a few jittering upwards before they finally came to rest.

Silence.

Silence; and a gentle nudge on Laura's arm.

Oh yes. The wife first, the daughter afterwards. She advanced upon the grave but shook her head against the proffered spade and knelt instead to pick one rose stem from a wreath. One red rose which she threw down into the grave and then stood back while the others were stirred to action, stood watching other flowers falling alongside the dirt, beauty amid the loam, life amongst the dead.

It was over, time to move away. Laura took a step forward, intending to link her arm to Jack's.

Too late: Margot had manoeuvred quickly, interposing herself between Laura and Jack. Deliberately, that's how she'd done it, and she couldn't resist a glance in Laura's direction, a glance that Laura saw was full of triumph.

And now, Laura thought, I am entirely alone.

'Come.' Steven's arm was round her waist. 'Come,' he gently said.

No, that was wrong, she was not alone. What she was, instead, was next.

CHAPTER NINETEEN

I'm next, she thought as the crowd filed past and as hands softened by age or by emotion pressed dolefully into hers. There were photographers as well, their flashes, released from inactivity, frantically discharging. She bent her head down, tolerating the attention, and when it was over she went and found the car.

They were waiting for her, the same trio; Margot, Jack and Steven. When she arrived they filed silently into the smooth, black limousine, and silently endured the journey back to Leo's house. No, not Leo's – Margot's house, for Leo had left it to his wife for the duration of her life.

His wife, who seemed now ill at ease, skirting conversations, an uneasy smile stuck to her pasty face. These were not her people, they were Leo's, and Laura's crowd as well, a glittering mixture. Officials and their masters – junior ministers, UN high-ups, ambassadors from multifarious countries – mingled with the artists, actors and academics who had come to pay their respects. A complex mix of wealth, power and fame was being stirred up her – and not a little business too.

'My dear, I am so sorry.' A Nobel prize winner whose talents Leo had once promoted squeezed Laura's hand. 'Leo was almost unique amongst mortals, a man who could tell the difference between good and bad. We are all the poorer for his going.' And then the dignified, white-haired man hobbled off, following a finger which had pointed out the unknown Margot, who stood there, nodding and smiling in that cramped way. While watching, Laura wondered what Leo had ever seen in her.

But of course she knew the answer. It was Judith, for in embarking on Judith's biography, Margot had taken on Judith's reflected glory. She was clever, was Margot, had used Judith to catch her man, and then, having succeeded, had annihilated Judith.

Yes, Laura nodded to herself, that's exactly what had happened. She felt her eyes narrowing, felt hatred creeping. And heard a voice hissing in her ear. 'Miss Weber,' it said.

When she looked up she saw it was one of the waiters who'd spoken her name. She frowned – she was not mistress of this house. 'Yes?'

'There's someone at the door for you,' he said and walked away before she had time to tell him that he was surely mistaken. She didn't want to talk to Margot – not now – so she went into the hall. There, standing by the open door, was a young man – a stranger in leathers and a helmet. A messenger. 'You must want Mrs Weber,' she said, going closer.

But no. 'I was told to ask for a Miss Weber,' he said, thrusting clipboard and pen at her. 'Sign here, please.'

She shrugged why not? and signed, and the next thing she knew he had removed the clipboard and in its place deposited a package. It was hand-sized, wrapped in brown paper, and it fitted her palm. She knew what it must be. Her hand curled round the package. 'Wait,' she called. He was down the stairs already and as she called out his foot kicked at his motorbike. Her voice was drowned by the revving of his engine.

She moved. 'Wait,' she shouted, but too late again: he had pulled out into the road, pressed his foot down and he was off, speeding round the corner, leaving her standing on the steps, package in her hand.

'Are you all right?' She turned: there was a man, a representative from a minor aid agency, standing framed by the doorway, his face bunched up in serious concern. 'Are you all right?' he said again.

She nodded. 'Yes,' she said. She was in sudden motion: walking up the stairs and on past him down the corridor until she was standing at the other end. He hadn't moved, the stranger; he was looking in her direction. 'I'm quite all right,' she said distinctly, using all her powers of calm. 'I just need a few minutes on my own.'

He went bright red. 'Of course,' he said and, turning on his heel, marched himself away.

The package – it lay heavy in her hand. She stared down at it, her mind blank, and then, suddenly, she was undoing the wrapping, noting absently as she did so how steady were her hands.

She had known what it would be. Of course. The tortoise: this precious gift that Leo had once, so many years ago, given to his Judith. The tortoise, sparkling in her hand and with it a crumpled piece of paper.

There was a table next to her: she laid the tortoise down and then carefully, carefully, unfolded the paper.

A few lines of unfamiliar writing, that's all she saw. Words, difficult to decipher. She peered closely, staring at the writing, until it started to make sense. 'To Laura Weber,' she read, 'even though it should not be hers. From a well-wisher.' A well-wisher? she thought and, sticking the paper in the pocket of her skirt, picked up the tortoise and began to move.

Into the living room, and straight to Margot. 'Margot,' she said abruptly.

Margot turned. 'Laura,' the word delivered on the crest of a gentle smile.

Which Laura did not reciprocate. 'I have something to show you,' she said.

'Of course.' Margot came closer. 'What is it?'

As if you don't know, Laura thought, but, seeing Heloise bearing down on them, she bit the words back. 'Come outside,' she said.

They were in the kitchen, the two of them. 'What is it?' Margot asked.

'A present.'

'A . . .' Margot began but stopped when Laura held out her open hand. 'A . . .' That was all that came out, in between some frantic gulping. Terror, it must be that, flooded her face, leaching out all colour. 'Where did . . .' she whispered, taking a step backwards.

'Where did I get it?' Laura's voice was loud and clear. 'That's my business.' She came a little closer. 'But what I want to know,' she said, 'is where it has been.'

'I . . .' Margot blinked and tried to move away, but she had already backed too far – she was pressed against the work-bench. 'I . . .' she stuttered.

'I know you hid it.' Laura said. 'And then, after that? Did you wash it well, hey, Margot? After you had used it?'

'I . . .'

'Did you?' She was so close she could see a vein in Margot's neck throbbing. 'Did you?' She wasn't thinking any more; her hand was rising, clutching at the tortoise, rising until her arm was quite extended. 'Did you?' She pulled it back, back into an arch, and then began to bring it . . .

'Laura!'

Laura. It startled her, making her drop her arm. She whipped her head around and saw Heloise, her eyes blazing, running forwards. 'What has got into you?' Heloise shouted and then she was upon Laura and wrestling the tortoise away.

Laura's hand went slack, the tortoise dropping from it.

'Were you trying to kill her?'

To kill her? Laura thought absently. But she's the murderer.

'Have you no sense of propriety?' she heard Heloise saying. 'To behave like this on the day of your father's funeral . . .' A pause only for a sharp intake of breath and then: 'How can you persecute poor Margot like this?'

Poor Margot whom Laura could see sidling away. *Poor Margot*. Laura felt own rage resurfacing, but Heloise was in full flood. 'How can you? Your father would be ashamed of you. No, worse than that, your father . . .'

I must stop her, Laura thought.

'. . . would have been so hurt. I cannot . . .'

Laura held up one hand. 'Stop it.' she said, quite calmly and watched satisfied as they both did stop – Heloise and Margot too. She looked at them, standing there; saw Margot, blinking furiously, wondering whether her luck had finally run out; and saw that Heloise was stirring, that words were re-forming in her angry mouth. Well Laura must get in first. 'While you fret about protocol,' she said to Heloise, 'Margot gets away with murder.'

A long silence and then, 'Oh, Laura,' and the outrage went. Heloise's face crumpled, she looked so sad. 'What makes you think that Margot killed Leo?' she said gently.

While something inside Laura began to ache. Don't go on, an internal voice said, don't go on – you'll lose her too.

She couldn't listen to that voice – not now. 'Margot has done nothing but lie,' she said.

Heloise's tone hardened. 'She's lied, has she?' She wasn't sad, not any longer. 'Well, tell me – which are the lies?'

Now – her chance was now. It might not come again. 'She said Leo went back to the office. But he didn't, he wouldn't have.'

Heloise shook her head. 'He did. The police said so. It was logged on the computer.'

No, she thought, it can't be. Leo never used the computer. And yet her conviction was dented.

'What else?' Heloise demanded.

She looked away. 'The jade,' she muttered. 'Somebody sent it back.'

Heloise's voice was determined: 'Margot? Did she send you the jade?' and when Laura remained silent, added: 'Can you prove she did?'

Laura shook her head. It wasn't her job, finding proof. She shook her head again. 'She killed him with it,' she muttered.

And heard a snort of suppressed laughter.

Or thought she heard one. But when she looked up, Heloise was staring at her unamused. 'Oh, Laura,' Heloise sighed. 'How could she do that?'

She remembered suddenly her own hand in the air. She did not want to think of it, not now, but Heloise was relentless. 'Have you imagined the scene?' she said, before hurling out a set of angry questions, 'Was Leo turned away? Is that what you think? That she came up from behind and felled him with one blow?' Her eyes drilled into Laura, demanding a reply.

'How should I know?'

'If you make such accusations you should know,' Heloise said. 'And you should know better, you should use your brain. You saw your father lying there. He was lying lengthwise, his head against the counter. If she had attacked him from the back he would have fallen the other way.

'So she . . .'

'No.' Heloise was shouting. 'Don't even say it. For if she had attacked him from the front, the bruise would have been on his forehead. And it wasn't, was it?'

No, she thought, remembering her father lying on the floor, a pool of congealing blood behind him. 'She could have moved him,' she said, shutting her eyes tight.

And heard another, 'Oh, Laura,' issuing from Heloise's mouth. 'Margot could not possibly have moved a dead Leo, not without leaving a trail. Your father was an important man – the police were extremely careful.'

Laura squeezed her eyelids tight.

Heloise's voice continued to pursue her into darkness. 'Leo had a heart attack,' she said.

A heart attack – but he never told me he was ill. She opened her eyes, just in time to see Margot walking quickly out. She felt tears rising. 'I'm sorry.'

A long silence and then Heloise nodded. 'It is time to let go,' she said.

To let go – if only she could. But no, 'I can't,' she whispered. 'Something happened that night – something wrong. I have to know what it is. I have to know if I could have stopped it.'

Another prolonged silence before Heloise shook her head. 'No matter how hard you try,' she said, 'you cannot bring back the past.'

Heloise had spoken so slowly that, hearing the gravity of her tone and the weight given to each word, Laura knew that Heloise was talking not about Leo but about Judith; about Judith's death and the moment of her dying. 'It's not the same,' Laura protested.

'It's not exactly the same,' Heloise agreed. 'But you've never given up wrestling with the past. It won't do you any good. It's over: you must accept that.'

Over, Laura thought, and wished it was. But Heloise was wrong: it wasn't over, it never would be, she would be haunted by the memory of her mother's act until her own dying day.

'Let go of death,' she heard Heloise saying. 'Choose life.'

If only, she thought. If only I could.

'Now come,' Heloise said. 'There are many people waiting for you outside.'

People, they kept flooding past her; people with their good intentions and their nicely phrased condolences. And then, finally, the last of them left and she could go home.

She pushed her front door open, feeling nothing but relief. 'Should I stay?' she heard Steven asking. She nodded and walked in. She was so tired, so very tired. She let her coat slide off and didn't stop at that. Each item of clothing she removed, one after the other, dropping them down until, having reached the bed, all she had to do was climb inside. And glance up once to see Steven following in her wake, picking up each item she had dropped.

'Good for you,' she said and closed her eyes.

She woke, hours later, suddenly, without warning, without knowing what had awakened her. She was sitting up, her heart beating furiously. Something – something had disturbed her. She looked round.

There was nothing to be seen, only Steven lying on his side, the duvet rising and falling in time to his soft breathing.

She heard the echo of a voice, Heloise's voice; Heloise slicing through her proof and through her certainty. *Let go*, she heard again and she felt what she had not allowed herself to feel then – her loneliness and humiliation as well. Let go. She had no other choice, she had to let go, had to join the soft voices outside the kitchen, see Margot circulating, deliberately avoiding her eyes.

No – she wouldn't think of it. She stretched out an arm. 'Hold me,' she said out loud.

He was instantly awake.

'Hold me.'

He sat up and he held her. She felt his large, familiar hands stroking gently at her hair. Her head was resting against his chest: she could hear the rhythm of his heart. She looked up.

He responded to her look, bending his head down, meaning, she knew, to kiss her on the forehead. But she tilted her head back and his lips met hers, when he hesitated she kissed him – hard, and felt him almost immediately responding, his arms tightening, his body pushing closer, the soft skin of his swelling penis touching at her leg.

And then suddenly he tried to pull away.

She would not release him. 'I want to,' she said, thinking vaguely that a pattern, where he was the one who always initiated sex, had been broken. 'I want to,' pushing her tongue into his mouth.

She felt her body burrowing into his, her breasts crushed against his chest. It was her desire that drove them on, her body that imposed its will on his, her voice that possessed the space between them. Her cries were seagull yelps carried on a gale of uneven breaths. As she listened distantly to them she felt, welling up in her, a desire so monstrous that it was an agony that must be assuaged. Hatred, that's what possessed her, moving her above him, rocking her and Steven too.

Except it wasn't really hatred, it was need. Need – to be joined securely to Steven. She felt it swelling, that longing, just as she heard the distant cries grow stronger and more frequent, as she felt waves of sweetness so intense that they were almost painful, as she felt all this rocking the very sinews of her body. She cried out again and again after that, her voice growing gradually softer until it had drained away.

It was finished with, the ugliness and the elation that had accompanied it. She lay stranded in its aftermath of sticky fluid, lay there for a moment unfeeling.

Steven's arm reached out, rested on her naked back. Steven's arm, strong and sure, covered in a film of perspiration, embracing her. She twisted from it, rolling away. He started and then relaxed. She watched him, lying there looking at her, smiling vaguely, his lids heavy. He's a stranger, she thought, and felt nothing. Her tongue touched her lip and it snagged against the skin, sticking momentarily.

She was suddenly restless. She looked again at Steven, saw his eyes were firmly closed. She did not want to lie by him. She must get up.

She got up and walking over to the window looked out. The night was hushed, no one about; and above the dark outline of the buildings she could see bare branches towering, blue against the artificial light. She shivered, feeling needles of cold air hitting at her. Winter was on its way. She shivered again, wondering what was next.

The answer came to her: *Hedda Gabler*, that's what was next. She would go back to work, as quickly as was decent, would bury herself in Hedda's pain and in so doing would stanch her own. She would go back and play Hedda as well as Hedda had ever been played.

She smiled. There was symmetry in all this – Judith, Leo, Hedda a threesome who diced with death. A threesome: Hedda, Leo, Judith.

Judith, Leo, and Hedda. And after that?

And after that, she thought simply, just as she had beside the grave, there will be me. For I, at last, am next.

Winter

1966

She stood on the edge of Judith's room looking in. She was gripped by an impulse to run away and yet she wasn't able to. She closed her eyes, shutting out the sight, but couldn't stand there, unseeing, for long. She opened her eyes again.

It was the same. The same – the thing lying on the bed, one arm sprawled down. The thing, pale as parchment, its arm lolling, slack, flaccid, loathsome. Bile swelled, surging up her throat, and for a moment she couldn't breathe. Get help, a voice was saying somewhere, get help, her own voice telling her to move.

But she couldn't: she was cleaved to that spot by a double fear – the fear that she was right, and also that she might be wrong. She couldn't move: she was stuck. She shut her eyes tight.

And heard a noise. 'Ummf.' Or that's what it had sounded like – coming from Judith's bed. She was wrong then, she must be. Forcing her eyes open, she took two steps forward.

And stopped. Had she really been wrong? The thing was as inert as it had been before. As dead.

But no, relief washed over her. The thing was not the same. It had moved and was lying face down now, sprawled across the centre of the bed.

'Ummf.' That noise repeated.

It was all right, it must be. She looked and saw Judith turning on to her back and saw the rise and fall of Judith's chest – of Judith's living chest. She smiled.

'What day is it?'

She had not seen Judith's lips moving. She jumped back in surprise.

'What day is it?' spoken through encrusted lips, in a voice still corpulent with sleep.

While Laura was in contrast high-pitched. 'It's Wednesday,' she said, hating her voice, too childish by far for her thirteen years.

'Wednesday,' she heard Judith muttering and she saw Judith's eyes slowly opening, the green gradually revealed. Except they were not exactly Judith's eyes: they were out of focus, gazing from the depths of a face too pale. 'Wednesday,' Judith repeated the word, adding: 'the day after Tuesday. So it didn't work.'

Laura turned, but Judith's voice re-called her. 'Wednesday,' she said. 'Which means your father is in Khartoum.'

Laura stared down at her feet. 'Addis Ababa,' she muttered.

'Of course.' Judith's voice was much strengthened. 'How silly of me. Khartoum was Tuesday.' And then she added something that Laura didn't quite catch, something that sounded like, 'I timed that right, he is still gone,' followed by a muttered, 'But she?' and then another notch up: 'What are you doing here?'

What are you doing here, *spoken as if in rage. Laura shivered.*

'Well?'

She turned. 'The . . . the dentist,' *she stuttered.*

And saw Judith's face softening and her red lips curling up. 'Of course,' she said. 'The dentist.' Judith was suddenly in motion, sticking one foot out of bed, groaning extravagantly. 'Come,' she said. 'Come and help your old mother out of bed.'

So Laura walked back and waited as her mother, who didn't really need help but who was trying to be nice, climbed out. Or maybe Judith had needed help – she stumbled halfway, her foot kicking at something. She leaned down, reaching for that something. A small brown medicine bottle, that's what it was. Judith straightened up, holding the bottle to the light, peering through the glass.

'Empty,' she muttered. 'No more . . . no more . . .' She shuddered; turned to Laura. 'A shot of caffeine is what I need,'

she said. 'Be a darling, put the kettle on, will you? And here' –
she shoved the bottle into Laura's hand – 'Throw this out on
the way, will you? The bin's beside the door.'

CHAPTER TWENTY

1992

She was lying sprawled across a plush red sofa, hearing the play's final lines. 'But merciful God!' she heard. 'One doesn't do that kind of thing.' And then the stage went quiet, each member of the cast motionless, waiting out the closing of the curtains.

A soft swishing of blue velvet and when that was over . . . silence, stretching on until it grew almost unbearable. At which point it was abruptly cracked as applause, so loud it sounded like torrential rain, descended; a thunderous torrent of approval and of something else as well.

Relief – that's what it was. The cast felt it too, they stood, half turned, staring at Laura, and on their faces was relief. Relief not that they had survived the play – for that was a foregone conclusion – but rather relief that, at last, Hedda had decided.

The curtain, it was opening, she must get up. There. She was on her feet and in the centre of the line. A hand was thrust into each of hers and as the line bowed down, a soft voice whispered, 'Brilliant.'

Brilliant. That was all, accompanied by a squeeze of Peter's hand, dry pressure against her soggy palms.

Another surging of applause and she was thrust into the forefront of the line, distant cheers joining the furiously clapping hands. She dipped her head, bowing, and as she did so beads of sweat trickled down her forehead, obscuring her vision, making the noise predominate. She bowed once, twice, a third time but still the sound did not abate.

And then the curtain was pulled shut and she saw her own

grin reflected on the faces of the others. In the wings they were also clapping, amongst them a triumphant Gareth who launched himself into the air, his fist punching upwards. 'We did it,' he shouted.

'*You* did it,' Peter muttered.

At which point the curtain was reopened and the line on stage rejoined. Laura's head dipped down, her eyes clear now as she saw a row of empty seats across the footlights, and in the distance the last bent back of a critic scurrying off to file his copy.

But this was not the time for critics. The rest of the cast pushed her to the front, making her take the brunt of the renewed applause. She bowed down low, using her hands to call them back, gesturing at the same time for the curtains to be closed. And finally it was done and she shook her head firmly and walked off the stage, walking fast as she heard the order to raise the house lights and the clapping which continued even after the audience must have known that there would be no more curtain calls.

'Congratulations, darling.' This from Gareth, his lips grazing her cheek. She nodded, increased her pace.

She was alone at last, under the shower, rivers of mascara and red rouge washing down her cheeks while Gareth's words of praise resounded. Hearing their echo, she laughed out loud. 'Congratulations' – just like that, after all the insults they had exchanged. Her laughter surged, blending with the water, washing her clean. She could afford to laugh. She had triumphed: after three proficient but uninteresting previews and two catastrophic ones, she had emerged upon the stage a true Hedda.

Except . . . she felt herself sobering up, remembering how close to disaster she had been. She remembered how it had happened, the horrified look on Gareth's face just before the play began as she had fled from him. I can't go on, that's what she'd been thinking as what she had spent so long repressing – her father's death and her reaction to it – came surging back. She had run away from it, running from her dressing room, and, for reasons that she had not completely understood then, had gone to stand in the wings.

The wings, she realized now, because she had been resisting the impulse to flee the theatre and because it was harder to escape from there. And so she'd stayed, breaking with convention, a Hedda who had watched the house lights lowering. Silently she had stood as conversation and uneasy rustling ceased, standing waiting out ten painful minutes as the ground was laid for Hedda's entry. Dressed and ready she had stood, feeling the tautness in the atmosphere as the first lines were scribbled into critics' notebooks. She had stood, enduring all of this and then suddenly she was on.

She was Hedda then, truly Hedda, doubt did not come into it. From the first words and the first gesture, as Hedda held out one imperious hand, she had known she could do no wrong. She *was* Hedda – not Laura acting Hedda, but the woman herself; a living, breathing, angry, charming, clever, fated, cynical moth playing with the bright flames of life; dodging, twisting, resisting and finally succumbing. What Laura had learned in life, what Laura had experienced, was selected by Hedda and then transformed. Everything – movement, thought, feeling – each one of these was utilized, sharp and accurate. And it galavanized the other members of the cast, her performance, giving them permission to shine as well, so what came out was a dance of death that each individual had joined.

A dance of death. It came back to her what she had thought before, that time before the winter. First Hedda, that's what she had thought. And then . . .

'Darling!' Maya bounced into the dressing room and, being Maya, whipped the shower curtains open, hugging Laura so hard that by the time she had let go she was thoroughly soaked.

'Serves you right,' Laura said laughing, grabbing a dressing gown. She was on the move after that, greeting each successive wave of people who came bursting in, popping corks, calling out, hats and coats mixing with the mounds of flowers which Laura's dresser dumped unceremoniously into water. Success: the smell of it infused the air, heightening senses and voices as well.

The crush intensified and Laura's facial muscles were hard at work, fielding compliments, exchanging jokes, kissing lips and cheeks alike. All of this did she endure, made high not by what others told her but because she knew that what she'd done had truly been special.

'Coming?' Peter's hand was raised above the chaos, his finger pointing to the door.

She waved, going behind the wooden screen and dressing quickly. Then she began to push through the crowd, smiling and nodding as escalating praise was heaped upon her shoulders.

The party was in full swing when she arrived. She had meant to go straight there but a crowd of autograph-seekers by the door combined with the chill freshness of the night air had diverted her. She had strolled first round one block and then another and another. It was just what she needed – physical activity without thought – and it was only reluctantly that she at last turned back.

So the party was in full swing when she arrived – she almost managed to sneak in unnoticed. Almost, but not quite: someone on the fringes called out her name, setting off a chain of recognition until the various dots of conversation faltered and heads were turned smiling in her direction, palm fluttering against palm.

She, who found applause bearable only if it was distant, blushed and play-acted her embarrassment, holding a coquettish hand against an open mouth at the same time as she bobbed down in an exaggerated curtsy. It worked, drawing an ironic titter from those nearest, breaking the air of stiff reverence. And as the amusement became more generalized, her own place in the centre diminished; conversations were lightly rejoined. She was free to choose her own company.

Or almost free.

'Darling.' Gareth strode towards her, a white-haired couple in tow. 'Darling, I'd like you to meet my parents.'

Gareth's parents – as if Gareth were not enough! She grimaced inwardly as she stretched out a hand. 'Pleased to meet you.'

'You were marvellous.' Gareth's mother was a sweet-looking woman whose smile was so generous that the lines of age around her eyes were momentarily extinguished. That smile warmed Laura and she regretted her impatience. Of course this was the right place for Gareth's parents: if Leo had been alive he surely would have come to this first night.

Leo. He had wanted her to play Hedda and now he was gone.

'Excuse me,' she said, cutting across Gareth's father's copious compliments, 'excuse me,' and turned and walked away. A waiter passed, bearing a tray of drinks and she grabbed for one of them, white wine, and took a slug.

'Yeuch.' It was sweet and at the same time slightly methylated – she couldn't drink it. She looked around for somewhere she might dump it.

A voice cut throught the commotion. 'Try this,' it said.

This – a long-necked bottle lunged into vision, a sure hand holding it. She followed the hand, up the arm, and found herself staring at a man. A man – Tom Hooper. She'd had a formal card from him, his condolences on her father's death, but now she was thrown back, suddenly, to their last meeting. I kissed him, she thought.

She was hypnotized, her self dissolving under his unyielding gaze.

He smiled.

This is a cliché, she sternly told herself. She wrenched her eyes away.

When she finally looked back, he was holding the bottle innocently out. If he guessed her inner turmoil, he gave no sign of it. 'May I?' he said and taking her glass emptied its contents into the base of a nearby palm. That done he poured out some of his wine. 'Try this,' he said.

She took a sip, looked up and nodded. 'Where did you get it?'

He shrugged. 'There's always quality hiding somewhere amongst the rubbish.'

Yes, she thought, and I bet you always know where to find it.

But he had moved beyond her, was staring, the wine forgotten. 'You were extraordinary,' he said. He had spoken softly but his sentence resonated long after it was over. Extraordinary – not a word, she guessed, that he would often use.

She was unnerved by how flattered she felt. No, she must not be dragged into this man's dangerous orbit. She made herself resist. 'Extraordinary,' she said smiling. 'Like some kind of exotic vegetable?'

His concentration did not waver. 'And what was so astonishing,' he said, 'was the knowledge that that's not all.'

'Not all?' Not all — what could he mean? She grimaced. 'What do you want? Blood?'

His face was deadly serious. 'I want only,' he said, 'what I know you have to give.'

He was serious and it frightened her; she wanted to diffuse the tension. She raised an eyebrow. 'Are you propositioning me?'

He smiled, the intensity of his concentration broken. He no longer seemed dangerous; he had returned into the shell of a handsome, sure-footed, easy-going man.

I'm safe, she thought.

'Would you like me to?' he asked.

She swallowed. She'd been over-confident. She had not disarmed him — but nevertheless he let her off the hook. 'Sex aside,' he said, 'what I was trying to say is that even though it was an astonishing, a virtuoso performance, I sensed, especially at the end, that you have even more to give.'

'More?'

He looked at her, a smile flashing across his lips.

'I . . .'

'Darling.' Oh no: Gareth again. She turned to see what Gareth wanted. And found that he was not alone, that Steven was beside him, smiling quizzically at her, embarrassed, unsure of how to behave. Her reaction was automatic: she dropped her eyes. Guilt — that's what she felt.

Guilt. She pushed it back, thinking that she had not even spoken to Steven yet — another rift. Another in a long line of changes that had begun on the night of Leo's funeral and that had gradually and without acknowledgement been accelerated; the distance between them growing so big that, looking at him again, he seemed momentarily a stranger. She didn't know what to say.

She didn't need to know. Gareth, domineering, insensitive, bluff Gareth was impervious to any tension. 'I was just telling Steven what a clever one you are,' he said.

She frowned. 'Tom thinks I didn't give my all.'

'Bloody film stars: what do they know?' Gareth said, while Steven smiled politely and turned as if he were about to go.

She couldn't let him — not like that. She stretched a hand out, touched him on the shoulder. 'I'll be with you in a minute.'

He smiled. 'I was afraid that you might be getting tired,' he said.

Tired — he was right. He was so considerate; she was tired and of course he assumed that he would be taking her home — he always did so. 'In a moment,' she said, thinking she must rid herself of Tom. She dipped her head in Tom's direction, saying, 'You're a hard taskmaster.'

'Takes one to know one.' He bowed lightly, returning her gesture and at the same time punctuating a mutual recognition that what had passed between them was not entirely over. And then he stretched across and shook Steven's hand. 'I'm Tom Hooper,' he said.

She didn't listen any longer. She stood between the two men, watching the third one, Gareth, grinning inanely, while she felt the aftershock of the spark that had passed between herself and Tom and thought that what Tom had said was true, that she had held something back. Not deliberately, not because the audience or Hedda did not deserve it, but because the time was not yet right.

'Great to have seen you again.' Tom's voice and gaze alike were casual, all hint of danger gone.

She smiled, 'And you,' she said and watched him ploughing through the crowd, heads turning to follow him. He's used to being noticed, she thought. Or said it perhaps, out loud, because Steven, whose eyes were also on Tom, nodded.

'There are so many people here, dying to meet you,' Gareth's voice intruded.

CHAPTER TWENTY-ONE

As the party grew increasingly unruly, Laura found her own mood improving. She no longer wanted to go home. She felt herself released. She was free, that's how it felt, freed from the looming sense of disaster that seemed to have been pursuing her since the autumn. It's Hedda, she thought, and nodded. It was Hedda who had been dogging her and who, finally, in one performance, had been vanquished.

'Laura.' Another hand thrust warmly into hers and, at that same moment, the whoops of excitement which had started by the door, spilled over. The first review had arrived. Looking across, Laura saw newspapers, their guts discarded, being passed from hand to hand, disconnected adjectives extracted randomly from them. 'Dazzling', someone shouted, to be one-upped by 'rare' with a 'remarkable' tagged on briefly at the end. A maelstrom of exhilaration was stirred up, hands shaken, bodies lifted, all shouting with pleasure and Laura at its centre. And, unlike other times, she did not feel diffident about the praise. I deserve this, she thought as strangers and friends alike jostled for her attention, for I am free.

'So' – Maya's face came swimming into view – 'how does it feel to be lusciously luminescent?' and without waiting for a reply added: 'Hard work for your agent, I can tell you – I'm having to beat them off.' Her hand waved in the general direction of a group of men, all serious film money, who were standing together.

Laura laughed. 'Don't be silly, Hedda's far too serious to interest them.'

But: 'Hedda Schmedda,' Maya scoffed. 'It's not Hedda, it's

you. You frightened them and what frightens a modern financier he eventually tries to buy.' She winked and almost leered. 'As they say, nothing succeeds like success and other such clichés,' and then, grabbing hold of her assistant who happened to be passing, she waltzed him away, her red hair frizzing out, her voice raised, singing.

It went on after that, compliments heaped one on to the other, until eventually it really was time to go. She turned. And saw Steven, there on hand, waiting patiently. Her eyes briefly misted over. She was filled with a sudden surge of love for him, for the way he had stood by her, tolerating her endless, boring suffering without complaint. She linked her arm to his. 'Come,' she said softly, feeling the familiarity of his skin, wanting to pull him close, to kiss him hard. 'Let's go.'

'Let's go.' It was she who had involved him in getting her home and she who soon regretted it. Sitting beside him in the car, passive in the face of his capable manoeuvrings, the misgivings that had recently made her feel so distant from him came flooding back. Her exhilaration and her love for him faded, replaced by rising irritation. It was instinctual, her reaction, she could barely put it into words. She only knew that what she was experiencing was a kind of claustrophobia.

She had tried to persuade herself that nothing had really changed and yet she knew that everything had. It was almost as if her perceptions had been turned upside down – what had once attracted her to Steven turning to its opposite, a focus, these days, for repulsion. What she'd called grounded now seemed utterly confining, what had been reassuring was now plain boring. Of course he hadn't changed, he was still practical, was Steven – and so uncomplicated it made her want to scream. She no longer even thought of him in bed. Her impulse in the party to kiss him hard had been a startling aberration which had quickly evaporated. For these days, ever since that night, in fact, that night of Leo's funeral, she had ruled out sex.

It wasn't something that she had thought about, or could even verbalize. It was an instinctive, physical reaction which verged occasionally on the nauseous. She didn't want him, it

156

was as simple as that. She didn't want him touching her, to feel his body next to hers, to feel her own desire stirring.

'We're here.'

She looked up startled and saw that, while she'd been lost in thought, he had drawn up outside her block of flats. Drawn up – not parked . . . Her eyes flicked across his face.

He was smiling and if he was saddened he had succeeded in concealing it. 'You must be exhausted,' he said.

She felt suddenly so grateful to him for his tact and his diplomacy. She nodded. 'I am rather,' she said and, reaching over, kissed him.

'I'll call you,' he said, and that was all before she was out and he driving away.

Shutting her flat's front door she leaned against it and breathed slowly out. Alone – at last she was alone! She felt herself smiling, relief surging through. It isn't Steven, she thought, it's anybody. I just need to be alone.

She was tired, but only physically; her brain was buzzing too frantically for sleep. She saw the answer phone flashing and thought, Why not? and going over clicked it on.

'Laura,' she heard a jovial voice saying: 'you're a genius.' And the voice went on, describing on tape and in detail the power of her performance, hyperbole piled on top of overstatement, sliding over the machine. And when it was finished, there was another and another, a string of messages, and although none of them were quite as wordy as the first the message was essentially the same: she had triumphed, that's what each and every one had rung to say.

It was over, finally, an electronic voice informed her of that, and she was well and truly sated. She put her finger on the wipe-out button and pressed decisively down on it. It's over, she thought, and I can go to sleep.

And then, just as the tape began whirring backwards, annihilating what had gone before, the phone began to ring.

The phone, in the middle of the night. Who could it possibly be? Anxiety possessed her: she sat staring at the ringing phone, frozen into immobility as memories of other times, of other phones ringing in the night, engulfed her. Bad news, a small voice told her, it can only be bad news.

Except – and she blinked – except she had no family left. No bad news could therefore be delivered. She reached out, snatching the receiver.

'Hello.' She heard a confident, slow drawl. 'I didn't wake you, did I?' Tom. It was Tom. Her hand began to shake.

'Damn,' she heard him saying. 'I did, didn't I?'

She swallowed. 'It's OK. I just got in.'

'Thank God.' A pause and then: 'I wanted to apologize.'

'Apologize?' It came out like a squeak.

Which he ignored. 'I overstepped the mark,' he said. 'I had no right to tell you that you could have done better.'

'I didn't . . .' she began, almost croaking. She coughed, cleared her throat. 'It was fine,' she said and then, because her mind had seized up, she said, 'fine,' again as if she were an idiot.

'That's generous of you,' he said.

She could think of no reply. She merely grinned inanely.

He filled the silence. 'I hope the rest of the run goes as well.' There was finality in his voice: he was about to hang up.

She knew suddenly that she did not want him to. What she had told herself such a short time ago was now exposed as nonsense. It wasn't that she just wanted to be alone, it wasn't that she was off sex per se. Not that at all.

And she didn't even care. I want him, she told herself. She didn't have time to think; she breathed in and on the out-breath heard herself babbling unplanned words. 'What are you doing tomorrow afternoon?' was what she said.

'Shall we meet?' He sounded amused.

Which made her even more embarrassed. Pull yourself together, she told herself, thinking also that she had gone so far she could not withdraw. 'A walk?' she said, and reassured by the fact that her voice was on an even keel she went one further: 'St James's Park?'

'Sure,' he said, and they discussed times and meeting places and then, after telling her that he was looking forward to it, he hung up.

Leaving her with the phone like a love-sick teenager, wondering what she would wear and what, if anything, she should do tomorrow to fill the time before her date.

Her date! It was ridiculous. She was an adult, not a teenager, and this was no date – at least not in the conventional sense. It was a meeting of like-minded colleagues, a short walk before the darkness closed in and she had to return to Hedda. No date, just a diversion.

A diversion, she thought and, remembering suddenly the flashing of Tom's eyes, she grimaced. 'Who are you kidding?' she said out loud.

CHAPTER TWENTY-TWO

She was already up and dressed when she heard the bell. The first of many bouquets, she thought as she went to answer it. It rang again: impatient florist, she thought as she opened up.

The young man on the doorstep was carrying a notepad, not flowers. 'Hi, Laura.' He was beaming. 'Paul James, Associated News. I wonder whether you would care to comment on this.' He thrust a tabloid at her. 'It's about your dad.'

Your dad, she heard, and glancing down saw the beginnings of a headline. AIDS BOSS, she saw.

She blinked. Aids – what did that have to do with Leo? She looked again and saw of course that she had read it wrong. What was really written was 'Aid' not 'Aids'. She read the headline, this time in one go: 'AID BOSS IN GUN SCANDAL,' she said.

She looked up. The journalist was smiling. 'Take your time.'

Her eyes were drawn inexorably back to the printed page. *The scandal which has dogged former UN supremo, Leo Weber*, she read, *will not die down.*

Scandal? What scandal?

She felt the journalist's gaze on her but made herself read slowly, concentrating on each word, on the brief resumé of Leo's life – his Prussian beginnings, wartime record, the praise which in his lifetime he had gathered – and then her own c.v. and Margot's as well.

And then, when that was over, she saw a sub-head: BE-TRAYAL, it said. Betrayal. *One sunny day*, she read, *a man stepped into UNESCO's New York office. His name was Ben Okalia.*

Ben Okalia. His name in full. The man on Margot's doorstep. Some of what he'd told her came flooding back: *It's about your mother*, that's what he had said, and other words as well: *your father, transit, worried, conscience*, all spewing out of memory.

Except, she thought, this article had not even mentioned Judith. She focused back on to it. *Mr Okalia*, she read, *had a strange story to tell. A story of false imprisonment and of Leo Weber's ties to an evil gun ring.*

She was reading fast now, speeding to the end. Ben, the article told her, had been charged with gun-smuggling and after a rigged trial had spent twenty-five long years in a black dictator's prison. When finally he was released, he had pointed fingers – hardest of all at Leo. At *Leo Weber* is how the article put it, *a one-time benefactor who, according to Mr Okalia, cruelly betrayed him.*

Leo's influential friends, it went on, would not listen to Ben. But Ben was determined and had travelled to Britain, fighting to have his voice heard; and then, at last, an inquiry was begun. An inquiry which now, with Leo's death, had been brought to a premature end. 'I am not happy that Leo Weber is dead,' he was quoted as saying. 'I wanted justice, not revenge.'

The article ended after that, save only for one final paragraph full of malicious innuendo, all about the downfall of a saintly reputation.

Laura's arm dropped, her eyes focused on nowhere in particular.

'Care to comment?'

'No.' She shook her head. 'No comment,' and, turning, went quickly inside.

There were journalists outside Leo's office also, a whole bevy who swooped on her. She shook them off. 'No comment,' she kept on saying, 'no comment,' as she pushed past them and, leaning hard against the bell, shouted 'It's Laura,' into the intercom. She heard a buzz; she was inside. The sight was so familiar, the rounded marble stairs winding upwards. The stairs, she told herself, were only an obstacle to be surmounted, and the quicker the better. Up she went, all thoughts shut off, her feet on automatic, up to the very top.

She was in the office. 'Dorothy,' she said to her back. Dorothy jumped, scattering papers. 'It's me.'

'Of course it is.' Dorothy was in motion, her arms flung out, pleasure and distress passing, in equal measure, over her face. Behind her there was chaos – papers scattered on the floor and spewing out of open files; cardboard boxes, full and empty, jumbled one on top of the other; and even on her desk there was tangled disorder.

Laura frowned. 'You're packing?'

'I'm making sure it's all in order.' Dorothy's reddened eyes were welling with fresh tears. 'I don't want to be accused of hiding anything.' She used her handkerchief to swipe ineffectually at her face. 'Oh, Laura,' she said, and broke down, crying now in earnest.

Laura put her arms round Dorothy, holding tightly, holding on as Dorothy's sobs resounded and her tears ran down Laura's neck, until at last the spasm of grief abated. Only then did Laura speak. 'What's going on?' she said.

Dorothy jerked away.

'What's going on?' Laura asked again.

'Ask him,' she heard.

'Him?'

'Jack,' Dorothy said. 'He's in Leo's office.'

Jack. It came back to her, echoes of the argument between Jack and Leo. Jack. She was no longer sure that he was her father's friend; she didn't want to ask him.

She was no longer sure of anything, in fact, except that this familiar woman in front of her had loved her father and her as well. Her crying had shown that. 'Can't you tell me?' she said gently.

But Dorothy's lips tightened so firmly that it felt almost as if a door had been slammed shut. In that moment Laura remembered what it was that Judith had used to call Dorothy: not secretary but 'secret aid agent', spoken fast, each word merging into the next.

At the time Laura had been provoked by what she saw as a criticism of her father into defending Dorothy. But now, seeing Dorothy's cold determination, she knew Judith had been right.

Dorothy pretended to be a family friend but her loyalty had lain exclusively with Leo. Leo and Dorothy; the boss and his faithful handmaiden. Judith was right: their relationship had been fortified by secrets.

Which left Laura wondering how far these secrets stretched. 'Did you know Leo had heart trouble?' she asked, and saw the narrowing of Dorothy's eyes – another confidence concealed. 'Never mind,' she said wearily and, turning, walked to Leo's office door, entering without knocking.

Jack was behind Leo's desk, his brows furrowed in concentration. 'Not now,' he snapped without even bothering to look up.

She stood there silent.

He raised his head. 'Laura. Honey.' He was on his feet, striding over. His arms, those arms that Margot had so recently appropriated, embraced her. They felt so safe. Jack – Leo's friend – so big, so reassuring; she couldn't imagine how she could have doubted him.

'I'm glad you came by,' he said. 'You didn't have too much trouble on the doorstep?'

So he knew the press was there. And yet he hadn't warned her of it. She moved away, looking at him straight. 'What's going on?'

'Laura, you don't look good. Come' – he held his hand out – 'sit down.'

But she repelled the hand. 'No, I don't want a seat. I want an answer.'

'An answer?' He was buying time.

She grimaced. 'Come off it, Jack,' she said. 'I'm not a child.'

His arms went limp. 'How much do you know already?' he asked, his voice soft.

Nothing, she wanted to say; I've been told nothing. But she didn't. She reached instead into her bag and withdrew the newspaper.

He had seen it already, that much was plain. 'Those assholes,' he said. 'It's all lies.' And he began tearing at the paper, shredding it into small bits.

She had no time for amateur dramatics. 'Who is Ben Okalia?' she asked.

No answer. Jack's head was hanging down, bits of newspaper strewn around his feet.

'He's the man you saw me talking to,' she stated. 'The night of the party.'

A nod, barely perceptible.

'That night I asked you if you knew him. You changed the subject.'

'Look.' Jack had raised his head. 'The man's sick; a psycho.'

A psycho. Dorothy had said the same. 'Let me be the judge of that,' she said, her voice hard.

'OK,' Jack nodded. 'OK.'

'So who is he?'

Jack sighed. 'He came from Algeria,' he said but immediately, frowning, shook his head. 'Or was it . . . It's immaterial where he came from. He was a modern nomad – had many bases. He and your father went a long way back. To the sixties.'

The sixties, Laura thought, when Judith was still alive.

'He was a kind of political fixer,' Jack was saying. 'We use them occasionally – especially in Africa where it's not always easy to find out where the real power lies.' He paused.

'And . . .'

'Leo liked Ben,' Jack said.

I am a friend of Leo Weber's, she heard Ben's voice saying. *An old friend.*

'I never trusted him. I tried to warn Leo, but your father was a stubborn man.' Jack lapsed into silence.

'And the guns?' she asked.

Jack's voice was much quieter than hers. 'It was in early 1967,' he said.

The year that Judith died.

'Ben was a go-between,' Jack said, 'who had been hired to ensure safe passage for a convoy of food supplies through a war zone. Leo was in charge of the operation and when he heard rumours that Ben was using the convoy to run guns he didn't believe them. But Leo was always careful and he had the convoy searched. They found crates of AKs, boxes of ammunition.'

'And so Leo reported his friend?'

'He had no option.' Jack was angry. 'He couldn't risk jeopardizing the operation. It was difficult for him but he did it.'

She nodded, knowing that Leo would always have done the right, the correct thing, no matter how painful. 'And Ben was gaoled?' she asked.

'He was arrested February 1967, sentenced two weeks later.'

'For twenty-five years?' she said, thinking that if what Jack was saying was true then Ben Okalia could not have been with Leo in Stockholm.

'You know how these things turn out,' Jack continued. 'Ben became a political hot potato and he was unlucky: one military coup after the other kept him incarcerated.'

'I see.'

'Leo never stopped lobbying for Ben's release,' Jack said. 'He was broken up by it.'

'Not as broken up as Ben, I bet,' she said and saw Jack glaring.

'Don't make the mistake of feeling sorry for Ben Okalia,' Jack hissed. 'Your father did enough of that and it nearly destroyed him. Ben Okalia is an asshole. He always was. He never stopped trying to destroy Leo. He said that he was innocent, that Leo was involved in the gun-smuggling.'

'And was he right?'

Jack scowled. 'What do you think?'

'I'm asking you,' Laura said, watching Jack's face flushing.

'Laura.' Jack was quite obviously shocked. 'Was your father such a stranger to you?'

Perhaps, she thought; perhaps he was. 'I'm asking you,' she said again.

'Of course he wasn't right.' Jack was furious. 'Leo would never have done that. Ben was up to his stinking neck in shit. Leo checked it all, found people who had seen him buying guns. Ben was just a sore loser. He played a dangerous game and he got caught. There was no way Leo could have rescued him – Ben should have known that.' Jack was in full flood now, readying himself for a fresh flow of invective when the intercom suddenly squawked incoherently. Jack seemed to understand it. He leaned across, flicked at its button, said, 'In a minute,' and then, turning back to Laura: 'So there you have it.'

'Not quite.'

He frowned. 'What's missing?'

'What's missing,' she said, 'is, if Ben is the slime you say he is, why did anybody believe him?'

Jack's face cleared. 'They didn't.'

'But . . .'

'Nobody *believed* Ben,' Jack said, loudly emphasizing the middle word, 'that's why you haven't heard about it – it was so unlikely it was kept under wraps. But, even so, they had to investigate. And that's where Leo fucked up. He was a stubborn man, your father, he refused to answer the charges. He wouldn't lower himself, he said. He didn't understand how mud can stick, how people can start worrying about it sticking to them as well. I tried to tell him . . .'

Yes, she thought, remembering, Jack had been trying.

He was looking at her, smiling apologetically. 'I'm sorry, honey,' he said. 'I've got to brief the press. Stay here, why don't you and leave when they're all in the conference room.'

She nodded and offered her cheek to him and let him kiss it and then she watched him walking away.

Except, as she watched him, she realized suddenly that there was something else she had to ask. She took one step forward.

'Wait,' she said. She watched Jack stopping, seeing how his shoulders hunched. He turned. 'What is it?' barely controlling his impatience.

'Did you know Leo was sick?'

She saw something crossing his face, a decision quickly taken.

She shook her head and spoke up before he could. 'It's too late,' she said and then, lowering her voice, added: 'too late for lies.'

'Yes,' he said, saying the very thing that she had dreaded. 'Yes. Leo told me about his heart. He was toying with surgery but decided against. The risks were too high.'

Of course Leo would have told Jack, she could see that now. 'Thanks,' she said. looking down.

His voice tugged at her. 'I'm sorry,' he said.

She looked up again, throwing him the semblance of a smile.

'He was probably trying to save you pain.'

She shrugged.

'Well,' Jack shifted uneasily on his feet. 'I must . . .'

'Yes,' she said. 'It's fine. Go.'

'I'll talk to you soon,' he said. 'I'll call you.' And then, as if he knew he would get no reply, he walked across the room and out of the door, closing it quietly behind him.

She stood there, in Leo's office, thinking only one thing: that her father was a liar. Oh, maybe not about Ben – maybe Jack was right and maybe Ben Okalia was mad – but that wasn't it. No. What got her, what continued to flash fiercely through her mind, was the knowledge that Leo had told both Jack and Dorothy that he was dying. Had told his colleagues but not Laura – his daughter, his only child.

She closed her eyes. She heard words, issuing from the past. *'You're going to die, you are, aren't you.'* Her own childish voice. And heard his answer, also, journeying through time. *'I'm not, I'm not,'* and once again: *'I'm not. I would tell you if I were.'*

She remembered what had happened after that, remembered how she wouldn't let it rest. *'Promise me.'* She had been almost hysterical. *'Promise me.'*

And he – what had he said? Oh yes, she remembered that as well. *'I promise.'* That's what he'd said, compounding this with the crossing of his heart. *'I promise that if ever I know I am about to die I will tell you.'*

I promise, and yet he had not told her.

And not only that, his other promises had also been empty. He, her father, Saint Leo, who stood for truth, who told her that she was his confidante and that he shared everything with her ... Everything – it was a joke! He had told her nothing – nothing of Ben Okalia – either in the then or in the now.

'What else?' She said the words out loud, addressing the room and Leo too. 'What else did you conceal?'

No answer came and she was crying. Her face was soaked, she must have been crying for some time. A tissue, she thought vaguely, I need a tissue, and seeing a box on Leo's desk she went over to it.

She sat down on Leo's chair and felt grief overtaking her. Her head dropped down on to his desk, her arms stretched out, sobbing. Sobbing while she smelt something so familiar, something – the hint of cherry – and it came back to her how they had used to be: she sitting on the floor, a bowl of cherries beside her, while he sat on his favourite easy chair, sipping cherry liqueur.

The cherries at least were real, she thought, and something else as well. His love – it had also been real. No one could have feigned that, not even Leo.

She was crying still but was no longer angry. All she could think of, as she sat, her tears staining the burnished surface, was how much she missed him – and how much she always would.

CHAPTER TWENTY-THREE

She had had plenty of time but somehow managed to be late; she was running as she rounded the corner of Trafalgar Square and turned into The Mall. Tom was waiting, turned away, but even from this distance she could see how relaxed and self-possessed he looked. She speeded up, railing against the indignity of her haste.

He knew somehow, he must have known that she was coming, for as she approached, and before she had time to call out, he had turned to face her. He was smiling. Lazily – that was the only way she could think of describing the way his mouth slowly uncoiled and the way the faint lines beside his eyes were crinkled.

'You've been running,' he said and, stretching out a hand, touched her gently on the nose. 'But you're cold.'

He was looking at her, his eyes glinting. 'Let's go and have a coffee first,' he said and he held the door of the ICA open for her, ushering her in.

They separated momentarily: Tom going to fetch coffee while she chose a table by the window and, sitting down, looked out. Time speeded up; she felt him suddenly beside her. She reached out; he picked up a cup, passed it over. Their hands touched, and in that moment she felt a sensation both pleasurable and frightening. And which, she thought guiltily, gave the lie again to her excuse that her refusal to make love with Steven came from a generalized lack of interest in sex. If this is uninterested, she thought, smiling to herself, then save me from being interested. She looked away.

Tom began to talk in an even, dispassionate voice of things

they had in common – work things, that is – and of people as well, making her laugh as he had once done before. I like this man; the thought suddenly overtook her. She smiled, looked out of the window.

'. . . rituals,' she heard Tom's voice in the distance saying.

Rituals? What had she missed? She looked back, smiling quizzically.

'The weirdest I ever came across,' Tom continued, 'was the actor who had to tie and untie his shoelaces ten times before going on. Drove the wardrobe people mad – they kept having to replace frayed laces – and since he had to do it in the wings, the stage managers were constantly tripping over him . . .'

Her stomach plummeted and she was gripped by unbearable anxiety. *The wings*: those innocuous, easy words. *The wings* – it came flooding back, the memory of how, the night before, she had stood and waited in the wings, waiting out the beginning of Act One. I'll have to do it again tonight, she thought suddenly. I'll have to.

She clutched her stomach. What if it didn't work? What if instead of calming and protecting her, her vigil only made her more nervous? The thought was too frightening. She felt her heart beating and as her vision dimmed she heard a strange sound, the sound of someone gasping for breath – herself, that's who it was. She made an effort, told herself that the solution was simple – she would not go to the wings until it was time.

But no: if standing in the wings had worked the night before could she change the routine now? What, she thought, what if I don't manage to leave the dressing room? Her throat was closing: she would soon be entirely without breath.

'Stage fright?' she heard Tom slowly asking. His face swam blearily into focus.

She nodded. 'I . . .'

'Relax,' he said.

'I . . .'

'No.' He stretched a hand out, touched her lips lightly with one finger. 'Don't say anything.'

'I . . .' She wanted desperately to speak. She couldn't.

'No.' He was on his feet, hauling at her. 'Don't try to talk. Trust me, I'm an expert.' He stretched over, grabbed her coat. 'Come on,' he said, 'follow me.'

Follow? She could not do that, her legs were jelly. Yet she did; he forced her to. He pushed her coat on and supported her out of the ICA into the cold air, across the road, through a gate and into St James's Park.

'Now run,' he said.

Run! She shook her head. Run? She could hardly walk!

'Run,' he said, 'come on,' and gripping her by the hand he began to pull her. 'Run,' he shouted, running ahead, hauling her after him.

He was wrenching at her arm, pulling at its socket. She felt it tearing. He'll have to stop, she told herself.

He didn't stop. 'Come on,' he was shouting. 'Come on.'

To protect her arms, she took one step forward.

'That's it,' he urged. 'Run.'

Another step and her legs were liberated. Run, she thought, as she saw others in the park, staring at them. She almost smiled. Tom must look like a madman, she thought, a persecuting madman, his eyes flashing full of menace.

'Don't smile,' he said. 'Run.'

She was in motion. Run she did, wildly, recklessly. Running to keep up with Tom and to overtake him as well; cutting him off, running ahead along the path and then zigzagging on to the grass. Running as fast as she ever had, as all she passed was blurred. Running . . . running until she could run no more.

'Enough,' she protested, her words emerging as one incoherent grunt. She threw her hands up and then went one further, throwing herself on to the ground. 'Enough,' she said, her laughter blending with juddering breaths.

He was standing looking down at her. 'Better?'

She nodded. And it was true, she did feel better. *The wings.* She tried the phrase out in her head but it only sounded vaguely ridiculous. The wings held no terror.

'Here.' He bent down, offered her a hand. She looked questioningly at him. 'You'll get a chill if you stay down there,' he said.

She had no energy to resist, nor did she want to. She took his hand, felt its warmth and strength enclosing hers, and then she felt his hand tightening and she was standing next to him. She knew that she would be able to go on that night.

But what Tom had done reached further than a mere performance. What Tom had done was save her from a greater menace.

After Hedda – she remembered thinking that. After Hedda – the thought had dogged her. After Hedda – me.

But now, looking into Tom's clear eyes, she was no longer so sure. Looking into his eyes, she saw salvation.

CHAPTER TWENTY-FOUR

Maya was already at the restaurant. Hearing Laura's approach, she looked up, scowling in mock despair. 'Your post-aerobics glow is sickening,' she said as Laura sat down. 'And now,' she continued, 'I guess you're going to order a small green salad.'

'On the contrary.' Laura stretched across and prised the menu out of Maya's hands. 'I'm ravenous. I suspect that only the cannelloni will do. But just in case . . .' Grinning, she began to study it.

A moment's silence and then: 'You're in a good mood,' Maya commented.

'Sure.' She didn't look up. 'Why not?'

'Aha!' Maya's voice was boisterous. 'Anything to do with a certain Tom Hooper?'

Laura lowered the menu, looking over its topmost edge. 'Why on earth would it have anything to do with Tom?' she asked, innocently.

'Just wondered,' Maya answered in a demure voice. 'How's it going?'

'How's what going?' Laura asked, mock stern.

While Maya smiled: '*Hedda*, of course – what else?'

Laura shrugged. 'It's fine,' she said and then wondered whether that was entirely true. She knitted her brow. 'I've been a bit flat during the last few performances,' she admitted – as much to herself as to Maya. 'I've had to rely more on technique than I should.'

Maya shrugged. 'Don't worry about it. Often happens on long runs,' she said and, putting her horn-rimmed glasses on, looked straight at Laura. 'Strong enough for the offers?'

'Sure.'

Bending down, Maya reached into her bulging briefcase. 'This,' she said, humping a great wedge of paper, bound and unbound, on to the table, 'isn't even the half of it.' She pushed her glasses to the edge of her nose and began rifling through the pile. 'Now, let's see,' she muttered. 'Clive drew up a list . . . ah yes' – she extracted a single sheet – 'here it is,' and passed the paper on.

On the paper was typed a list of jobs – almost every manner of proposal: a couple of features, a mini series for Carlton, a Screen 2 plus a few others, TV one-offs and more – all neatly catalogued. 'Clive's done a good job,' Laura said.

'Don't sound so surprised,' Maya replied, 'Clive's not only gorgeous, he's also hardworking,' but then, in response to Laura's raised eyebrows, added: 'No, no. He's far too young – even for me.'

At which point the waiter arrived and they ordered – Laura, as she had predicted, a hefty cannelloni while Maya went for the green salad accompanied by a bottle of Chardonnay.

'Quite a list, hey?' Maya said after the waiter had gone.

Laura nodded. 'Not bad. Any preferences?'

Maya frowned. 'There's a lot of junk, of course, but amongst it a few that deserve serious consideration. You know the kind of thing – good directors, solid ideas.' With that she began to talk Laura through the options. She didn't look back at the list: she was completely fluent without it, her encyclopaedic memory and fierce intellect both shining through.

When the cannelloni arrived Laura ate, listening all the while to acerbic descriptions of the rejects and slick summations of the other possibilities. 'As usual we must guard against typecasting,' Maya concluded. 'We can't have you restricted to suicidal roles. Maybe it's time for comedy.'

'A suicidal comedy perhaps?' Laura suggested.

Maya grimaced. 'There is one,' she said. 'Clive's listed it amongst the wacky.' She paused, sipped at her glass and then continued. 'There are so many offers – do a preliminary scan, see what you think and after that we can discuss them in more detail.'

Laura nodded and held one hand over the top of her glass to prevent it from being filled while with the other she took the proffered scripts.

'So,' Maya announced, 'business over.' She dropped what was left of the paper into her open briefcase. 'And now for the really serious stuff,' she said. 'Did you hear what Michael did to Miriam?' And with that she was off, doing the thing she did second best, gossiping with all the attention to detail and to personality quirks for which she was renowned.

Laura listened happily, working her way through her food, listening to Maya's caustic tales of love, jealousy and betrayal, thinking that this world, which was also hers, seemed at the moment very distant. But then, she thought laying down her fork, of course it would be distant. Her world had, by necessity, been drastically reduced, restricted by the demands of work into a rigid sequence of stage, bed, and exercise.

'The capacity of some people to deceive themselves,' Maya was saying, 'continues to astonish even me.'

Laura smiled. No only 'some' people, she thought, realizing that there was another vital ingredient in her life which she had just left out. Another ingredient: Tom. Stage, bed, exercise and Tom she thought wryly, although not necessarily in that order.

Her face must have shown what she was thinking – either that or Maya was a mind-reader, for she stopped in the middle of a complex anecdote, picked up her glass, poured the last of its contents down her throat and said: 'So tell me – are you sleeping with him?'

'With whom?' Laura asked – as if she didn't know.

'As if you don't know!' Maya said.

Laura smiled, shook her head. 'No,' she said. 'I'm not.' It was the truth. She hadn't slept with Tom – not yet.

'I haven't seen a lot of Steven recently,' Maya said.

'Haven't you?' Although Laura's voice was non-committal, the look she threw in Maya's direction was fierce.

Without effect – Maya pressed on. 'It's not over, is it?' she asked.

'Over?'

Maya was exasperated. 'You and Steven,' she said, sighing heavily. 'Is it over?'

Well, thought Laura. Is it? She looked across the table and, seeing Maya waiting expectantly, said the first thing that occurred. 'Things are fine,' is what she said.

'Are they?'

'Yes,' she said, thinking in fact the opposite, that things were far from fine. 'We've both been busy,' she said briskly, blocking out such doubts. And it was true, they *had* both been busy. She smiled. That was, she reminded herself, what she had always liked about her relationship with Steven: that within it was a great measure of freedom. And besides that . . .

She never got to find out how she might have finished that thought because Maya's voice intruded. 'Be careful,' Maya said.

Be careful? Laura thought. Why should I? What she really wanted to be was reckless. She had had enough of care. She spent it nightly on the stage, carefully husbanding her energy, parcelling out a measured dose of Hedda. She opened her mouth to tell Maya so.

But once again Maya got in first. 'You can't keep running,' she said. The word brought back the memory of Tom standing over her, his hand outstretched. She frowned, looked at Maya, taking in the gravity of Maya's face, waiting for Maya to say more. But all Maya did was repeat herself. 'You can't keep running.'

What does she want of me?

Maya did not move.

This is too heavy for me, Laura thought. She smiled. 'You only say that,' she said, 'because you don't know how fit I am,' and she followed the sentence with a wicked wink.

It worked. Maya's face softened as she gave up the uneven struggle. 'You always were a stubborn one,' she said fondly. 'And now I suppose you're going to punish my bossiness by devouring a three-million-calorie dessert in front of me.'

Laura could not resist the challenge: teasing Maya, she ordered a chocolate mousse. When it arrived she raised it lovingly to her lips, lingering over each mouthful until Maya, laughing, begged for mercy.

'You can't have mercy,' Laura said, 'but' – she pushed the dish at Maya – 'you can have the mousse.'

They drank coffee and more coffee after that, until they were sated and Maya protested that she must get back to work. She had already paid: now she yawned, stretched and got up reluctantly. 'When you've had time to look through that lot,' were her parting words, 'let me know what you think.'

*

They were in the café in Kenwood, the only customers. The conversation had petered out and Laura was relaxing into silence. What crossed her idle mind was that it was strange how her relationship with Tom was centred almost entirely on the outdoors. In parks, that's where they met; in parks and on riverbanks and even once, when he was accompanied by his small niece, in a playground. There were so many things that they had never done together – they hadn't gone to the cinema, nor to an exhibition nor, even briefly, to each other's flats – but they had covered most of London. She nodded; an outdoor affair – that's what she was having.

An outdoor affair, she thought, because the indoors was too threatening.

'What are you thinking?'

She smiled and selected a convenient lie. 'I was thinking about work,' she said, pointing to the pile of scripts that Maya had given her. And then, to reinforce the point, she picked one out. Or meant to pick – she fumbled the move and, losing her grip, dropped it.

Tom was quicker than she: he retrieved the script, glancing at its top title as he handed it over. *'Blue Screens,'* he said. 'I'm looking at it too.'

'Catchy title,' she commented dryly.

He smiled and nodded in agreement. 'Although,' he said, 'it's a lot better than the title deserves. The plot's punchy, the dialogue adequate and the director attached is somebody I respect. You should read it.'

'I will.'

'We might even end up being in it together,' he said.

She did not think before she spoke. 'I don't like to work with ...' she began, ... *with somebody I'm involved with*, was what she nearly said but at the last minute she stopped herself.

Not that it really mattered. Tom's eyes were sparkling. He knew how she'd been planning to finish the sentence.

She did something then that she never, ever did: she blushed. She felt her face grow hot, felt heightened colour moving through it.

He smiled, and in the moment's silence that followed the gradual fading of his smile she wished that he would say something. Not just anything but something definite. She wished that he would make the first move.

'More tea?' he said.

She nodded and while he walked up to the counter, she sat there thinking that he would never make the first move. She knew he wouldn't: if she wanted to shift their relationship from friendship into something other, then she would have to do it.

Watching Tom returning bearing a single cup, she saw something she hadn't recently noticed: a hint of danger, that's what it was. He challenged her in a way that Steven – nice, normal, gentle – had never done.

Steven. She must not think of him.

'Your tea,' Tom said. 'Black, no sugar.'

She didn't want it, not any longer. She stood up. 'Let's walk instead,' she said.

So they walked out through the glass doors into the stone-covered eating area and out some more until they were facing the bleakness of Hampstead Heath in winter. Tom stopped and she linked her arm to his, feeling its strong familiarity, and feeling, too, their mutual awareness of the contact. And as she did so she realized that she had been wrong. She did not want Tom to make the first move.

For if he does, she thought, the chase will be over. And the chase, she thought, feeling how light and yet how firm was his grip, the chase is where Tom excels.

CHAPTER TWENTY-FIVE

She had planned to spend the time before she was due at the theatre catching up on correspondence but, having dressed and cleared away her breakfast things, she fixed instead on other, more energetic tasks. She started small – loading the washing machine, unstacking the dishwasher, passing a cloth across some random surfaces – but she had soon graduated on to bigger things. A full spring clean, nothing less. She started scrubbing behind what was rarely moved: the cooker, the fridge and, very ambitious this, her vast array of books.

It was several hours later before she – her hair tied back and now quite dusty, grime streaking her hands and face, her clothes spotted by detergent – even thought of stopping. She paused looking round, expecting order. What she saw was chaos. The place was cleaner, that much was true, but it was also more untidy.

'That's enough,' she said out loud and, finding several big black polythene bags, began to fill them all with rubbish. When that was done she was relieved to see the flat restored to equilibrium. She stood at its centre wiping her forehead with the back of her hand, looking around her smiling. Only one task left, she thought – disposing of the trash. After that she would reward herself by soaking for a long time in a bath.

She picked up the bags and, leaving the front door open, walked down the iron stairway and to one extreme of the central courtyard. The dustbins were kept there, in their own enclosure, surrounded by a high wooden fence. She unlatched the gate and walked in, heading for the huge bins. Thinking longingly of clean, warm water she lifted up her arm.

And then: 'Miss Weber' she heard, hearing also the clicking of a latch.

Miss Weber. She knew immediately who it was. She turned.

She was right. It was Ben Okalia, leaning against the gate.

He tilted his head in the direction of the bags which now were lying by her feet. 'I sincerely hope that the jade tortoise is not amongst all that?'

'The jade?'

He was even thinner than the last time: when he frowned the outline of his skull was almost completely exposed. 'So – her stepmother hasn't seen fit to confide in her?' he muttered as if Laura wasn't there. But then, raising his voice, he spoke directly to her: 'We meet again.' bowing slightly.

She didn't answer. She watched, mesmerized, as he straightened up, seeing how his mouth had been twisted into an approximation of a smile.

The smile was suddenly annihilated. 'And at last we are alone,' he said.

Alone, and he was blocking her escape. He planned this well, she thought.

He nodded satisfied. 'I must apologize for ambushing you in this fashion,' he said, 'but on the previous occasions of our meeting you have had friends to protect you.'

Friends. It sounded vicious issuing from those cracked lips. What Jack and Dorothy had said about Ben was true – he was mad. And bad as well, she thought, seeing him ogling her.

He started talking then, dropping his voice gradually until she found herself straining forward. 'You have many men friends,' she heard. 'You are a popular woman.' A shrug. 'But, of course, you deserve such tribute. You are beautiful and talented – as was your mother.'

He smiled again, so full this time of malice that she moved involuntarily backwards. He had sensed her panic and was patently enjoying it. For a moment all he did was eye her, slowly, up and down. 'But you are more modern than your mother,' he eventually said. 'Mrs Judith Weber had times only for one man. You, Miss Weber, you are different.' His tongue shot out, lizard-like, licking at his lips before being quickly retracted. 'Take Steven Barker. He loves you – no? And Tom

Hooper as well; he is very interested. But more dangerous, that one,' he said, 'do you not think?'

She was up tight against the metal bins.

'I have done my research well, have I not?' she heard.

He was trying to scare her, quite deliberately. She took a long breath in. She would not be scared. Breathing out, she met his eyes. 'What do you want?' she asked, her voice as hard as she could make it.

But he was impervious, continuing as if she hadn't even spoken. 'My hope for you,' he said, 'is that the man you eventually choose – and I have faith that you will one day settle down – will treat you better than your father treated your mother.'

She opened her mouth, instinctively, intent on rebutting what he'd said. But she snapped it shut. Don't, she told herself, don't give him any reason to continue.

He didn't need a reason, he was thrust forward by his own mad logic. 'Your father had different standards of loyalty than I,' he said. 'I read his many, most excellent obituaries. A lover of humanity, that's what they called him, is it not?' He paused and, looking at her, leered. 'Oh, certainly Leo loved humanity, especially,' and he lifted his hands and made a quick motion in the air, sketching out a woman's curving shape, 'especially the ones with big, what do you call them, tits.' He smiled and repeated the word: 'Tits,' his teeth closing over the final 't', spittle spraying out. That over, he came one step closer. 'Leo was with a woman, you know,' he said. 'That night your mother died. She knew of course. He was not always discreet.'

No, she told herself, don't listen. 'What do you want?' she whispered.

This time he chose to answer her. 'Justice,' he said. 'I want justice.'

Justice, not revenge, she remembered. That's what he'd told the newspapers. Except it was a lie: what this man wanted was revenge.

His words confirmed it. 'I have to go away soon,' he said, 'Your father's friends will have me deported. But before I go, I want Leo Weber to suffer some of what I have endured.'

Leo? She frowned. How could he? 'Leo's dead.'

That made Ben angry. 'You think me mad?' He was upon

her, close enough for her to smell the acrid staleness of his breath. 'I know that Leo is dead, but I am a religious man. I know also that he is watching.' His eyes were red and bulging, looming up. 'When I was imprisoned, I lost my wife. She could not tolerate the disgrace. I never saw her again.' There was no sadness in his face, only fury. 'Leo lost nothing, but now he will: now he will feel what it is like to lose a daughter.'

She was trapped by his mad logic and by his hatred, she could feel it piercing her. A movement – he was so close she couldn't tell at first what he had done. She saw his calloused hand almost touching her face and then he moved away, and she saw what it was holding – a blade.

A blade, thin, silver, shining, sharp, glinting. She gasped.

He flicked his wrist.

She did not have time to think. She closed her eyes. Like that. Shut. Tight. And waited.

And waited, feeling nothing but another vague movement.

And hearing something then.

'I am not a violent man,' she heard, and heard an echo also: *a violent man*. Her eyes reopened. She saw that he was no longer looming and that his knife was gone.

Gone – but he had used it to slice through one of the plastic bags. Rubbish: old stale rotting food, crumpled paper, leaking pens, jagged tin cans, balls of dust; all this and more cascading out.

We kicked his foot at it. 'Your father was rotten,' he whispered, 'the worst kind of hypocrite.' A sudden acceleration; words spilling out so fast that her ears were having trouble separating one from the next. 'Leo would do anything to enhance his reputation. Anything.' His eyes were twitching, out of control. He shot his hand up, held it to one eye, physically stopping the movement. 'If I was guilty then so was Leo. He knew that the only way to ensure safe passage for the supplies was to barter it for guns. He was shocked that I took profit for my work but he was paid for his, paid in the only currency that he valued – esteem.'

A sudden silence, and then more words, much slower. 'Leo could have saved me. But he didn't, he didn't. I knew too much about him, you see.' Another pause while Ben looked under heavy lids, sated almost. 'I knew.'

I knew, whispered on the wind. *I knew* and he was by the door, bobbing briefly down. 'Enjoy the jade, Miss Weber,' he said. 'Although that too was wrongfully acquired.' And with that, having bobbed down once more, he pulled the door towards him, walked through and was gone.

Leaving her standing in the midst of debris. She was no longer shivering, she had gone beyond that. She was cold, so cold – cold as the grave. Her thoughts came curt and distinct: that she must leave the place; that Ben Okalia was gone; that she must clear up the mess – separated each one by blank space.

She didn't clear up the mess, she left it. She walked through the gate, across the courtyard, up the stairs, and into her flat. She was in fast motion. She kicked off her shoes and automatically, not thinking really where she was going – not thinking anything in fact – went towards her bed. Too fast. As she passed her bedside table her arm brushed against it and a glass of water was knocked off.

'Shit,' she said and almost kept on going.

But there was glass and water on the floor and her foot was hurting. 'Shit and double shit.' She stretched down and touched her toe and saw that when her hand emerged, it was reddened by blood. Her chilled immobility had gone, replaced by curses streaming out. Anger fed itself on anger. Her trousers were wet, of course, and, mopping up the mess, she cut her hand.

Her hand. She held it up against her face, wet against a different kind of wet – she hadn't realized she was crying. She was crying; she sat down on the floor. This is absurd, she thought as tears coursed down her cheeks, thinking of what Leo had done to Judith. He had brought her mother to the brink of death and then provided her with the means. But no, it's absurd, she repeated, seeing the man's face looming, his eyes popping, the intensity of his hatred making him grotesque. She could not believe anything he said. He was mad, that's all.

Her tears dried up. Just like that. One minute she was raging and crying at the same time and in the next she was calm. She stripped off her clothes, stuck a plaster on her hand, pulled a hairbrush through her hair, doused her face with cold water and dressed herself again, still calm, still quiet, not thinking. There was no need for thought. She dressed herself knowing what she would to; knowing that she would, instead of calling for a taxi, take the tube to the theatre; would arrive early for a change; would mix with the other members of the cast, be normal just like them.

Yes, she nodded, at the door already, holding it, preparing herself to let go. Yes, that's what she'd do. She moved her hand.

And then heard a voice, not her own. A voice ringing in her ears; a voice, her agent's, Maya's voice.

She frowned, and the words slipped out of grasp. Her frown deepened. What was it Maya had said? What was it?

You can't keep running, that's what Maya had said.

You can't keep running. Well, what did Maya know? Laura took one last look around her flat, seeing it clean and neat and orderly and all hers. She lifted her hand, clicked off the light switch, walked through and closed the door.

CHAPTER TWENTY-SIX

At the tube's entrance hall, as she was putting money in the machine, she smelt the unmistakable stench of urine. The source was soon located – a knee-high stain was spreading on to the floor.

'Disgusting, isn't it?' a voice said. 'Bloody pigs,' the woman, a stranger, continued. 'That's what they are.'

There had been no menace in the woman's voice, only shared disgust, but grabbing her ticket, Laura fled. Down the escalator she hurried, down the corridors, and as she went the stench grew stronger. Rotting food, human perspiration, and faeces it seemed as well; axle grease and something else, the sweetness of of an artificial fragrance that was perhaps the most offensive – all this assailed her. She broke into a run, running full tilt, her hands grasping at her neck, holding on so tight that she began to gag.

And all the while Maya's voice pursued her: *You can't keep running*.

She loosened her fingers, increased her pace. The noise as well – it was unbearable, savage drumming against her brain. She felt a scream rising – she pushed it back. If I start now, she thought, I'll never stop. She was at the top of a rank of steep, dark stairs, her momentum carrying her down. Too fast, too uncontrolled: she slammed against a wall.

'Are you all right?'

She didn't stop, she was in motion; hearing the screeching of brakes, she skidded on to the platform. Just in time – the train was waiting. Into it she jumped while behind her doors slid shut. And then the train moved off, she swaying to its beat.

*

The time between station and theatre was blank; lost in a whirlwind of fear. She remembered handing in her ticket, and the next thing she knew the duty commissionaire was thrusting an overblown bouquet at her. Her hand went out, automatically, to receive it and in that moment she glimpsed her watch face. Six-forty-five. She gasped. It was six-forty-five – she had lost four hours, had a mere forty-five minutes left. Her mouth widened: she must hurry.

She took one step but as her foot touched ground she stumbled, possessed by panic. If she took another step – she was convinced of this – if she took another step – calamity would descend. She stopped.

'Laura,' she heard.

Footsteps running towards her. 'Laura. Thank God,' and the stage manager's face swimming into focus. 'We've been frantic. Where have you . . .' The voice tailed off.

It's that bad then, Laura thought.

It was that bad. The stage manager grabbed her by the elbow. 'Let's go to your dressing room.'

'I can't,' she said. The stage manager was stronger than she. She was hauled bodily along the corridor. 'I can't,' she muttered.

She was in her dressing room, in a chair, surrounded by faces; each vaguely familiar; each, bizarrely, in a different stage of make-up. A cacophony of voices reverberated, faces swaying in and out of focus.

'*What happened?*' and '*Is she ill?*' and '*What can we do?*' swirling past her. She didn't want to listen. She clamped her hands against her ears, hard and fast. 'Laura.' Somebody was shaking her, pulling her hands loose. 'Laura. Speak to us.' No. She wouldn't listen. She wouldn't speak. 'Laura.' She felt hot breath against her neck.

Hot breath – as Ben Okalia's breath had been, its poison seeping through her pores. She couldn't bear it. Pushing the hand roughly off, she stood. That made things worse – the clamour escalated. She couldn't bear it; she must put a stop to it. 'Shut up,' she tried but it emerged a feeble whisper. She took a deep breath, tried again. 'Shut up.' This time a scream of rage.

Which worked: silence.

She knew what she must do. 'It's OK,' she said in an even voice. 'It's OK. Just stage fright. Thank you, everybody, for your concern, but I think you'd better go.' She smiled again, her lips stretched uncomfortably over an array of teeth. 'I have to get ready, you see,' she said, glancing studiously at her watch, hiding the fact that her vision was so blurred that she could make out neither the numbers nor the hands. She pointed at the door.

And they? What choice did they have? None. They filed obediently out.

Closing the door behind them, she collapsed, slithering down the length of the door's surface until she reached the floor. Her mind was blank. She lay slumped against the door, concentrating on her breath. For an age she sat, only breathing, until at last her vision cleared.

And then she heard a voice. I have to get ready, she heard. She frowned. *I have to get ready*. It was her voice. She stood up, dressed, sat down again (in front of the mirror) and began to apply her make-up. Another loss of time and space, and then a knock upon her door. She turned and saw the stage manager's face appearing, blanching and then, just as rapidly, withdrawing.

Looking at the mirror, Laura saw that her own face, so recently powdered, was now all streaked by tears. She sat there stolidly, watching the tears coming, gushing so heavily that as regularly as she wiped them off there were others to take their place.

She heard the door opening. 'Seven twenty-five,' a quiet voice said against a background of frantic interlocution. '*The understudy?*' she heard, and '*A short delay?*' She neither spoke nor turned.

They didn't try consulting her again. They made their own decision. What they did was close her door and start the play. They didn't even tell her. The first she knew of it was when she heard lines sounding over the backstage intercom. My understudy must be ready, she vaguely thought. The door opened. 'Ten minutes.'

Ten minutes – they were expecting her to go on!

That's all it took. That's all. She knew she must go on. She looked in the mirror, repaired her make-up, nodded gravely when she had finished. I'll wait in the wings, she told herself. It worked before. She left the room and walked slowly and evenly along the corridor. Arriving backstage she tucked herself into a corner of the wall, listening as Act One proceeded.

The panic, when it came again, was unendurable, experienced as a physical agony. It gripped her, making her want to scream. She ground her teeth together but the pain was stronger than her jaw. It was going to destroy her. Escape, she must escape. She clawed her way out, cleaving through sticky air, barrelling past astonished stage hands along the corridor until she reached the Ladies.

There was an old tile floor there, a cold tile floor. She flung herself on it. Down she went, spreadeagling her body across the tiles. Her mouth was moving – she was sucking in her cheeks, clamping them between her teeth and chewing on them. She clutched the coldness, making the hardness of the tiles resist her body's dissolution.

And there she lay until it was no longer necessary and until she was calm. That done, she got up, brushed her clothes, walked back towards the wings. She had time only to register relief and disappointment, passing in equal measure across the face of her understudy, and then she was on the stage. 'Good morning, my dear Miss Tesman' she heard her own voice saying.

It was an experience she never wanted to repeat, but an experience all the same. She powered through the first half, her lines spilling out without recall to conscious thought.

The last lines of Act Two had come: '. . . with vineleaves in his hair,' she heard herself saying and then she was off and in the wings.

'Fantastic,' Gareth said. 'But perhaps a little slower . . .?'

She circumvented Gareth and, going to her dressing room, found Peter there. She didn't mind, she stretched out, pulled a tissue from the box, blotted methodically at her lips while Peter filled the space with trivial conversation and a smattering of gossip. They've chosen wisely, she thought – of all the people involved with *Hedda Gabler*, Peter's the only one I like. She relaxed, let his words flow over her.

But then a single sentence jarred. 'Dedicated b.f. you've got,' she heard. B.f.? she thought. Of course: b.f., boyfriend. She nodded absently. 'I've lost count,' Peter continued. 'Is this his third or his fourth time?'

She frowned. 'He?' she asked, thinking that she must have forgotten that Tom was coming.

'Steven,' A pause – a reassuring smile. 'He's out front.'

No, she thought. Not Steven, surely?

Peter's voice went rattling on. 'I saw him sitting in the auditorium when I went to have a pee. He was next to Margot.'

'Margot?' she said, sounding gormless.

'Yes,' Uncertainty flitted across Peter's face. 'Margot – your father's wife.'

She nodded, reassuring him, thinking *Margot and Steven together*.

The nod was more bravado. She closed her eyes as everything she had kept at bay came swirling back. *Leo was with a woman, you know*, she heard, and then a part repeated: *a woman, a woman, a woman*; a litany pounding her. Betrayal, she thought, that's what happened, blind betrayal; and she imagined them together, the man and the woman, entwined, twisting in mutual passion, while somewhere a cry of pain was lost. Betrayal – and this time, I its victim. 'Laura?' she heard. 'Are you all right?' A distorted voice saved her the bother of replying. 'One minute, Miss Weber,' it said.

She gave the performance of a lifetime, not more nor less than that. Anger, that's what had coaxed it out of her, the white heat of anger which was Hedda's driving force, the same anger which she had used, once, to good effect during a rehearsal. When it was finished she took the final bow and walked calmly off the stage and as she moved Hedda was sloughed off. It was as simple as that. One moment she was Hedda and in the next she had been returned to her own skin.

Her exit, however, was not as smooth. A throng of people had collected backstage and now they swarmed around her, jabbering excitedly. She tried walking more quickly but they were so eager to get close that they blocked her exit. It was frightening: their faces distorted, looming out at her, their bulging eyes prodding at the last remnants of her self.

'A *tour de force*,' the phrase was whispered in her ear.

'Magnificent,' she heard someone else saying.

Their words were insects clawing at her, adhering to her itching skin. She could not stand it: she must get away. 'Excuse me,' she said as compliments accelerated. 'Excuse me.' She saw a tiny space in front. She took a step. Too late: the crowd oozed itself together, cutting off escape. She was in a tunnel, a musty grotto composed of overripe human flesh and softening and soured human smells. It pressed against her, sucking away her breath. She closed her eyes but the stench worsened – all around decay was multiplying.

They were suffocating her. She felt her head spinning as blackness intruded. She pushed forward. A foot crunched down on hers. She sucked her breath in, spoke between gritted teeth. 'Get your fucking foot off,' she snarled.

The violence of her voice wrought transformation. What was once a mass of pulsating flesh became a disparate group of sullen individuals. Feet shuffled, eyes turned away, while into the silence one lone voice intruded. 'Never turn your back on a compliment,' it said.

Your back? she thought and looked around her, trying to locate the cliché. No one claimed it. Instead, 'Come on,' someone said, 'she doesn't want us here. Come on. Let's go.'

'I'm sorry,' she said. 'I'm tired.' Muttering quietly amongst themselves, they let her pass on through.

She walked feeling their eyes on her, walked slowly, keeping her head erect, making straight for her dressing room. And then at last she was inside.

A clear voice spoke again. 'Never turn your back on a compliment,' it said, and suddenly she knew who had spoken. Judith. '*Never turn your back on a compliment,*' Judith had said. '*For it might be used to stab you.*' And having said that Judith had bent down to Laura's level and had flicked her finger once across Laura's chest. 'You were wonderful, darling,' she had whispered.

You were wonderful, a mother had whispered to her five-year-old, and the child, dressed in satin ballet shoes and a gushing tutu, had wondered why tears had sprung into her eyes.

'No,' Laura said. She would not think of it. She shook her

head, shook memory away; and then, opening her eyes artificially wide, stared into the mirror. She was staring at an image of a self she did not know, at a gaunt, misshapen face and at green eyes as cold and unfeeling as tarnished steel.

At eyes which had seen too much.

Which had seen Steven and Margot, whispering to each other as Laura took her bow. Whispering, perhaps, but it had been dark out there and what looked like a whisper could easily have been more than that, could have been a concealed embrace.

'No,' she said again.

She picked up the telephone, dialled Steven's number. She would tell him, tell him what she thought of him.

Three rings: always three and then his voice was heard. 'Hello,' he said, 'you have reached two . . .' She let her mind go blank while his voice droned on, supplying endless boring details of when and where and how often he listened to his answer phone. She waited it out and yet, when the bleep finally sounded, she did not leave a message. What she did instead was use her index finger to disconnect the line and then use it once again – this time to dial another number.

CHAPTER TWENTY-SEVEN

When her taxi drew up outside the block of flats, she saw Tom waiting in the lighted lobby. She got out, paid, and climbed the stairs. He held the glass door open for her. She walked in, brushing close. She shivered.

'It is cold,' he said. 'Come. Let's go upstairs.'

Past a uniformed porter, into an upholstered lift and up to the sixth floor they went. His apartment was opposite the lift. He turned the handle, ushering her in.

'Tasteful,' she commented as she stepped into the living room, for tasteful it was, its walls white, and the carpet too, its furniture two large fawn sofas and a matching armchair, all lit by elegant cream lamps standing on glass tables.

'A drink?'

She shook her head. She did not want a drink, she wanted . . .

She shook her head a second time thinking that she really didn't know what it was she wanted.

She turned. Tom was still standing by the door. She forced herself forward, chose the armchair, ensconced herself in it and then, feeling his eyes on her, turned her gaze aside.

She was looking at a photograph, silver-framed; a portrait of a young boy, six or seven years of age. She would have recognized those features and those blue eyes anywhere. She looked up amazed. 'You have a child?'

Tom nodded and then was finally in motion, coming to sit in the middle of the sofa opposite. As she watched him settling down, she found herself wondering why the picture had surprised her. She should have suspected a child somewhere in the background – most men his age did have one. 'Do you see him often?' she asked.

Tom shrugged. 'As often as I can,' he said. A pause and then: 'He's with his mother in the States.' He stretched his arm along the sofa, settling comfortably into the silence.

She in contrast sat still, her back erect. She couldn't meet his gaze: her eyes travelled upwards and beyond him, focusing in the end on a black-and-white photograph of New York which hung on the wall above his head. As she continued to look at it, her mouth twisted into a semblance of an ironic smile.

What she was thinking was that she had been a fool.

She wasn't smiling any more. She nodded. A real fool who'd deceived herself into thinking that she knew Tom. It was total bullshit. All she'd really known were the intangibles – the way his eyes crinkled when he smiled, the way he liked to walk and think, the way he hid his thoughts. As for the rest, the many details of his life (and of his life before she had met him) of all that she was ignorant.

Her lips had lengthened; she was frowning now. There were so many things she wanted to ask of him, important things like why he'd left the States and what he was doing here and whether he ever planned to return. So many things she did not know. She opened her mouth.

'What are you doing here?' he asked.

What are you doing here? It was delivered mildly but it stung. She blinked and looked more closely at him, wondering if he was joking. He stared back, absolutely intent. She tried to make light of it. 'Don't you want me here?'

But he faced her down. 'Come on,' he said, refusing still to smile. 'You know I do.'

She dropped her eyes; turned her hands palms upward and began to examine them.

'I need to know what it is you want,' she heard him saying.

She nodded, thinking of course that he was right – it was only fair that she be straight with him.

But – and it was a big but – she didn't know whether she could.

'Otherwise . . .' he said.

He left the word hanging in the air and, a moment later, she heard his body shifting. It was now or never, she must say something. She opened her mouth, preparing herself to tell him – to tell him about Steven and Margot. Yes – that's what she should do, she should describe how she had felt when she saw Steven's lips brushing against Margot's ear, and saw as well Margot's triumphant smile. She took a deep breath. 'I . . .' she began and then again, 'I . . .'

'Yes?' He was impatient.

'I did it,' is what issued, involuntarily, from her mouth. She looked up and straight at him. 'I did it,' she repeated. His eyes were on her, a question playing there. 'I played Hedda,' she said.

I played Hedda. As if that in itself was explanation! *I played Hedda* – a ridiculous pronouncement since of course he knew that she played Hedda almost every night. She sucked her breath in, waiting for his laughter.

He didn't laugh. What he did was ask a simple question. 'Did you?' There was a peculiar timbre to his voice. Sarcasm? she wondered and looked up sharply. His face was serious. He was nodding and she knew then that he did not find her ridiculous and knew also that his tone was far from sarcastic. He understood! He understood that she had not played Hedda as she did every night but had played her differently, as only he had guessed she could. She felt tears welling. 'This is . . .' she began. And could not finish, for what was there to say? That this was embarrassing? Absurd? Shaming?

'Difficult,' he said, finishing the sentence for her.

Yes, she thought, that's what it surely is. Difficult. And worse than that.

'We try so hard,' he said, as if this was part of some conversation that she was privy to.

But he had lost her. 'Try?' she asked.

'To get it right,' he continued. 'To get it more than right.'

Oh, that. She nodded.

'And when it happens,' he continued, 'when we finally win an audience's trust, and an audience's love, then we discover how ephemeral is the satisfaction. They clap, we bow and then it's over. We are separated for ever and, while they go home strengthened perhaps by what we have given them, we are . . .'

Nothing, she thought.

'. . . still the same,' he said. 'And tomorrow and tomorrow' – he grinned in conscious self-parody – 'all the performances after that stretch in front of us, each one as big a challenge as the last. Unless . . .'

She interrupted him. 'Unless,' she heard herself saying, 'that performance was the last.'

'Yes.' He nodded gravely. 'But it never is, is it?'

Maybe, she nearly said, maybe it is for me.

She didn't say those words, she used other ones instead. 'I'm scared,' is what she said.

'I know.' He was leaning forward, stretching out his hand. No. She shook her head. How could he know?

'I'm scared,' she said. 'I'm scared, I'm scared,' over and over again, her words interspersed by tears until, after a while, the tears predominated, driving out the words. She sat, crying, trying to stop herself crying, and thinking as well that she had come here, late at night, precisely to do this – to cry on this man's soft furniture. 'I . . .' she tried to say.

'It's all right.'

No – it was not all right. Her tears fell heavier, flooding down her face.

He leaned back, resting against his fawn sofa, waiting as if expecting her tears to abate. They never will, she nearly told him.

But, at long last, they did.

He waited for a moment longer, making absolutely sure. She did not, could not look at him. She heard a movement and then, into her soggy palms, a bunch of tissues was delivered. She smiled blearily, used the tissues to swipe at her face. 'I must look dreadful,' she muttered.

'I've seen worse.' His eyes were twinkling.

No, she thought, don't laugh at me. She closed her eyes abruptly. And heard a movement in the air and one word as well. 'Come,' she heard. He was standing in front of her, his hand held out. 'Come,' he said again.

She didn't stop to think. She put her hand in his and then she was on her feet, standing next to him, smiling shyly. She tried to make a joke of it. 'Thank you, kind sir,' was all she could think of to say.

He brushed her nervousness gently aside, just like he brushed a last tear off. 'I won't bite you,' he said.

'Oh.' She pouted, feigning disappointment. 'Are you sure?'

Which made him laugh. 'You are impossible,' he said, and then, folding his hand over hers, he led her from the sitting room and down the corridor.

They were in his bedroom and she just had time to take in the king-size bed and array of cupboards opposite when he kissed her. He did so gently, putting his hand around her shoulder, nudging her closer as his lips brushed hers. Brushed hers and brushed the words and the resistance that was carried on the words away with it.

His arm gripped stronger and at the same time she moved in. Their faces bumped. She pulled away. What am I doing here? she thought.

'The final humiliation,' she heard him saying. 'Teenage nightmare come true: our first kiss and our noses clashed.' His face had softened and in his eyes there was a question.

'It happened to me once, you know,' she said, 'on camera. I was so nervous ...' And as she began to relate this past embarrassment, she saw him relaxing. She concentrated on her story, embellishing its details so grotesquely that he started laughing. His laughter ensnared her, too, and then it flared up between them, swelling until they fell backwards on to the bed.

It ended, her laughter, quite abruptly. She turned her head to look at him and as her gaze touched him his laughter also faded and, facing her, he was quite still, his eyes boring into hers. It wasn't funny, not any longer – it was deadly serious. They moved together, their arms stretching for each other, and they began to make love.

It had taken so long to get to this point that she had built the occasion up, thinking that if it ever happened it would be momentous – a fitting end to an old-fashioned courtship and, as well, a dramatic day. But it didn't turn out like that, not at all. Instead, it was easier, far easier than she had imagined it would be; it was more like an extension of their earlier conversations and of their laughter – frivolous, uncomplicated and fun.

There was passion there but it was detached and harmless. Their bodies came together lightly, easily, their desire channelled on the act itself rather than on something else, something bigger than their combined embrace. The unfamiliarity of his body, its litheness when compared with Steven's, was a joy to her but the contrast did not make the act more dramatic. Gentle, that thought in the midst of it, is how she would later describe it to herself. Gentle and it got no rougher. When it was over she was left with a deep sense of calm and a liking for this man. She turned on her side, smiling softly at him. And fell asleep.

She was dreaming: dreaming she was a girl again, decked out in a short-sleeved, brown-checked, knee-length dress and white bobby socks. A girl of twelve or thirteen perhaps with the body of an emergent woman clashing with the gaucheness of an adolescent. A girl whose mother should still have been alive and working downstairs. But in this dream she was a girl whose mother was already dead, a girl who was treading carefully upstairs in a stranger's den, walking across a whitened floor. A girl who knew exactly where she was headed but who walked in dread of what she was about to discover.

She saw it, in the corner of the room – the thing. It isn't, she thought, so frightening, it's merely familiar – 'Façade', her mother's most famous sculpture, made when her mother had been pregnant with her. Her mother's sculpture and a sculpture of a mother-to-be, a mother hewn from darkened granite, a rounded, smoothed-out but, at the same time, jagged thing. She – the girl Laura – feeling hot, leaned her weight against the sculpture, and leaning felt the coolness, almost clamminess, of its touch. She didn't like that; she let go, stood back, frowned.

'They named you rightly,' she said.

Or thought she said but as she heard the words repeated she thought that this was, surely, not her voice. It couldn't be – not hers, it was a man's voice which had spoken. 'Rightly,' the last word resounded and it was too deep for her. She frowned, tried another. 'Façade,' she said.

Façade, an octave deeper than she could possibly have formed it. It wasn't her voice, it couldn't be. She shook her head, looked uneasily about her.

She felt something moving. Almost unobtrusively she felt it, something nudging cold against her. She looked at the sculpture and saw that it was still and innocent. No – not innocent, it never was that, not with its harsh grey shadows jutting into black. She looked at it and frowned. 'I never liked you,' she told it.

And at that moment the movement was exaggerated. Something lashed out. Like a whip it struck her, a many-tentacled whip, shooting out from inside Façade, shooting out and grasping her and she knew then that it was not a whip but a hand – her mother's hand, her dark, angry, vengeful mother's hand which had come to claim her.

'No,' she cried.

The hand had hold of her. 'No,' she cried again but lost her balance. She was falling, plummeting into darkness, into the place where Judith had long lain. Into death.

'No,' she cried again.

She was awake. She felt a hand restraining her. 'No,' she said, more weakly now.

Tom was next to her, his hand gripping one of hers. Seeing her eyes opening, he let go. 'It's all right,' he was saying. 'It's all right.'

But he was wrong. It wasn't all right: it never would be. She shook her head.

'It was only a dream,' he said. 'It's over.'

But it wasn't, not a dream. She had seen Steven and Margot together. Not a dream – she didn't have such dreams. She shook her head again, rolled away from Tom, rolling herself out of bed. 'I have to go,' she said.

She saw him wince, saw pain crossing his face, but there was nothing she could do to console him. She had to go, that was all. She walked across the bedroom, began pulling clothes over her head.

'Laura.'

She turned to look at him, saw him naked, a stranger with pleading eyes.

'Don't . . .' he began but stopped when he saw her shaking her head.

'I have to go,' was all she could think of to say.

CHAPTER TWENTY-EIGHT

She had no idea what time it was, knew only that it was very late.

'Sleep well, love,' the taxi-driver called as he pulled out.

Sleep well – her lips curled at the very thought. She swivelled round. She was on the top step facing a front door more familiar even than her own. But no – she shook her head – she would not think of that.

She was on the top step, immobilized by a lethargy which, creeping in, anchored her body to the ground, her bones so heavy that she could not budge them. She stood there, still as the night, willing herself to move. She would lift her hand, that's what she'd do. She gritted her teeth, telling her hand to obey.

Nothing happened. She frowned. 'Come on,' she muttered angrily.

It worked: she lifted her right hand, jabbed out an index finger, poked it at the bell. Short and sharp the gesture and she heard its curt response: a shrill ring.

Nothing. The house remained shrouded in indifferent shadow. She nodded – of course, one ring was not enough to distract them from their passionate embrace.

Well, no problem: she would give them more than that! She was in furious motion, using the flat of her hand, smashing hard down. And after that she did not let up: she followed through with all her weight, leaning against the bell, her ear resting on the door, listening to the long, high monotone.

Success! A light clicked on, high in the house. Now the die was cast.

The wailing of the bell had used up all her anger. She was composed. She heard tentative footsteps, far away at first, gradually coming closer. She turned, concentrating on a Primrose Hill which was resting in darkened tranquillity, bare tree branches reaching stiffly up to oxygen. She breathed out, saw her breath curling grey against the blackness of the chill night air. She was calm, prepared for anything.

'Who's there?' she heard an anxious voice inquiring.

She didn't bother answering – Margot could easily see her. Yes, there it was, a rattling as Margot lifted up the cover to the door's eye and there it was following through – a muffled recognition.

The door opened and she heard her name. 'Laura,' coming from Margot's deadened mouth. Margot was wearing a dressing gown, a worn blue candlewick affair covering her nakedness, white legs sticking out from below. Her nakedness – did she have no shame?

The thought propelled Laura forward. She pushed past Margot and through the door and then down the hall, her feet whipping already against the first step.

'Laura!'

She was climbing the steps, two, no, three at a time, her legs stretching out effortlessly as Margot's ineffectual voice tried to hold her back.

'What are you doing?' Margot was puffing from the exertion. 'Where are you going?'

Laura snorted. *Where are you going?* The question as pitiful as Margot's loss of breath. It was obvious where she was going. She was going upstairs, that's where.

'Laura. Stop it. Laura.'

Laura, Laura . . . Margot's twittering voice pursued her, the name repeated with a few words on either side. She closed her ears, shutting the incantation out. She did not, would not, let Margot slow her down. She was turning now, nearly there, rounding the corner.

'Laura!'

She smiled. Margot was using and reusing her name deliberately, as a way of forewarning Steven. Except it was too late – she had reached her destination, was at the doorway. She took one further step, breached the entrance.

And stopped abruptly. The bed was empty, its only occupants inanimate – a dark blue duvet roughly pushed aside, a pile of pillows all bunched up.

Doubt, the first hints of it, crept in. She shook her head, shaking doubt away. She was right – she knew she was. She must be right, Steven must be here. She heard a sound. Her face cleared. Of course – that was the answer – he was hiding. In the bathroom – that's where he was.

'Laura!' Margot was almost upon her.

Well, damn Margot, let her rot. She strode across the room until she was at its other end and throwing her weight against the bathroom door. It wasn't locked and her own momentum carried her in. Down she almost tumbled, losing her bag, hearing it go skittering across the hard tile floor. She pushed her hand out, broke her fall, ended up half leaning against the bath. Her breath was coming heavily, long-drawn-out gasping.

But no, she was wrong, it wasn't just her breath – it was hers and Margot's. She turned, saw Margot standing by the open door, illuminated from behind.

'What do you want?' Margot asked.

She saw an image then, a memory from the past of herself inside this bathroom, her face framed by a mirror, her hand reaching out.

Margot took one step nearer. 'What do you want?' repeated harshly in the half-gloom.

Laura's answer, the one she had planned to give, came automatically. 'I'm looking for Steven,' she said.

'Oh, Laura.' Margot shook her head mournfully. 'Steven isn't here.'

She knew that now: of course she did. 'Why on earth should he be here?' she heard Margot saying.

Because, she nearly began, because ... But the rest of the sentence deserted her. She stood motionless in a dismal world wondering vaguely what it was that had fuelled her certainty, and wondering also what words she had been planning to pronounce. What could she possibly have said? That she knew Steven was here because she had seen them together at the theatre? Or was she going to be more honest than that? Was she going to tell Margot that she knew Steven was there because she had slept with Tom?

Margot reached out a hand, clicking on the light. What Laura saw was herself through Margot's eyes – what she had become. A fool – that's what. She snorted, leaned down, retrieved her bag and began slowly retracing her steps. Which meant, of course, that she was heading straight for Margot. And at that moment the balance of power changed. Alarm flashed across Margot's face, its dull pallor infused with temporary colour.

Alarm, yes, – but something else as well. Laura took a closer look. Guilt – that's what she saw etched on Margot's face. She looked some more and nodded – Margot was trying out a synthetic smile.

'Come, Laura.' Margot's hand touched her arm.

Margot's warm hand – she jerked it off. And as their flesh was separated she realized what she had come to say. 'I want to know the truth.' Yes, that's what it was.

'The truth?' Margot's stiff smile was in place.

Well, Laura would soon be rid of it. 'About the jade,' she said.

Margot thin lips jerked. 'The –'

How theatrical, Laura thought. How melodramatic. 'Yes,' she said, 'the jade. I want to know where it went, and how you got it back.'

'It didn't go any –' Margot began.

But Laura was not having that: 'Oh yes, it did,' bringing her hand down to her side, and slapping it for emphasis against her leg. When Margot winced, Laura came one step closer. She had Margot now; she would not let her go. One step and Margot was in her orbit.

They were facing each other head on, these two women, Leo's women. They were facing each other as they had never done before, their breath mingling. So near were they that depth of vision had gone. All Laura saw were Margot's eyes, weak hazel in a sea of white. She widened her own eyes, let them drill into Margot's and saw Margot's whites shimmering with moisture. She frowned. She would not let her eyes reflect back Margot's weakness. She frowned and her gaze clutched more intensively.

It was too much for Margot. Her mouth moved and out of it crept one single word. One word, a name: 'Ben.'

'What?' Laura was belligerent.

Margot's eyes dropped, fixing themselves numbly on the floor. 'Ben Okalia took the jade,' she mumbled.

Ben Okalia. 'He took it?' Laura said slowly, emphasizing each separate word and her disbelief as well, although in the back of the mind she remembered what had been written on the note, and remembered also how his parting words to her had echoed that. 'When?'

'The night of Leo's death.'

Oh no – this was preposterous: it could not be. 'Before?' she asked, sarcasm dripping. She dropped her voice – a fitting contrast. 'Or after?'

The question had at least some impact. Margot's head shifted; she raised her chin, her eyes – no longer puppy-dog moist – looking at Laura, her mouth firmly closed.

So Laura had to speak again. 'Did Ben take the jade before or after my father's death?' she asked.

'Before.' There was a tear running the full length of Margot's cheek. 'If I had known how insane Ben was, I would never have let him in. But he fooled me.'

Yes, thought Laura, and me as well. But she would not, could not, let herself pity Margot. 'Go on,' she said, harshly.

And Margot did. 'After Leo went back to the office Ben turned up. He must have been watching, waiting for Leo to leave. I let him in. I didn't know, you see. I let him in. I shouldn't have. He went up to Leo's study.'

'And took the jade?'

Margot nodded.

'While you stood quietly by.'

That gesture again, that single nod. Laura was smiling. It's so unlikely, she thought, I might as well get the full breadth of it. 'So how come he sent it back?' she asked in an amiable voice.

Margot's breath was one great shudder. 'He came back once after Leo's death. To gloat, I think. He hated Leo, you know, with a force of hatred that would never be buried. He wanted to destroy him, would go to any lengths to do so. He said you and I were legitimate targets; that he had lost the ones he loved. He scared me. I suppose I wanted to scare him back. I told him that you had noticed the jade was missing and that I was going to tell the police that he had stolen it. I must have frightened him – that's why he sent it back. The truth is, I wouldn't have told the police. There was no point – Leo was dead. Ben's vendetta upset Leo but Leo was ill – he was going to die anyway. So what was the point of dwelling on any of this?'

What was the point? Laura thought, feeling a needle of anger, a small, bright white light twisting her guts. 'The point, as you so blandly put it,' she said, her voice dripping venom, 'the point is that the jade wasn't yours to give away. The point –'

'Ben said it was his.' Margot cut right through Laura's rage.

'It wasn't Ben's,' Laura said. 'It was Leo's until he gave it to Judith and after that it was Judith's.'

But Margot shook her head.

'It was,' Laura insisted.

Another shake, another disagreement. 'Ben told me that it had belonged to him, that it was a family heirloom, given, in friendship, to Leo to keep for as long as the friendship lasted. Ben said Leo had betrayed him and that, by the rules of friendship, the jade must be returned. He wouldn't leave without it and so I gave it to him. I thought Leo would understand – he didn't care much about possessions.'

No. Laura shook her head. No. Leo would have minded for the jade was Judith's.

'Ben said it was his,' she heard Margot repeat. She heard momentary doubt and then Margot's voice was strengthened. 'When Leo came back and saw that it was missing, I knew by his response that what Ben had said was true.'

In that moment Laura saw again into the past; a different hand, her daddy's comforting hand, stretching out and turning and in it a palm-shaped parcel. 'It's beautiful,' she heard.

It's beautiful: hushed words whispered, carried along the trees of time, spoken in her mother's melodic voice as the wrapping had fallen away.

'No,' she shouted the word out.

And then, as her denial rang out, she knew that what Margot had said was indeed the truth. It came back to her, all of it; what she had not understood then. It came back to her how Leo had folded her inside his arms and how, as she had told him it was Judith's birthday, she had felt his muscles tensing.

The lie wasn't Margot's, or Ben's either, it was Leo's. It was Leo who had forgotten Judith's birthday; who had given the jade in guilt; who had covered his lapse by giving to Judith what had never been bought for her. Poor Judith: it must always have been like that – Leo, nimble on his feet; Leo, the skilful negotiator playing one side in a civil war against the other, reeling in emotions and responses which would suit his ends. What chance had Judith had against that? Poor Judith – she had been so pathetically pleased that Leo had remembered.

Poor Judith. If this was true then so was all the rest. Leo had betrayed Judith – from the beginning until the end. And her, Laura, as well; and Margot, who was waiting there.

'Did Ben tell you that Leo knew about the guns?' she asked.

A nod.

'And was that also true?'

'I don't know what happened,' Margot whispered. 'I don't really know.'

That *really* was the giveaway: of course Margot knew! But Laura did not press her. There were other more important things to discover. 'Who was it?' she asked. 'That Leo was sleeping with?'

And once more got the same answer. 'I don't know ...' Margot began before faltering. Her mouth was opening and closing, indecision written all over her face, while Laura, watching, thought of Judith; thinking, No wonder. No wonder that ... She had no need to complete the thought. She lifted her eyes, seeking Judith out.

But Judith was gone. The space where her portrait had always, always hung was now empty. Laura looked fiercely at Margot. 'You threw her picture out.'

'I packed it away,' Margot gently corrected.

Gently ... What right had Margot? What right to patronize? Except, and she felt her shoulders drooping, what did it matter? What Margot did, what Margot felt – it was all irrelevant. What mattered now was something other, something much bigger than Margot. Her eyes were stinging. She reached out a hand.

Margot's distant voice reached her. 'Laura, are you all right?'

She did not answer, had no answer now to give.

'Come, Laura,' she heard Margot saying. 'Sit down. I'll get some water.'

1967

'Water,' fourteen-year-old Laura heard. She looked up, staring into the other's eyes, seeing her own green pupils, darkened by shadow, reflected back.

Silence – until Judith blinked. 'Some water would be nice,' she said.

Some water, Laura heard, grateful that the silence had been broken, thinking that her mother had been so nice, had brought her freshly squeezed orange juice. It was Laura's turn now: she nodded shyly: turned to go.

'Lots of it,' Judith's voice pursued her. 'A jug.' Judith sounded calm, as if what had gone before the juice – the rage, the frenzied cries against the world, the unceasing sobbing – as if all that had been illusion.

It's over, Laura told herself. Her mother, the best mother in the world, had returned to her skin.

'Darling?'

Judith was waiting, she must hurry. She left the room and, tripping lightly down the stairs, went into the darkened kitchen.

She left the light deliberately off; she liked the kitchen in its half-shadow, moonlight filtering through. Padding over to the cupboard, she withdrew a jug and, holding it under the cold tap, filled it almost to the top.

An ice tray – that was next. She took one out and banged it against the metal sink, dislodging individual chunks. These she put into the jug and then was ready: she stretched up, grabbed a glass and, putting it and the jug on to a tray, carried the lot upstairs.

Judith was in bed. 'A tray,' she said when Laura entered. 'Now that's what I call service.' Sitting up, she took the jug and glass. 'Be a dear and put the tray on the dresser, will you?' she said.

Laura complied, but as she turned she heard a sound. 'Oh,' she heard – Judith sounding nonplussed. Turning back she saw Judith frowning but as she watched her appearance was neutralized. 'Ice.' Judith eventually said, deadpan. She smiled, wiping the last remnants of – what was it? – dismay, perhaps, away. 'How very considerate. And now . . .'

And now, Laura thought, coming closer.

'And now it's time for bed.'

Bed. Of course. Judith must be tired. And so, of course, was she. She turned.

'Good night, darling.'

Good night. She was dismissed. She did not turn again, she walked out of the room, softly closing the door, and made her way upstairs. Into her bedroom she went, and into bed, laying her head down, smiling in the darkness. She was so sleepy, so very sleepy, and so so happy to be in bed. It's over, she thought, Judith's rending pain. Her mother was now calm and would be all right tomorrow and all right the day after that, because Leo was due home soon.

She fell asleep thinking, stupid, misguided child, that it was over.

She woke once in the night – blearily opening her eyes. It was no longer dark, she vaguely saw, seeing how round the sides of her drawn curtains soft light was glimmering. Dawn had come already, but early dawn – the world was hushed. She lay in bed, dazed, more asleep than not, hearing ringing. The telephone, she thought.

But surely not, for if it was the telephone, her mother would have answered it.

No. The ringing stopped. No, she thought, not stopped – it had never been. That's it, that must be it. She had imagined the noise. She was drowsy, so drowsy, her eyelids drooped and then she was asleep.

CHAPTER TWENTY-NINE

1992

The orange juice, Laura thought, that's why I slept so late, why Heloise had to shake me awake – because Judith drugged it. She made sure that time, Laura thought, that what had happened before, me waking her, would never reoccur.

'Here,' she heard a gentle voice saying. 'Here. Drink this.'

Judith's voice; Judith watching the juice sliding down her daughter's throat and smiling in satisfaction when it was gone.

But Judith was long gone. Laura blinked. It wasn't Judith she had just heard. It was the same room but Judith was dead.

'Here.' The glass was thrust at her.

The glass contained not orange juice but water. Seeing it Laura was pulled back once more into the past. She didn't want to be – she shut her eyes against memory – but it was too late. She could not close it out: that hand, stretching for a glass; that hand, her mother's hand; and those eyes, her mother's eyes; knowing what they were doing. She drugged me first, Laura thought, but that wasn't enough. Afterwards she made me bring the water.

The thought was almost unendurable and it filled her with a savage rage. 'She made me bring the water,' she shouted, lunging out, knocking the glass away. The water drenched her and brought her to her senses. She saw Margot standing there, astonished.

She didn't try and explain. Margot was no longer important. Nothing was really, not any more, for Laura had lost everything. Everything: her countless childish inventions, like the fact that her parents loved each other, and her as well; or that her mother had been too full of creative pain to live; or that her father was honest, strong and true. All of this which had once been her doctrine, shoring her up, now all of this was gone.

In its place had come reality, laid bare, and with it the knowledge that the death, which she had told herself was Judith's dreadful act, or her fear for Leo's end, was not in fact anything to do with her parents: instead it was, and had always been *her* death.

They came welling up inside: her grief, her mother's anguish, her anger, her father's lies, and she could evade them no longer. What she had struggled to believe – that she was a successful actress, capable of sustaining good friendships and long-term lovers – none of this mattered because she was something else entirely, had always been. What she was was plain Laura Weber, the daughter of a suicide and a traitor, her being defined solely by her parents. She turned.

'Laura?'

She turned and began to walk. Down the stairs she went, watching blankly as one foot replaced the next and the next one after that, as she got closer to the ground floor and to going out.

'Laura.'

She shrugged, shrugging Margot's concern off. It was all one stupid device, she thought, my entanglement with Margot, a way of hiding from the truth. The truth, which was, she thought – she saw her hand go out – that she had never been alone – she was turning the doorknob – that behind her the giant shadow of Judith – the door was open – the grim heritage of Judith's pain, mighty and overpowering, loomed.

The fates were helping her now. She walked out of Margot's house and saw a taxi passing by. Up her hand went automatically and when the taxi stopped she climbed inside, mumbling her address in an unfamiliar voice. And then she sat, eyes open but unseeing, as London flitted past, as north gave way to south, as the taxi moved closer, closer to her end.

She had known how she would do it, had always known. Pills – that was the only way. Judith had taken them; so would she.

Not that things were otherwise equal – Laura had to work much harder for her pills, collecting each one from a different source.

'So what?' she said.

So what, out loud. She meant it. It made no difference, none of it. Her pills would work as well as Judith's.

She was sitting on the bed, her legs dangling as if she were a child. But she was no child. She never really had been one. She stretched her hand out, blindly locating the shelf, intent, at last, on getting on with it. But then she paused. Something, she thought, is missing. She frowned, and realized what it was. Liquid to help the pills go down.

Water. She'd been shown the way: water was best. She rose. 'A glass of water, then,' she said. And went to get it, feeling very calm.

Calm. This fact had haunted Laura. For twenty-five years she had wondered why her mother, who had chosen death, why, at that point, she had been so calm.

Now, finally, after twenty-five years, Laura understood.

It was simple, the answer. There was no longer any need for tension. All that thrashing about, all that trying to pretend it was worth continuing, was for the living. Now that tension could be banished, and that fear as well. Death was irrelevant. What Judith had wanted, what Laura wanted, was not death but silence; not death but the absence of pain, of struggle, of ever-impending defeat.

Death beckoned.

But she would not die like Judith. She would allow some variation. Not for her the sunlight streaming on to her pale corpse. Darkness that is what she craved. She put the glass down.

She would have darkness. She began to move through the flat turning the handle on each separate blind until the outside was expunged. That done, she went to the kitchen, used the kick stool to reach up to a high shelf, pulled the white jug down, and, going over to another counter, began to fill it.

She watched the level rising thinking that she would die a modern death, her pills helped by way of filtered water. Filtered water at room temperature – no ice for her.

Ice. Judith had been surprised when Laura brought iced

water, which would have slowed down the process. Her surprise must have concealed a curse. Judith had cursed her daughter just before she died.

'So what?' Laura said as, leaving the kitchen area, she clicked off the light.

She was on the bed, her hands working fast, removing books and laying them to one side. Reaching the pills, she took great care with them, decanting a group into her hand. Carefully she laid them upon the wooden surface, returning for a second and even a third batch. She had retrieved them all. She was finished; beside her lay a loose mosaic manufactured from the things that would deliver peace.

She let go her grip on a bottle and watched as it dropped down to the floor. And frowned. Why had she dropped it?

Immediately the answer came – another image from the past. Her sight of Judith's first attempt came back to her, the vision of the thing that once had been her mother and of the thing's pale arm lolling over the bed, pointing at an empty bottle.

This phantom – it had always walked beside her. But now she had no need of it. 'Go away,' she told it gently. 'Go away.' And smiled for she was about to banish it for ever. She leaned over and picking up the bottle placed it down beside the pills.

Her last moment would be tasteful. She savoured the prospect, arranging it to suit. She took the pills, one by delicate one, and laid them out in an orderly line, colour-matching them so that this unstrung necklace of death, its beads of yellow, baby blue, of bright reds and darker blue, looked right. And then, when that was done she popped the pills inside her mouth, one by one, sipping water to drown their bitterness. One by one, slowly but determinedly, until she'd had them all. And then, just as she had done twenty-five years ago, she laid her head upon the pillow and waited, calmly, for sleep.

It drifted up on her, that last sleep, drifting through last thoughts. Of ringing – she heard it once again, coming from the past. The ringing of the telephone that she had always thought she had imagined.

She was imagining it now, not then. For she understood, at the last, the final piece to the puzzle. Leo. It was Leo who had been ringing. That's what he'd meant when, as the ambulance had gone screaming off, he'd started shouting. 'I phoned,' that's what he had shouted, 'I phoned.'

He'd phoned – in the dead of night.

She nodded. Of course he had. He had phoned knowing that something was wrong and, not receiving an answer, had taken the next available plane, arriving at his home two days in advance of schedule. Two days early but still too late.

1967

Stretching across Leo's desk, Judith's arm inadvertently hit the table lamp. It fell to the floor and lay there, its beam shining in her eyes. She didn't pick it up, she was possessed only by what she was doing, searching Leo's desk, opening drawers and scrabbling inside, rummaging through the layers of neatly categorized files.

He was so meticulous, was Leo. If he really was having an affair, the evidence would be catalogued there.

But no – another drawer, another failure. She raised her head and saw the letter lying on Leo's blotter, a scruffy piece of paper on which a few malicious lines were written. Her eyes were drawn to its end: from a well-wisher, that's how it was signed. She shook her head, wondering why a stranger would write to a wife about her husband's infidelity and then sign himself a well-wisher.

An affair, she thought, almost laughing, it was nonsense anyway. Leo wasn't the type. He was far too angelic, too faithful and, apart from that, too occupied with saving the world.

And even if she'd misjudged him, even if he had a woman in every bloody country that he visited, would she really care? She shrugged – she didn't think so, could even sympathize with Leo finding uncomplicated consolation elsewhere.

But she continued, anyway, because the task itself – invading a place that had previously been sacrosanct – had calmed her, forcing the demons into temporary retreat. Temporary only, she was sure of that, and when they came back she knew they would be even more malevolent, but nevertheless she was *determined to enjoy this slight respite. It makes a change, she thought, to follow Leo's trail. What usually happened was the opposite – Leo tracking her, viewing her work as a way into her psyche.*

One more drawer to go. She opened it.

She saw a shoe box. That wasn't Leo's style. She pulled it out.

And then, after she had removed the box's lid, all thoughts fled. There were the things she had been craving: pills of all shapes and sizes, colours and cures, numbers beyond her wildest dreams. She dipped her hand in, scooped up a random bunch, licking her lips, seeing some she recognized and some she didn't. I can sleep now, she thought, I can . . .

And heard a sound. She whipped her head round.

It was Laura, standing in the lighted doorway, staring, staring as if she knew.

But if Laura knew then Judith was lost. 'What do you want?' Judith's words came rasping out, a muted echo of the raging that had earlier possessed her.

Laura flinched. 'I . . . I . . . couldn't sleep,' she stuttered.

Well, neither could I, Judith thought angrily, thinking that Laura had no idea what not being able to sleep was really about. Real sleep: how she longed for it and how unobtainable it seemed. Ever since that last attempt they had kept all drugs, even a single sleeping pill, from her.

But now all that was changed. Now resting under her hand was the means.

'Mummy?'

She looked up, saw Laura again. Laura who had come the time before, and who had roused her then from sleep. Well, Judith had learned her lesson. I'll plan it well this time, she thought; send Laura to a friend.

But no – she shook her head, gripped by sudden urgency. Only a few hours ago when Leo had phoned, she had not been able to disguise her mounting panic. He must have heard it, he knew her so well. He must have known that she was once again possessed by despair.

Despair – such a paltry name for what she regularly experienced. It was deeper each time it came and this time, she knew it, it would be even worse; this time the madness that was descending would never, ever leave her.

She had only one chance, then, one way out and it was here, in front of her. She must do it – now – before Leo returned.

Leo – she remembered what had panicked her. Leo who thought, poor darling, that he could save her. She'd heard it that very evening in his voice; how he was planning to try and do just that. Although he didn't say so, she knew that at this moment Leo the superman would be moving heaven and earth to get back to her side.

But she couldn't stand that. No matter what Leo said, she knew that she couldn't endure it. Not again. She must act, now, must end this agony and, in so doing, save all three of them from further torture.

She nodded, suddenly completely sure of herself, knowing exactly what she would do. She would take the pills that very night, before Leo could get back and, at the same time, would stop Laura from interfering. She turned. She had so much to think of suddenly. The letter, she must destroy that first off, and then she must get the box. And Laura – she must find some way of quieting her. She nodded. The pills – there were enough, she could spare a few.

She smiled. 'It's warm in here,' she said. 'You go to the bathroom, wash your face. I'll squeeze you an orange juice – that should help.' And then, when her daughter had gone, she turned again, grabbed the letter and the box, closed all the drawers and left.

She was thinking nothing as she left, nothing as she hid the box under her bed and went downstairs, and nothing as she pushed the letter into the sink's disposal system, hearing it churning up. She felt nothing but vague anticipation as she dropped two small white pills into a glass and poured fresh squeezed orange on top.

CHAPTER THIRTY

1992

There was a time before and a time afterwards, and they were entirely separated. The time before encompassed almost her whole life: her childhood, happily remembered (and yet it could not really have been happy); her adolescence, hardly begun (wiped out by that one horrendous act); her adulthood, a passing into modern life. And then this, this final humiliation: the beginning of the time afterwards.

And because what went before had all been pure illusion, the after was emergence into almost unbearable reality. In pain and harsh light it was born, faces swimming into vision, tubes and retching and a throat bruised by rough handling. Groaning, there was that as well, her own or somebody entirely other's, she never did find out. She was an object on a conveyor belt, human baggage to be emptied and funnelled out. She was tired, so tired, but they wouldn't let her sleep, they kept on shaking her, prodding her with foolish questions. And then, when they had squeezed the last drop of resistance from her, only then did they leave her in peace.

In peace – she had a room to herself, a cheerless hospital enclosure with sludge-yellow walls, a white side table bending on spindly legs, a narrow metallic bed. In peace – she lay on her back, staring unseeing up at the dingy ceiling. Her mind was blank. Not quiet, not blocking off unwanted thoughts, but blank as if the slate had been wiped clean.

Not for long though: the door opened and a succession of intruders began streaming through it. Tom knew enough about her to stay away, but Steven came. Steven, still officially her partner, fretful, endeavouring to produce a blend of smiles and light conversation and, at the same time, to avoid mention of her dreadful act. She almost found herself feeling sorry for him. His eyes, moist and bewildered, were filled with unspoken hurt, showing clearly what he was really thinking. But she had no strength to pity him and found she could not deal with him, could answer his unspoken questions only with a sullen silence, so that when finally a nurse ordered him out, she was as relieved as he.

A bevy of brisk professionals – nurses, doctors, social work-ers – followed. She could not bear it. She closed her eyes stubbornly against this scrutiny of strangers and eventually it worked: she managed to banish them all. She kept her eyes closed, drifting in and out of sleep, occasionally checking she was still alone. Time passed. A tray of food was produced and, after it had all congealed, removed, to be replaced in turn by another, similar tray. The day was artificially marked out: the blind opened to admit a filtering of murky daylight and then, as it began to fade, shut again. Monotony – that's what she experienced – a monotonous routine of starched aprons, bright smiles, empty chit-chat passing over her head. All these flitted in and out of her consciousness, each as superfluous as the last. Until, that is, she opened her eyes and saw a familiar figure.

Heloise, it was, sitting quietly beside the bed. Heloise, en-grossed in contemplation of her hands, her head bent so low that all Laura could see was the top, her soft grey hair tied in a central bun, stray wisps flowing down. As Laura lay there, watching Heloise's serenity, her eyes began involuntarily to close.

Not for long though. A vision, a recent memory of Heloise erupted and in an attempt to evade it she snapped her eyes wide open. But the vision pursued her into the light, this sight of Heloise ferociously in motion, spinning across the room, her mouth stretched in a silent scream.

Of course – she knew what it must mean. It was Heloise who had driven her from death, who had hammered on the door, who must have found someone to break through and who, shaking Laura and shouting her name, had summoned the ambulance.

But wait! Laura frowned. How it could have been Heloise? She lifted her head. 'Was it you?' she asked. Heloise recoiled, her intertwined hands jumping apart. 'It was you, wasn't it?' Laura did not bother waiting for Heloise's reply. 'How? How did you know?'

Heloise blinked and Laura, watching, saw faint lines running across the surface of her heavy lids. A sigh, and Heloise began to speak. 'I was awake,' she said, her voice coming at Laura as if from a long way away. 'I heard you ringing Margot's doorbell. You pressed hard, you know.' She smiled vaguely but before the smile could gel her knitted brow had disposed of it. 'I got up, and waited, wondering whether I should check on Margot,' she said. A pause, another elusive smile. 'I didn't. I knew that you would never harm Margot. But after I saw you leaving I could not persuade myself to go back to sleep. I lay awake all through the night until I could no longer tolerate my own inaction. I tried to ring you . . .'

The ringing, Laura thought.

'. . . and when I got no answer, I came round.' She turned her head and her voice grew more distant. 'I could not let it happen,' she said. 'I could not . . . not . . .' Her head jerked back, she was looking now straight at Laura, her eyes glistening. '. . . Not again,' she said.

Again, Laura thought. I am not even original.

She shut her eyes. Silence in the room while outside it the world went on. The bustle of a busy hospital, that's what she could hear, and then she incorporated that into the background and it was nothing; nothing stretching into eternity, nothing . . .

She was drifting back into sleep when the silence was ruptured. She heard a scraping of a chair against the floor, abnormally loud. Heloise had abruptly risen. She's going, Laura thought, hearing footsteps moving from the bed. She opened her eyes, in time to see Heloise by the window, pushing the blind aside. A faint glow of yellow light, diffuse and bleary, flared, starkly outlining Heloise's profile.

Laura frowned. A solitary figure, lit by artificial light, a figure standing by a window – where had she seen that before? A shadow against the dark night: as the image rose, she forced it back, swallowing it and with it the stiff lump that had formed in her throat, swallowing both hard down.

'It was foggy then also,' she heard Heloise muttering.

Foggy, she thought, was it?

'The night she . . .' A pause and then Heloise stamped her foot down on the hospital linoleum. 'The night that Judith killed herself,' she said. She twisted her head round, glanced at Laura.

Who did not really see her. Who could not see her because she was too busy remembering how, almost a year previously, she had been that solitary figure. She – she had awakened to a distant sound, a siren slashing through a foggy night. Yes, she remembered thinking that it was foggy. A foggy night – she had thought then that some outside noises had disturbed her but knew now that this was wrong. It was Judith, and what Judith had done, that had reverberated. Judith who had been waiting in the grave until the time was right, and when it was, Judith who had shot her hand out, pulling her daughter to her.

Her daughter, whose eyes were welling with fresh tears.

No – she would not let them fall. She blinked, driving them away.

'I let it happen once,' she heard Heloise whispering and then she heard the sound of the blind clicking into place. She glanced across, saw that Heloise had turned from the window, was staring at the bed, her face fiercely determined. 'I will not let it happen again,' Heloise said.

Which brought a vague smile to Laura's lips, the movement tugging at her insides. 'You think you're so powerful?'

Her feeble humour fell on stony ground – Heloise's eyes, hardened to slate-grey, repelled it. And Heloise now proved herself stronger than Laura who, finding that she could not meet the intensity of Heloise's stare, dropped her eyes.

But Heloise persisted. 'No, my Laura,' Heloise said. 'It is you' – she stressed the pronoun fiercely, and the second time she stressed it all the more – '*you* who are powerful.'

Laura was so tired. She closed her eyes. 'Some power,' she muttered.

But Heloise's voice pursued her. 'We are going away,' she heard Heloise announcing.

'We? There is no we,' Laura said, and then, having made that clear, she turned over and almost immediately fell asleep.

CHAPTER THIRTY-ONE

There was a side to Heloise filled with the very opposite of her usual gentle self, and it was this side which, in the next few days, was paramount. She was indomitable, a virago capable of beating back all comers. Friends and foe alike were repelled, their good wishes and demands equally renounced until everybody (including Gareth at his most belligerent) ended up bowing to her will. *We'll go away*. That's what she had said and so it was arranged. Laura's understudy was to play Hedda, Laura was to leave. Laura said no – she did not want to, could not, she insisted, go away – but then she found herself packing and installing herself and her luggage in Heloise's car.

Their end point was on the edges of Exmoor, a small cottage with two tiny bedrooms, a damp bathroom, and a living room furnished with faded floral cast-offs. Laura hated it – or at least she hated it at first. Not for long. She had no real energy to sustain hatred. She was completely empty – of nourishment and of emotion as well. When she stood by the window (her most strenuous activity) staring blankly out, she watched an unyielding nothingness, a heavy grey sky weighing down a flat, bracken-covered land. On into the distance it extended, this harsh terrain. She was empty and it felt better that way. She stood and looked and little came to break the silence.

Even Heloise was complicit, restricting conversation to the minimum, using words as mere shorthand notification (to call Laura to the table, for example, and, after an interval, to release her from it). Where it was possible she relied on gestures, running a bath and placing a towel in Laura's hands, bringing tea to show it was time to get up. And otherwise she was just there, that was all, just always there, near Laura.

Not that Laura minded. It was fine. Everything was. Fine. She didn't want to speak, she didn't want engagement; the dullness suited her.

Except it didn't last for ever. One afternoon, Heloise's voice cracked the silence. 'It is time,' she announced.

Time? Laura thought vaguely and glanced down at her wrist – without effect since there was no watch there. She wondered vaguely what had happened to it but then forgot to follow through. It didn't matter, none of it did. She dropped her hand and continued staring out of the window.

'The inaction is congealing your brain,' she heard Heloise saying.

She stayed quite still, staring at a landscape stretched out, unrelenting, and if she thought anything at all it was that she had no remnant of a brain left to congeal.

'Tomorrow we will go for a walk,' Heloise said.

No. Laura shook her head but so lethargically that the shaking was almost imperceptible. She stood, wiping out the echo of Heloise's voice, thinking vaguely that although it was still light outside, she was weary. She was weary, she must sleep. Picking up the book that she carried everywhere but never opened, she trudged out, making her way slowly to the small room nestling under the eaves that she considered hers. There she felt safe, because there Heloise's instructions could not reach her. She closed the door, got into the narrow bed, pulled the quilt over her head, shut her eyes and waited, patiently, for the onset of merciful sleep. It did not keep her waiting, not for long, and it never disappointed her. In sleep she lay swathed, unmoving and unavailable.

A hand was shaking her. She grunted and tried to move away from it. But the hand would not let up and: 'It is time,' a loud voice said.

No – she wouldn't listen. 'I'm tired,' she muttered, turning from the voice.

But Heloise yanked her back. 'You have slept for more than fourteen hours,' she said and, as if Laura were weightless, hauled her out of bed, dropping her feet down on the cold floor. 'Wear something warm,' was her final instruction before she left the room.

*

They were sitting at breakfast as they had done each morning, but the silence was continually breached. 'We are going out,' Heloise announced.

Those words again. Laura's hand stopped in mid air. 'Now?'

'Later. When we have finished breakfast.'

Later – oh well, that was all right. She couldn't worry about later: she existed only in the now. Her arm continued on its way, picking a piece of toast from the rack and depositing it on her plate. Slowly, her hand moving through the sludge that enveloped her, she began to scrape her knife across the toast, covering it with a thin layer of butter.

But Heloise would not leave her alone. 'It is good to see you interested in food again,' Heloise said.

Good, Laura thought, is it? and the knife dropped out of her slack hand.

'Laura!' Heloise's voice was curt. 'Don't be so childish.'

She pushed the plate away, looked challengingly across the table and said the first words that came into her head. 'What's the problem?' she said. 'Scared I'll starve myself to death?'

To death. The phrase issued out unexpectedly, slicing through Laura's protective mist.

And because the mist had been breached Heloise's voice was made deadly. 'What did you say?' She sounded so fierce.

But no, Laura told herself, that's not what mattered. What mattered was that she had betrayed herself, and the haze, which had once been a fogged mass, was suddenly clarified and it, her only defence, was drifting off.

No. She wanted her protection back. She squeezed her eyes shut.

'Laura!'

She squeezed harder. 'Leave me alone,' she muttered. 'Stop watching me.'

'Laura. I am not . . .'

'Stop watching me,' the words stabbing out in a flash of rage. She shook her head so wildly that it inscribed a frantic arc. She shoved her hands up to her face, covering it with extended palms, covering it so hard that the continued shaking rubbed her cheeks into skin, pressing it taut. Dry sobs, that's what she began to hear, the dryness of her inept anger reverberating in the ineffective dark.

The sobs were pointless. She despised herself. She ended them abruptly, let her hands drop, looked at Heloise. 'You don't have to worry,' is what she said. 'I'm a failure' – her voice was loud, too loud – 'even at suicide.'

A silence stretched between them, but it was too abrasive to be of comfort. A silence as arid as Laura's heart.

And then, at last, Heloise broke the silence. 'I am not worried that you will try to kill yourself. What terrifies me' – she paused and smiled so sadly that Laura felt herself aching – 'what terrifies me,' she said again, 'is the depth of your depression.'

Depression – Laura knew all about it. Judith's black despair had been strong enough almost to annihilate her daughter.

And strong enough also, to annihilate itself – but only until this moment. For until this moment Judith had stirred up powerful memories – of anger, certainly, but of other, more life-enhancing visions as well. Judith had seemed once to have been wild and wildly creative, an impossible free spirit, a woman with a burning passion, an animated, mighty woman – not this other person, this languid figure, wasting miserably away. Not this poor inept figure that Laura had inside her and now remembered; Judith sunk in bed, her black hair strung out across a grimy pillow, her wan smile, pathos warding off a much stronger emotion, a depression so desperate that it had eclipsed not only her vitality but her daughter's too, and Judith, climbing slowly out of bed, sparking a sudden hope in her daughter's heart which ended when Judith would go, numbly, to stand by the window and gaze outside.

'Come.' Heloise was clutching at her elbow and half lifting her. 'Come. It is time.'

They were outside on the moors, the sky above them unrelenting, so heavy that it looked as if the horizon had been summarily cut off. On their left a wire fence, to their right clumps of bracken – muted orange and bitter brown interspersed with dulled, grey-purple heather – all of this stretching merciless and across it a chill wind sweeping.

Laura was so cold that she was almost numb, yet it was

coldness of a different kind – on the outside, rather than the in.

'Why did you say that?' Her voice was puny against the blowing of the wind. She tried to raise it, but only managed to turn it up a fraction. 'Why did you say you're not worried that I'll try again?'

'I felt it,' Heloise answered softly, 'when I walked into the hospital room. I looked at you and for the first time, the first time in twenty-five years, I realized that the shadow had gone.'

'The shadow?' Ineptly she echoed Heloise's words.

'The shadow of death,' Heloise said. 'Judith's death.' She dropped her head and her fingers were laced together, just as they had been at the hospital, interlocked but trapped, weaving one inside the other. 'We did wrong,' Heloise said softly, 'we misunderstood, thought that you were too young . . .'

Too young. Those were the words that Leo had once used. And she – she had silenced him. *Would he have told me then?* she thought. *Would he have told me what he did?*

'We congratulated ourselves,' she heard Heloise saying. 'And, patting you on the head, we told you how brave you were, how well you were doing. And all that time we did not look – really look – at you.'

We did not look, Laura heard and thought that it was true. All her life since Judith's death people had averted their gaze. It would happen in so many ways: a stranger, say, on being introduced, would blanch and look away and she would know that death, Judith's death, had intervened. Or worse still: someone, innocent of what had happened, would ask politely how her mother had died and the countdown would begin. It was inevitable, no matter how she told it, no matter what tone of voice or which expression she employed, it would always end in the same way, in the sudden, horrified withdrawal by the questioner.

'I suppose,' she heard Heloise saying, 'we could not bear to look, we could not bear to see that your mother, your foolish, anguished, talented mother was shining out of you. We did not look.'

We did not look – an expression of collective guilt and collective responsibility, and yet the blame was not universal. It wasn't Heloise's fault nor any of Judith's other friends nor strangers either.

It was Leo's fault, Leo who had wept so long, whose grief could not be stanched. She would remember it always, how her father – the one she needed, the only one who could have helped her – how he had lost himself in his own misery; her father whose cheeks were always salty-wet, his tears rubbing at her words, whose grief was so entangled with guilt that there was no room for anything, for anybody, other.

With guilt for he had abandoned Judith and his daughter as well, knowing that they needed him. The lies he must have told – and the ones, which, according to Ben, he did not even bother to say. Leo the great, Leo the great saviour of humanity – this Leo was his family's oppressor. Judith's strength was drained by work and rage and by her husband's lies. Judith had no one to be her champion.

'Leo.' She shouted his name out 'Leo.' Her voice was bitter, driven by a surge of bitter anger. 'He betrayed Judith. He . . .'

'No.' Heloise shook her head. 'You cannot blame Leo.'

The jade, an image of it turning in Judith's cracked hand – it was so clear. 'He lied.' Her cheeks were wet, tears falling like hot rain. 'He lied to her.'

'Perhaps he did,' Heloise said.

She looked across at Heloise. Perhaps? There was no perhaps about it. Leo had lied. She was gasping through her tears. 'He killed her.'

'No.' Heloise was quite calm. 'Whatever it was that Leo did, he never killed your mother. If he was unfaithful, well, there are many things that could be said about it, but murder is not one of them. What your mother did, she did because of who she was – and who, perhaps, she couldn't be.'

'But all she wanted was the truth.'

'The truth?' Heloise murmured looking at Laura, her eyes in hard focus. 'Your mother faced a truth too harsh for most of us. She called herself a coward and yet, even though she knew it might fatally wound her, she continued seeking for inner truth, travelling in her mind to places that had the power to terrify. She was damaged but she used her disability. I am convinced that her unflinching honesty was the well-spring of her talent. But we were not like her and sometimes the truth felt dangerous. If Leo lied, he was not the only one. I too, I remember lying to your mother . . .'

And I as well, thought Laura suddenly. I lied when she asked me if I was all right, lied when she sought reassurance.

She could not stem the flow of tears. 'It hurts,' she whispered, 'it hurts.'

'Yes,' Heloise said. 'It hurts. And perhaps it always will.'

They stood together at the edge of the cliff. Laura looked down on to the expanse of water, deep, grey, and infinite. She saw it was churning furiously, high grey waves shedding dirty white dashes, the top swell surging against the wind. She took one step towards it, stood tight against the land's tip, on the boundary that separated land from sea.

She lifted her foot, but instead of going forwards went back. Her flirtation with death was over.

Running, that's what she'd always done, running from the knowledge of her mother's deed, her father's pain, her own complicity. Hard and fast she'd run, her head bent against the ferocious storm, her mother's eyes sparkling in faked delight, her mother's lips set to an easy smile. Running – and her profession had been an intimate part of the race. Tom had been wrong. He'd given her the easy answer, the one that she preferred, that what she was seeking up there on the stage was an audience's love. But it wasn't true, she knew that now, for what she had been chasing was a brief respite, a resting point in her desperate sprint. And it had worked, it had worked fine, she had gone from strength to strength until the moment when she had overstretched herself, had fallen into Hedda's arms. Hedda, her nemesis. Like Hedda she had finally been defeated.

Except, unlike Hedda, death was no longer an option. She only had one chance and it had gone. She had used up her pills, and more importantly had used up her rage, the part of it at least that knew no boundaries; that could, when pure, have launched her off the cliff even knowing about the splattering of blood and splintering bones. But now that side was subdued.

And yet, she thought, if I do not die what other option do I have?

Her eyes filled with fresh tears. 'I can't,' she whispered. 'I can't go on.'

She had spoken softly, but not softly enough for Heloise

who was standing within touching distance. She stood on the cliff side, looking across, waiting for Heloise's next move.

What Heloise did was something Laura did not expect. What Heloise did was smile. She smiled and then stood silent, looking out, and only after a long, long time did she turn and finally speak. 'To know that you cannot go on,' she said, 'that is the beginning.'

CHAPTER THIRTY-TWO

After that moment on the cliff, Heloise began to talk more freely. Of Judith – that was her subject – of Judith and Judith's early life and the death that had always stalked her. Of Judith's parents as well, especially her father – his constant rejection and his final momentous fury when she told him, just after the war, that she was going to marry Leo, a German and much richer than the Cohens. Max never forgave his daughter, never talked to her again. But Judith had no other choice, Heloise said. She had to marry Leo, not only because she loved him (which, Heloise quickly said, she genuinely seemed to do), but because he seemed to offer her a chance of escape from the demons that had always haunted her.

'And it was a real chance,' Heloise said. 'Leo loved her deeply and he believed in her. While Max reviled her art and Rachel didn't understand it, Leo encouraged her to take it seriously. She took the plunge, throwing herself into work, and the misery seemed *momentarily* to lift.'

Momentarily – Heloise stressed the word – for the reprieve was not long lasting. The change came slowly at first, the surface of Judith's new-found happiness being only gradually chipped away, but then, when the outer layer had been removed, Judith began the redescent into her own interior hell.

'It wasn't easy to deal with,' Heloise said. 'Neither for Judith nor for your father.'

'So he sought consolation elsewhere,' Laura said, stating it as a fact.

But, to her surprise, the shaking of Heloise's head was quite determined. 'No,' Heloise said. 'Leo did not have affairs.'

'He must . . .' Laura began.

'I would have known,' Heloise loudly insisted. 'If Leo had been sleeping with other women I would have known. I started a neighbour but we became good friends. I knew him well: he did not know how to practise deception. He was an honourable man.' She paused and grew serious and then, very softly, added something unexpected. 'Perhaps too honourable,' is all she said, but Laura, watching, saw such sadness crossing Heloise's face that she did not interrupt.

When Heloise finally spoke her words came out painstakingly slowly. 'Perhaps if Leo had been less compassionate,' Heloise said, 'Judith might not have felt so guilty about what she was doing to him, and that in turn would have relieved the pressure on her.' Another pause, before Heloise shook her head. 'No,' she said, shaking her head again, stressing that she must be wrong, 'it would have made no real difference. Judith was lost already. We tried to help her, all of us, but we had no access to whatever it was that really troubled her. And as things changed . . .'

'When she had me,' Laura said. 'It was me, wasn't it?'

A sigh, 'Truly, it is difficult to know what . . .' Heloise began.

'Which means yes,' Laura said.

But: 'No,' Heloise said. 'It wasn't you – would never have been you. If anything, it was the responsibility of mothering. Judith did not feel that she had the resources to be a good mother and this distressed her – more than I can tell you. But' – Heloise's voice was suddenly adamant – 'your mother loved you.'

Loved me? Laura thought. And her last act – was that also love?

'Her love was perhaps too terrible,' she heard Heloise saying.

Yes, Laura thought, too terrible for me. The thought was new but it was the truth. Judith *had* loved her – had loved her almost to the death. Laura closed her eyes, felt her breath come shuddering out. Judith: a haunted figure, her fierce creativity and her dread destruction locked in perpetual combat; a woman swaying between two polarities, between perfection and absolute neglect. Judith: her mother, victim not perpetrator. She could hardly bear it. She closed her eyes tightly.

'More.' That's what she remembered shouting: 'More, Mummy, more,' shouting it as she soared higher and higher up into the air. *More* – that's what Judith had always struggled to give, more of herself, more of what pleased her daughter. And yet with each successive throw, Judith had grown increasingly exhausted, her smile tensing at the edges. *More* – that's what Laura had asked for one time too many, and was met by silence and an angry bump. She had gone too far and she found herself on the floor, alone, deserted by her mother. And the irony of it was that she could never have had more. How could she when she never had enough?

Tears, they were welling – she fought them back. I can't cry about it, she thought, because it isn't really sad, it's something else, it's . . . She looked up, put her thoughts straight into words. 'It's pathetic,' she said.

'What is?'

'What's pathetic,' Laura said, smiling bitterly, 'is that I'm almost forty and it has only just occurred to me that what I want, that what I have always wanted, is my mother.' She swallowed, lowered her head and, looking down, saw the faded carpet, blurred flowers blending with the grime, and she wondered how Judith, with her genius for pattern and her acid tongue, would have described this carpet. And as she puzzled over this she thought as well of the many, many times when she had wanted Judith's voice to describe to her the world; had wanted – oh so badly – had wanted Judith. But Judith had been dead.

'I miss her,' she said.

'Of course you do,' she heard Heloise saying. 'After what Judith did . . .'

'No.' Her head whipped up. 'It's not because she killed herself,' she said. She dropped her head again, and with it her voice. 'It's not because of what Judith did,' she mumbled. The tears could no longer be dammed – they swamped her eyes. 'It's because,' she stuttered as they began to fall, 'it's because . . .' She couldn't go on. Language was a worthless way of describing how she felt, made worthless by a string of missed opportunities and by fated undertakings.

She thought about it, about her parents, Judith and Leo, locked in their own misfortune. About Judith, who had married

Leo to escape her father only to discover that what she had really tried to escape was embedded deep inside her. And about Leo, as well, doing what Leo had always done best, stretching out a helping hand, promising to use his strength to pull his Judith out. Leo who could help thousands, even millions, but not the one he truly loved.

Clarity – that's what their daughter now possessed. The pieces of her family jigsaw slotted into place. She saw them, the three of them, united in a macabre dance of death, moths dashing themselves against a light from which, because it was internally powered, there was no real defence.

But what's the use, she thought, of knowing this all by hindsight?

Her tears had diminished. She pulled a tissue from the box that Heloise held out and wiped it across her face. 'What makes me sad,' she was finally able to say, 'is not the fact that Judith killed herself, but the fact that she died . . . she died too soon, before I was ready to let her go.'

Heloise nodded gravely but answered with a question. 'Do you think that people ever can die exactly at the right time?'

She had been so tired but found now that she couldn't sleep. She lay stretched the full length of the narrow bed, staring up at the skylight, waiting in vain for the embrace of unconsciousness. She heard faint noises, water turned on and off, and Heloise's footsteps coming closer, pausing by her door, passing on. A click and the light in the hall was extinguished, another movement and Heloise's door was opened and then shut again. Laura lay, her hands folded on her stomach, warding off thought. For a long time she lay as the darkness intensified, as the night was given over to the muffled sounds of small animals, the distant barking of a lone dog, the hoot of an owl, the scurrying of rodents.

And then, finally, when even this activity had ceased, she decided to get up. She reached across and pulled her dressing gown on. I'm hungry, she thought.

Yes, of course, that was it. She was only hungry. Walking over to the door, she opened it quietly, crept downstairs, thinking all the time that she must feed herself.

The fridge was packed with a huge variety of food. She

made her own selection – salamis and other cold meats, slick black olives and shining red peppers, green artichoke hearts and small yellow slivers of cheese, all of which she arranged carefully on a plate. And then, closing the fridge door, cutting off its yellow light, she began to move towards the table.

When she turned, she saw Heloise, standing in the doorway, stock still, staring, her eyes drilling into Laura, her expression inexplicably hostile.

'Heloise?'

A moment's silence before Heloise shivered. 'I was not sure . . .' she began, and then, abruptly turning, muttered, 'I thought I heard a noise,' and began to walk away. 'Good night,' she said, tossing the words over her retreating shoulder. 'I'll see you in the morning.'

Laura stood silently watching the hallway until long after Heloise had disappeared from sight and then, when she was ready, she returned the plate untouched to the fridge, went upstairs, lay down on her bed and fell asleep.

She woke suddenly. Light was streaming through the skylight and she could hear movement down below. Heloise, she thought. I'll join her, and, having bathed and dressed herself, she went downstairs.

Heloise was at the table and her 'Good morning,' was so cheerful that for a moment Laura thought she must have imagined their night encounter. But then, as she reached out for the milk jug, she happened to glance across the table. What she saw etched on Heloise's face was ominous. It wasn't antagonism – it wasn't strong enough for that, but something other – apprehension perhaps? Yes, that was it, apprehension combined with weariness. She frowned. 'What is it?'

Heloise did not immediately reply. What she did instead was put her cup down, carefully placing it at the centre of its saucer.

Laura's eyes focused on Heloise's hand. She saw dark spots upon them – She's getting old, Laura thought – and then she noticed something else – that Heloise's hands were shaking. 'Hey,' she said softly. 'How bad can it possibly be?'

Heloise's question came hurtling out. 'Are you pregnant?'

As bad as this, Laura thought. Her mouth was open. No, she told herself, no, I'm not pregnant, but even as she mentally worded her denial, she knew it was false. She shut her mouth.

'When I caught sight of you last night,' she heard Heloise saying, 'standing in the darkness, lit only by the refrigerator, I realized that your body has been changing. It has a look about it . . .'

A look – of course. And of course she was pregnant and far enough advanced that it was already beginning to show. She sat still, wondering how she could possible have been capable of such self-delusion. Somewhere, somehow she must have known about it, for only pregnancy explained her many symptoms: her spreading body, her endless nausea, her exhaustion. She closed her eyes, as she sometimes did when trying to remember lines, and now, instead of a printed page, a calendar emerged, there in her mind's eye, the months stretching back into the past, the days unringed.

Not Tom, she thought. No, it wasn't Tom's this baby, it came from further back than that. It was Steven's. She could date the very moment of its conception. The moment was the aftermath of death, four months and some days ago, the last time that she and Steven had made love – that moment, the night of Leo's funeral.

'You must go and see a doctor.'

She blinked. 'A doctor? What for?'

'Do you want this baby?'

The words wedged themselves in the forefront of Laura's brain: *Do you want, do you want,* repeating over and over again, buzzing through her head. *Do you want this baby* – Heloise's accursed neutrality at the fore. Of course I don't, she nearly cried, I don't want this baby, unplanned, unloved, brought on to this earth by me, no, I don't.

But what would be the point of saying that? It was too late, too late. 'It's too late,' she said.

'Perhaps not,' Heloise said. 'It is possible to arrange a late abortion, and in your circumstances . . .'

She means after my failed suicide, Laura thought.

'. . . I imagine that we could find a sympathetic doctor if . . .' a long pause and then Heloise completed the sentence: 'if that is what you want.'

Laura's eyes were stinging. She shut them tight. 'I don't know what I want,' she muttered.

And heard Heloise's distant reply. 'You must find out.'

She opened her eyes but, finding Heloise's gaze on her, she looked away. How do I find out, she nearly cried, I who have spent my whole life running? How am I expected to know what I want? She didn't say the words. She asked instead another futile question, knowing already that Heloise would not answer. 'Do you think that I should abort it?' she asked.

She had thought, had known, that this was a question that Heloise would reject. She was wrong. For Heloise did answer, slowly, searching out each separate word. 'It is a decision only you can take, my Laura,' she began, and then her voice grew stronger. 'But if you decide to have this child,' she said, 'don't do what your mother did to you.'

Laura was so tired. 'I don't know what you mean.'

Heloise sighed. 'Choose life,' she softly said.

'I have!' She was shouting – at herself as much as anything, and at the way new tears came flooding down her cheeks. 'I've told you and I spoke the truth. I will never try to kill myself again.'

'But that,' Heloise said firmly, 'is not the same. You have to do more than reject death. What you have to do, before you bring a baby into this world, what you have to do is choose life.'

CHAPTER THIRTY-THREE

Choose life – the words stayed with her, reverberating through her skull. She didn't want to, she couldn't, she wanted to get up and walk away. Or go to sleep – yes, this would be the best – to sleep and, waking, find that it had all been a bad dream.

But even as she thought these things, she knew that they were fantasies. Her body was already alien. Lying in the bath, she saw her nipples darker than they had been before, a slight swelling of her stomach apparent. She shut her eyes but it didn't work, not any longer, There was no way, no way that she could shut this out. She had so little time before everyone would refuse to cut this thing, this growth inside her, out.

To cut it out – it was shocking the way she phrased it to herself but that's how she thought of it sometimes, that a merciful blade would excise this wound and relieve her of the risk of bringing a child into the world and in so doing of destroying both of them.

For what if the darkness returned? She had told herself and Heloise as well that she would never try to kill herself and yet what if it was out of her control? What if she found herself gripped again by a self-destructive rage, and what if this second time she had a child as well?

No – she could not take the risk. She could not be a mother, she could not. She must abort the foetus. She nodded. Her mind was made up. She reached for the soap.

Except – her hand was stopped as she listened to an interior voice – *you are nearly forty*, that's what the voice was saying.

Forty – so soon would her time be gone. If she did not have this one, this child-to-be, she would never have another. So if she did not . . . if she did not have this baby she would always be alone.

No. She would not, could not think of it. She could never have a baby for that reason – to gratify a selfish need for love. No – she had no other choice. Her only choice was death – death to the foetus. Only in that way could she do what Heloise instructed, could she choose life.

She had decided. Down she went, down under the water, her body and her head as well, her whole self sunken, hearing a vague knocking and another sound as well.

It was her name. She came up, gasping for air, heard it again: 'Laura,' and a rapping of Heloise's knuckles upon the door. She pushed sopping hair from her eyes. 'Yes.'

'Coffee's ready,' and Heloise's retreating steps.

'It's Sunday,' Heloise announced as they sat together in the small sitting room. Laura smiled, her thoughts elsewhere. 'I got two weeks only from Gareth,' she heard Heloise saying, 'they are over.'

Her smile froze. She looked quickly down, stared blankly at the sludge of coffee which lined the bottom of her cup.

Heloise's voice pursued her. 'You do not have to go back,' Heloise said. 'You can break your contract completely.' A pause and then: 'But if you do go back, you will have to finish the run.'

Laura nodded, knowing already that those were the terms of the deal which Heloise and Maya had struck with Gareth. Her eyes lifted and began to wander aimlessly around the room, looking at the yellowing of the floral wallpaper, at the patches of damp which had penetrated its corners, at the shabby carpet, threadbare where it intersected the furniture, and as she looked at all of it what she thought was that at least this place was safe. She'd wasted time, despising the tackiness of it, but now she wasn't sure if she was ready to leave its faded protection, or ready to face the light, bright, jagged edges of her flat and – for that matter – of her life.

'You can say no,' Heloise said.

That is what Steven had wanted her to say, almost a year ago. Perhaps if she had listened to him, perhaps if she had done that, things would have been different. Except, of course, she had refused to listen to him then for the same reason that she must now say yes: because Hedda was part of her and because she must face Hedda. She smiled. 'I'm going back,' she said.

Which was what Heloise had been expecting. 'And Steven?' was all she asked.

'I will see Steven,' Laura replied, 'after Monday's performance.'

Backstage again in the most unfamiliar of familiar settings. She stood silently, waiting to go on, hearing the lines that were embedded in her consciousness, seeing familiar movements repeated and yet seeing also how they were strange. Two weeks – she had been away two weeks and someone else had taken on Hedda and that alone was enough to change everything. She could sense it, even just walking into the theatre, the way each actor had adjusted to fit a new combination and the way they were waiting watchfully to see how they must re-adjust to her return.

And of course there was a double burden for the cast and public had been told that she was suffering from nervous exhaustion – a phrase that everybody knew meant serious trouble. They were wary of her now and what greeted her entrance was a minefield of embarrassed sensibilities, of glances aimed sideways, smiles partially off-beam, greetings which although meant to be casual were delivered on an undercurrent of intensity. It was impossible to know how she should react. No – that wasn't quite true. What was almost impossible was the knowledge that she must not try to reassure them. There was no point: they wouldn't trust anything she said; not now, not for a long time. And so she had no other choice but to endure their apprehension.

It was almost unbearable and the rehearsal, which Gareth had insisted on, was an unmitigated disaster, lifeless and awkward, and then there were the hours in between, the waiting, her anxiety mounting as the time to start drew nearer.

And now it was finally upon her. *'I think she's coming,'* she heard and she walked alone on to the stage, her hand outstretched.

She survived the performance.

No – that was wrong: she did more than that. It was almost like the last time but more secure. The brilliance, that flash of something extra that she had shown on her last night, that was gone. But what had come to take its place was something perhaps even more precious – a sympathy and a real understanding for this impossible Hedda Gabler. She played Hedda now as if she was human, not superhuman, and she felt the rest of the cast relax. She was a star, no doubt about it, but she was one of them as well, a Hedda who also gave them space.

And a Hedda, she thought as her hand linked to two others of the cast and she bowed her head down, a Hedda who was pregnant – and who also had denied it.

The curtain began to close. She and Hedda had been separated. The cast stood back, not speaking, watching as the audience was shut out. Separated – they had been too merged before and now that merger was gone.

The curtain was opening again and she stepped forward, a pace ahead of the others. She was in the present suddenly, able to take in what was happening, to hear the applause as it came raining down. And to hear as well that the applause was slightly different. She glanced back, checking to see what was going on and what she saw was that the cheers was coming from behind as well. They had not moved forward, the other members of the cast, they were standing in their semi-circle and they were beaming quite openly, beaming and clapping their hands together.

'Bravo.' From more than one mouth it came and the tears that welled in her eyes were reflected in their faces as well, tears of relief and tears of belonging.

She blinked. 'Thank you,' she mouthed. Even above the clapping they knew what she was saying and as one they moved and linked themselves to her, tugging gently at her hands, smiling as they took their last collective bow.

'Thank you.' She said it again out loud as the curtain stayed resting down on the dusty stage. They knew exactly what she meant, they nodded and clapped her on the back and then did what they must have known she also needed – they left her, walking away to their separate dressing rooms.

There was one more obstacle to overcome that night, one more – Steven. She had arranged to meet him in a restaurant and now she headed there disconsolate, knowing what she must do and kicking against the knowledge.

She arrived to find him already sitting at a table, his head turned away. She stood for a moment watching him, and what came to her was how familiar was his profile – familiar and once so well loved. The curve of his forehead, that slight bump that seemed to grow larger when he was tired, that curve that she had often used to stroke: the sight of it almost destroyed her resolve. She had loved this man, perhaps still did love him, so why – why was she so sure that it was finished?

He looked up suddenly and spotted her; smiled and began to rise. She did not know what to do: she was terrified, she nearly fled. But no, she knew that she could not do that.

'Hi.' His hand was out and she felt it touching her, enclosing hers, and she felt a longing – a longing for a return of what they once had.

'Here.' He was holding the chair, waiting for her to seat herself.

'Thank you.' She sat and watched him returning to his place, watched how as he sat he flicked his hair to one side in a gesture that was painfully familiar.

He picked a menu up, held it out to her. She shook her head. 'You order,' she said, knowing that he would get it right. He knew her so well, did Steven, knew her appetite and the kind of things she could eat after a performance.

And more than that, she had leaned on him. He had been her rock, grounding her. She watched him ordering, saw how courteously he dealt with the waiter, using the same care with which he greeted everybody. Everybody – and she more than they.

And now she was going to hurt him.

She had to. She had to say it; she had to say it now.

She blurted the words out. 'I'm pregnant.'

Steven's face was suddenly gaunt and bloodless, blanched parchment-white. It frightened her, this transformation, this loss of composure from a man who was never at a loss. She acted without thinking, reached across the table, grabbed his hand with hers. 'Steven . . .'

He moved his hand away. 'Is it mine?'

She had the opportunity to undo some of the hurt, to heal. She took a deep breath in, prepared to tell him yes.

But if she did, they would be tied to each other by duty. She shook her head, no.

It was the answer he had been expecting. 'And are you going to keep it?' she heard him saying.

'I don't know.' She could not face that stare. She turned away.

And heard his voice pursuing her, his voice that was filled not with anger, but with sadness. 'You know that if you keep it,' he said, 'I can't have anything to do with you. It would hurt too much.'

She nodded now, looking down, thinking she was a fool to have driven him away. She wanted him back.

Perhaps, perhaps it was not too late. She glanced up quickly, and then the waiter was upon them, sliding a plate neatly in front of each. When he left, she held her tongue.

'It's over,' Steven said.

A part of her wanted to protest. No, she nearly cried, no, it isn't over. And yet, that part of her which had always railed against her fate was gone. She would not cry out. She looked across the table, smiled sadly. 'You were my sanity.'

He nodded, dropped his head. She saw him swallow, felt her eyes welling with tears. 'I'm sorry.' He nodded and blinked his eyes rapidly together and she saw that his lashes were wet. 'I'm sorry,' she said again.

He looked up, straight at her, smiled, looked and only after a long time spoke. 'I know,' he said.

She frowned. 'What do you know?' she asked.

'That you have to find your own sanity now.'

It was her turn to drop her head. She felt his words stabbing her. She opened her mouth.

She saw hope flaring in his face and in that moment she knew that she must not speak. Although the security Steven offered was tantalizing, it was also bad for her, she had spent too long hiding behind rocks. It was time to come out.

She took a deep, deep breath. It hurts, she thought and as she thought it, Heloise's voice returned to her. *Yes, that's what* Heloise had said, *it hurts. And perhaps it always will.* Those same words, spoken only a few days ago, yet now Laura heard them differently. For she knew now what Heloise had been trying to get her to do – to accept the hurt, and to accept that there might be nothing, nothing she could ever do to change it.

She let her hand rub gently across her eyes and then she tried a half-smile.

And he, he picked his fork up, spearing a tomato. They ate, in silence, both of them picking at their food until neither could keep up the pretence. Was it to be their last act of togetherness? They pushed their full plates away.

'Well.' Steven looked up.

'Well . . .' She smiled.

He did not return her smile. What he did instead was rise, pushing himself so violently up that the chair fell backwards and hit the floor. 'I'm sorry,' his voice was thick. 'I'm sorry . . . I have to . . .' He didn't say anything other than that. He walked away, his shoulders hunched, past an astonished waiter and the watchful gaze of all the other customers.

CHAPTER THIRTY-FOUR

She couldn't keep the baby. She wasn't strong enough, not to have it alone. She forced herself into action, making and keeping appointments, seeing doctors who told her that her suicide attempt would not have harmed the baby, and doctors who nodded kindly when she wept and who said it was all right, she had come in time. They would make it easy on her, they said, as easy as was possible, and they slotted her in on the Sunday coming so that, if all went well, she would miss only one performance.

Maya and Heloise were magnificent, dealing with Gareth, saying she did not know what (not that she was pregnant – she had forbidden them to tell him that) to get him to agree to her taking another day off. After that there was nothing left to do but wait. Five performances, that's all she had, five, and then she would admit herself into hospital and grit her teeth and lie, withdrawn, while what had to be done was finished.

She was on the fourth performance. Friday: she went on stage as she had done each successive night, numbly, and, on stage, as had happened every night, she was changed into Hedda. It was different from before: what had almost destroyed her – her dragging onstage the outside world – was now over. Only as Hedda did she feel safe, her other troubles sealed away, as this new Hedda whom she had found and fixed inside her.

It never lasted though. Each night she walked towards her dressing room buoyed up by Hedda's will but by the time she arrived that part of her was gone. The change came physically – her shoulders slumped and she felt again the weight that she was carrying. So it happened every night, this one being no exception.

Except it did turn out differently for as she neared her dressing room she saw a familiar figure. Tom, it was Tom leaning against the wall, watching her approaching, the expression on his face ureadable.

An image was suddenly illuminated: Tom's skin rubbing against hers, his body moving inside hers. She felt her stomach lurching. 'Hello,' she said, her voice quite flattened.

His voice in contrast was controlled and apparently unconcerned. 'Hi,' he drawled. He stood there, relaxed and easy, watching her come closer.

She slowed herself down but was already too close and soon – too soon – she was upon him. He smiled. There was nothing friendly in the lazy curling of his lips. She steeled herself, stretched out a hand, turned the doorknob. 'Do you want to come in?'

'Sure.' He watched her opening the door and walking through and then he followed and closed the door behind him, standing by it, waiting.

Waiting for she knew not what. She pulled out a chair. 'A seat?'

He shook his head and, having shot one more ironic smile her way, he stayed motionless, watching her.

Too much attrition – she couldn't take it. She turned away, pulled out the other chair, sat down on it and, grabbing a handful of tissues, began to wipe the make-up from her face.

Her gesture had an effect. Looking into the mirror, seeing her face transformed from overdone into something much more pallid, she also saw Tom walk over to the chair and seat himself on it, his legs straddling the seat, his arms resting on its back. His shirt sleeves were pulled up and she saw the hairs upon his arm and remembered . . .

'You're angry,' she said.

He nodded.

Angry – of course he was. 'I'm sorry.' What else was there to say?

He nodded again, looked straight across and what she saw this time was the startling blueness of his eyes, warmer than she had remembered them. She waited dully, knowing that whatever it was that he had come to say, it could not be good.

But what she had forgotten was how adroitly Tom could dominate a silence. She had liked this about him once, the fact that although he could weave an intricate tapestry with words, he was able to withstand, and even to encourage, their absence. He did it now; he let the silence build up, despite the waves of her anxiety. He must have felt them but he withstood them and then, just at the point when she was finding the silence almost unbearable, he broke it. 'It doesn't do an ego much good,' is what he said. 'To hear that you went from my bed to . . .' He left the sentence hanging in mid air.

To Margot's, she vaguely thought, and then realized that of course this is not what he had meant. 'To kill myself,' she said.

He didn't flinch.

She could not wait, not any longer. 'I'm sorry,' she said, wearily thinking that it would never end, this continuous apologizing. 'But please,' she said, 'please believe me that what I did that night was nothing to do with you.'

He smiled, his expression softening, the skin at the side of his eyes crinkling. 'That's exactly it,' he said. His smile was wistful. 'The fact that it had nothing to do with me doesn't do my ego much good,' he said, sounding almost fond.

And at that moment she couldn't help herself. She, who had thought herself so heavily defended against hope, felt her expectations rising. Is it possible, she caught herself thinking, that he's offering me an olive branch? She looked again, saw that he was still smiling – he was, he was offering a way out! She felt her spirits soaring. She had no doubts – she must take it. She must take it because she liked this man, he was her equal; he was, perhaps, even her future.

She opened her mouth.

Wait, a voice whispered.

Wait. She had done that too often, had acted without thinking, and had ended up enmeshed in a tangled web, struggling for release. She shut her mouth against her own words of hope.

As for Tom – he understood, knew exactly what the tightening of her lips meant. He got up abruptly. 'It's a pity,' he said.

'A pity?'

'That you couldn't . . . that you didn't feel . . .' He shook his head. 'It doesn't matter,' he said and began to walk towards the door.

Don't go, she nearly called out, don't go.

Perhaps he felt her unspoken words for he was walking as if in slow motion, his back rigid, showing, perhaps, that he was waiting for her to call him back. She held her tongue and watched as he reached the door, opened it, walked through and turned.

He nodded, one last time. 'See you around,' he said.

He was gone. And she – she had a curious reaction. She sat trying to face what Tom's departure meant to her, trying to work out whether what he had offered could ever have been accepted, and yet the more she sat, the more her thoughts began to wander. She sat quietly for a few minutes and then stretched her hand to the phone. She pulled it to her and then she began to dial a number as familiar as her own.

CHAPTER THIRTY-FIVE

The cemetery gates were huge, stately curving wrought-iron which had been pushed open, and beyond them gravestones stretched into the distance. Laura did not go in; she stood beside the gates, waiting. They had arranged, she and Margot, to meet here but she had wanted to spend time alone by Leo's grave, and so she had come early. It hadn't worked out like that – after a short, aimless exploration of the immediate vicinity, she realized that she did not know the way. They unnerved her, her confusion and her realization that she had not visited Leo's grave before, but she pushed all that aside. She stood by the gate waiting for Margot, thinking that tonight was the last performance before her abortion. By this time tomorrow it would all be over.

She kicked the thought away. A bright red Mercedes convertible pulled up, a window opened and Margot looked out. She did not, however, get out. She leaned across and opened the passenger door. 'It's quite a walk,' she said by way of explanation.

Of course, Laura thought as she climbed into the car, that's why I couldn't find Leo's grave, because it's deep inside the cemetery's sprawling grounds. She remembered now, as she pulled the door closed, remembered thinking, at the time, that the funeral procession seemed to take for ever.

She saw Margot looking at her. 'I'm glad you came,' she told Margot.

Margot nodded and then turned her attention to the front, driving through the gates and along the winding roads, steering the car easily, turning efficiently to left and right, confident as to their final destination. Beside her Laura sat thinking that Margot was lucky, that at least she had something to occupy her hands. Because even though it was Laura who had requested this meeting, and this particular meeting place, she was beginning to feel profoundly discomforted. Silence – she could no longer take it, especially this silence, too strained to be endured. She opened her mouth, said the first words that came into her head. 'Nice car,' she said.

And saw Margot's fleeting smile. 'Our' – Margot hesitated, flicked her eyes guiltily in Laura's direction and then started again – 'Leo's Citroen,' she said, 'felt too big for town driving.'

Not *ours* but *Leo's* – she was being so careful. Laura clamped her teeth together, biting back irritation. Don't start a fight, she told herself: it isn't Margot's fault. And of course it wasn't – Margot was not to know how Laura had changed, was not to know that the fury which Laura had once felt for Margot had now evaporated.

'It's round this corner,' Margot said.

And yes, now it came back to her, the memory of that tree beyond the grave, its branches bare as they had been the last time. But wait – she frowned, she was confused, had assumed somehow that more time had elapsed since Leo's death and that the tree might already be in bud.

Even as the thought came to her she saw it was ridiculous. She smiled in grim contempt at her own stupidity. How could she possibly have misjudged the time when inside her was growing a thing as constant as the passing of time itself, a thing whose development mirrored the progress of each separate day, a thing which had been started a few hours after she had been in this place.

Life and death, she thought, so inextricably mixed. But that was wrong. She shook her head, thinking, Not life and death but death and death – that's what she was facing.

Margot's question reclaimed her. 'Shall I come out with you?' Margot asked.

She shut her eyes. 'Of course,' she said. Of course Margot should come out – that's why she'd asked to meet her here.

They both got out of the car, began to move towards the grave, walking side by side towards the ugly mound of earth.

A mound which, as they came closer, Laura saw had a small bunch of flowers upon it. Anemones – Leo's favourites. Only Margot would have put them there.

She stopped abruptly, held out her hand, halted Margot's forward motion with a touch. 'You've been here recently?'

Margot turned. Her eyes were clear. 'I like to,' she said. 'It makes me ... it ...' She didn't finish the sentence. She swallowed, turned her head away, swallowed again.

While Laura, stepping closer, said: 'Margot,' and with the urgency of her pronunciation managed to tug Margot's eyes back.

To tug them back, but for a purpose she did not really understand.

They were facing each other, a fraction apart, breathing the self-same air. Deadlock, until Laura realized that this had happened once before, at this very place; that once before their eyes had met and had almost merged. Except it was different now. For now when Laura looked into Margot's eyes she saw not a pale reflection of herself, but the other. A separate person – the woman whom Leo had married. Margot, who had been a friend and who slowly had been transformed, by the force of Laura's inner rage, into a dreaded enemy. Laura dropped her eyes.

And heard Margot speaking. 'It was true what I said that night,' Margot was saying.

That night? Laura vaguely thought.

'I don't think Leo did have affairs.'

Laura nodded, thinking that what Margot said was probably true, that Leo had been faithful, but thinking also that it didn't really matter.

Margot seemed driven to continue. 'And if he knew about the guns,' she said, 'then he guessed late on. He felt guilty about Ben – that much I know – not because he was involved but because he accused himself of naïveté. He should have known, he said.'

Laura stretched out a hand, touched Margot lightly on the wrist. And finally found the appropriate words. 'I seem to do nothing but apologize these days,' she began.

'It doesn't matter.' Margot was smiling and at the same time lightly shaking her head, warding Laura off.

But Laura had to go on. 'I am sorry for what I did to you,' she said. A pause and then: 'I felt driven to it.'

'I know.'

No. Laura shook her head. 'You can't know,' she said, 'nobody can – not until I do.' She paused, expelling her anger, her need to explain. It wasn't important, not any longer. She took a deep breath. 'what makes me really sorry' – she shut her eyes, willing the words to form, shut them against the angry denial and against the part of her that didn't want to say them. And then she snapped them open – 'What makes me really sorry,' she said, 'is that we are no longer friends.'

There – she was finished. She had done it, had said what she had really meant. She was so relieved, was released from stiffness, heard her breath coming out in great gasps. And saw in that moment, reflected in Margot's eyes, the tears that were welling up in her own.

Laura responded, purely instinctively. She closed the space between them, coming right up to Margot, coming up and putting her arms around her and hugging her tight. Tight she held the other woman, for what seemed for ever, feeling Margot's breath shuddering and Margot's tears beginning to soak through her coat. Her tears, or Margot's, she was no longer sure which.

'I miss him.' That's what Margot was saying. 'I miss him so much.'

And Laura realized how much she also missed Leo: her father, whom she had tried so hard to put on a pedestal of perfection and thus never to have to question.

But now she knew that he wasn't perfect. Infuriating Leo – pushing his daughter into greater ambitions, helping her in the only way he knew how. He had done the same for Judith, had tried to help her by helping her to work. And if it was true that, in the name of saving Judith, he had pushed her too far, well that was Leo. He only had one way; to face suffering head on and move through it. No wonder then that he couldn't help his wife, for the suffering that she endured could not be solved by charity, by money, by moving forward from the past.

And, she thought, Leo did something else as well – more important than perfection – he loved me.

'I miss him.'

Her hand went up, stroking Margot's hair, 'I know,' she whispered. 'I know.'

And so they stood, holding on to each other, until at last Margot's tears diminished and gradually died out completely. Silence – and then Margot pulled away and Laura let her go until they stood again, separated but smiling at each other.

In silence until Margot spoke. 'Thank you,' is what she said and then, putting her hand into her pocket, withdrew the jade. 'You left this at the house,' she said. 'I thought you might want it.'

The jade. Laura had no doubt about it, no doubt that it was hers. She reached across, plucked it from Margot's hand. And said, then, words which came easily. 'I'm pregnant,' she said.

Margot's eyes flared.

But before Margot could say anything, Laura got in first. 'I'm going to have it,' she said.

She moved away from Margot's sharp intake of breath. Her boots crunched spiky grass as she went to stand by Leo's grave. She stood looking down, thinking that what she had said was true: she was going to have the baby. Her thoughts went no further than that. She stood, unthinking, staring at the ground. It was very quiet. She could hear the sound of her own breathing and, above that, something else: an ambulance's distant wail coming closer. She had heard its siren call before, but now, as the sound swelled, she let go of it. She stood, half smiling, savouring the stillness of the hardened earth.